So much love for you, Merry Christmas do
my personal jingle bell. Happy Reading
— Yashi

STANDING
WATER

TERRI ARMSTRONG

G000163378

STANDING WATER

Published by
Pewter Rose Press
17 Mellors Rd,
West Bridgford
Nottingham, NG2 6EY
United Kingdom
www.pewter-rose-press.com

First published in Great Britain 2012
© Terri Armstrong 2012
ISBN 978-1908136008

The right of Terri Armstrong to be identified as author of this work has been asserted by her in accordance with the Copyright, Designs and Patents Act 1988

British Library Cataloguing in Publication Data
A catalogue record for this book is available from the British Library

All characters appearing in this work are fictitious. Any resemblance to real persons, living or dead, is purely coincidental.

Cover design by www.thedesigndepot.co.uk
Printed and bound in Great Britain by
TJ International Ltd, Padstow, Cornwall

ACKNOWLEDGEMENTS

I am enormously grateful to Henry Sutton for his sound advice, practical support and unwavering belief in my work. Other great teachers who have supported me in developing my writing are Deborah Robertson, Lisa Selvidge and M.J. Hyland.

Huge thanks also to friends, family and others for their advice and support:

In the UK:

Tish Kerkham, Miranda Yates, Carol Lurch, Mike Bannister, Tim Bannister, Jeni Acelas, Bev Broadhead, Paul Smith.

In Australia:

Lindsay Armstrong, Natalie Chambers, Ivy Heptinstall, Shire of Mount Marshall, (Bencubbin, Western Australia), Shire of Yilgarn (Southern Cross, Western Australia).

For Tim and Max

'The man who never alters his opinion is like standing water,
and breeds reptiles of the mind …'

William Blake
The Marriage of Heaven and Hell

1 Mourning

On the way to the funeral Hester started to cry. Neal, driving the ute, glanced across at her. He reached over and squeezed her hand, too tightly. The tears wouldn't stop. She pulled in jagged breaths and held a tissue to her face. Without warning Neal swerved the ute into a gravel siding, throwing her against the door. He kept the engine idling.

'For Christ's sake, Hester. We'll be there in five minutes.'

'I know. Sorry.' She had to pull herself together. She turned her head to look at the roadside scrub, focused on the pale, thin limbs of a top-heavy mallee tree.

'Wasn't even your bloody mother,' Neal muttered.

Further up, a branch sagged with the weight of clustered pink and grey cockies. It would be a good idea for the boys to draw, she thought — they could spend a day or two on their favourite birds, talk about colours. They were at the General Store today. It was good of Graham and Lou to have them.

The cockies launched from the tree in a noisy squabble, spraying across the blaze of blue sky. The branch they'd left juddered and bounced before it settled.

Neal pulled the ute back onto the road. His hand was not steady on the gear stick. Hester dabbed water from a plastic bottle used to fill the radiator onto her puffy eyes and tried to settle her face into some kind of composure.

A black ribbon circled the crown of Jean O'Brien's hat, crammed onto her grey curls. Bill O'Brien was bare headed for the occasion, like the other men. They looked startled and wary without their wide-brimmed cover, Hester thought, like chooks due for the chop.

Bill shook Neal's hand. Hester shuffled closer to her husband, stirring up a puff of dust with the cheap black shoes that squeezed her sweating feet.

'A good un, your mum was,' Bill said. 'A real good un.'

Jean nodded. 'Lucky she had you, eh? Knew she'd left the farm in good hands.'

'Hmmm.' Neal lifted his chin and squinted into the excruciating November light. A cluster of mourners milled nearby, digging car keys out of pockets and trading news in the shade of straggly gums. He had decided there would be no get-together after the funeral, no send-off for Marjorie. He'd been irritated with Hester when she'd suggested it.

Hester gave the farmer and his wife an awkward smile. She brushed Neal's arm with her fingers.

'Hard, these days,' Neal said eventually.

'Too right,' Bill O'Brien agreed. 'Hard times. Bloody hard times.' He paused and shifted his shoulders in his too-tight button-up shirt. 'Salt in my top paddock, did you know? Poor damn sheep'll have nowhere to go soon. Reckon you could come out and have a look one day? When you got time.'

'Course. I'll have a look.'

'Ta, mate.'

Lizzie and Colin Bohan were the last to go. Tears had riven gullies through the powder on Lizzie's sun-ravaged face. It was the first time in six years Hester had seen her wear make-up.

10

'If there's anything we can do to help. Anything at all.' Lizzie took both of Hester's hands in hers for a moment, then pulled Neal's lanky frame towards her to kiss him on the cheek.

Colin shoved his hands into his pockets. 'Good turnout, eh? Shame Dom didn't make it.'

Hester noticed Neal tense beside her at the mention of his brother.

He went out early as usual the next day, as if nothing had happened, as if Marjorie was still down the track in the kitchen of the Big House, making the scones he sat down to every afternoon. Neal had lived there at the Big House before they were married; he'd seen his mum just about every day since.

The morning jabber of birds had barely begun. Propped up in bed, watching him move in the early light as he pulled on his work pants and buttoned the shirt she had washed and ironed, she asked if he was alright.

'Yep,' he said. Nothing else. Just 'yep', as though she had no reason to ask.

She heard the blur of the ute's engine as he drove off. He would spend the day somewhere on the farm, with the dog and the rifle.

The boys were grizzly and tired. For once, she didn't take them swimming in the dam. Instead she tried to keep them busy at home, stood them on steady chairs at the kitchen table with two wooden spoons and a mixing bowl. They stirred butter, sugar, flour and eggs. She let them make a mess. They cut out shapes — a heart, a star, a plain circle, an animal that might have been a pig — with tin cutters that Marjorie had given her, years ago, and laid the biscuits on a tray. She used a tea-towel to flick open the hot catch of the oven and slid the tray in, feeling the blast of heat on her face. She'd loved the wood stove when she first came, revelled in the constant rituals of chopping, lighting and stoking. Now it just felt like work. She'd suggested a change — gas, electric, even oil, but Neal would not hear of using anything else.

'Still works, doesn't it?' he'd said. And that was the end of it.

After tidying up she made icing with the boys, two colours, yellow and red, as well as the plain white, while the biscuits were cooling. She found an old jar of hundreds and thousands in the cupboard. The boys decorated the biscuits, spreading and dripping the icing, scattering the hundreds and thousands. She sat at the table across from them, watching the movement of their small, clumsy hands, their bobbing mops of dark hair, thick and needing to be cut. With a frown and purse of his lips, Billy, almost five, worked to create a face on a round biscuit. When he was concentrating he looked so much like his father. They both seemed more like Neal than her. Alex, a year younger than his brother, copied Neal's slight limp sometimes — she wasn't sure if he was deliberately trying to be like his dad, or if it was some unconscious thing. She was glad they had not inherited her pale skin.

Billy stopped and looked up at her, his face becoming clear and open. 'I'm making you, Mummy.'

She smiled and told him that was nice, but she had no energy to do more. She could not seem to rouse herself. For the first time in years she craved a cigarette. She picked a splinter out of her finger, then got up to open the louvre windows above the sink, even though she knew it would let in the fine red dust that settled on every surface and would hardly make a difference to the temperature. It was a big room — the wall between the kitchen and the dining room had been taken out sometime in the past, before her — but always hot. So damn hot.

She leaned a hip against the cool metal of the sink and looked out over the expanse of dry ground in front of the cottage, the double-fronted tin shed and tall, graceful salmon gum with the tyre swing Neal had rigged up for the boys. The windmill next to the house rasped and creaked with some imperceptible movement of wind. She doubted Neal would talk to her about his mum and what he was feeling. When they were first together she'd been happy that he expressed the bare minimum and asked little. She had preferred it that way; silence suited her. Now, she understood the depths of his inability. Emotions and thoughts built up inside him, then forced their way out, uncontrolled. That was how he was. He didn't mean anything by it. He loved her.

His brother should be turning up at any time and he hadn't said a word about that either. It worried her how much he was holding in: his mother's death, the pressure of waiting for the rain, not knowing whether the salt, despite his best efforts — and he was good, the best farmer in the district, no doubt about it — would seep up to poison the water and stain the

13

farm white. And now his brother. *That stuck-up bastard*, as Neal called him on the rare occasions he mentioned him at all.

Dom. He'd always sent books for the boys, every birthday and Christmas without fail, with neat inscriptions on the inside cover: *Lots of Love From Uncle Dom*. The presents had come through Marjorie, so Neal could not refuse them; it would have meant making a scene, upsetting his mother. She presumed Marjorie thanked Dom on their behalf. Her mother-in-law had only ever said good things about Dom. She'd often spoken proudly of him — his work, his flat in London, the exotic places he'd visited. Hester felt a pinch of guilt every time a new book turned up. Neal might hate his brother and perhaps with good reason — she really had no idea — but she was grateful for the books.

She filled three plastic cups with water from the filter barrel on the cupboard next to the sink and splashed green cordial into two of them. She gave the cordial drinks to the boys and sipped at the cup of water. There was plenty to do but she felt restless, couldn't get started. How much, if anything, did Dom know about her? He and Andy had been best friends — they'd grown up together, the Bohans' farm was only a couple of kilometres away. Andy had talked about Dom a lot. But that was a long time ago. She didn't know when they'd last been in touch.

She put on a CD of kids' songs for the boys and dried the dishes. Billy, distracted from his biscuits, murmured along to Incy Wincy Spider and made the hand movements that went with the song:

Incy Wincy Spider climbed up the water spout

14

Down came the rain and washed poor Incy out ...

She wondered if he even remembered what rain was.

For a while she wandered around the room with the tea towel slung over her shoulder like a waitress with no customers, before tapping out footsteps on the battered lino of the hallway to the room at the end. Neal's room. She stood in front of the door. Neal was never around anymore. He shut himself up in the room when he wasn't working on the farm or giving advice to someone else on theirs. He could talk about farming; he didn't have a problem with that.

She hadn't been in the room for a long time — six months or more. It had become, somehow, Neal's domain, his sole territory. Out of bounds. 'Daddy's in his room. Don't disturb him.' She'd hardly noticed it happening.

The room was a kind of office, a tacked-on lump at the back of the cottage, but crowded with beautiful objects; a heavy Jarrah desk from the Big House that Marjorie had given them when they were married, along with a set of matching drawers and a cupboard where the guns and rifles were kept on a special rack. Neal's grandfather had made the rack himself. There was an elegant brass desk lamp and a big leather swivel chair.

She leaned against the wall next to the door. She wanted to go in, to sit in the quiet room, the space Neal occupied without her, but he would not be happy if he found out. It was risky, asking for trouble. She closed her eyes. When they were first married it had been different.

She puts Neal's cup of tea down on the desk and he smiles up at her from the paper he is scribbling on, calculating the cost of sheep spray, or the amount of fence wire he needs for a repair. She sits on his lap and he holds her and twirls the chair around fast, so she giggles and clings to him. They kiss and sometimes have sex right there in the chair. He strokes her hair and whispers, I'll finish this later. They take the ute as far down the back paddocks as they can get on the rutted tracks, then walk to the farm's one remaining stretch of solid bush, dotted with salmon gums, thick with mallee and fat wattles, their bunches of pure yellow brighter than the lights on Hay Street at Christmas. Neal pulls her by the hand like an excited boy keen to impress, delighted to be sharing all he knows and loves, clearly explaining what he wants to, though he doesn't say much. He snaps a thin piece of branch from a jam tree and the sweet smell makes her mouth water. They stand still and watch a hoard of bright green parrots clatter away through the tops of the gums. At the dam, they lie in the shade of the windbreak trees and eat ham sandwiches and Granita biscuits. Sometimes they strip off, watching each other, and launch themselves into the big square spread of water, laughing like children, feeling the sun bite deep into their skin.

She could hear the boys singing along, out of time, to the duck song on the CD:

The one little duck with the feather on his back,

He led the others with a quack, quack, quack …

They rarely did anything together now, her and Neal. She had let him go, allowed him to sink into a world of his own. She wanted to comfort him, bring him back to her, make him understand that it could be the way it was before. Was it too late?

She wanted to go into his room.

As she touched the cool metal of the door handle there was a noise from the kitchen, a crying screech, a wail that tingled panic through her. She ran down the hallway, burst into the kitchen

'What? What's happened?'

'Billy took my bickie,' Alex sobbed. 'My best bickie!'

'Said he can have this one.' Billy shoved a star-shaped biscuit towards his younger brother with a sticky hand. Alex batted it away.

'Come on, you two.' She was calm with relief. 'Your biscuits are great. Let's do some more. Make a nice surprise for Daddy.'

That night, Billy had trouble getting to sleep. Hester lowered herself onto the edge of his bed and watched his flushed face in the glow of the night-light as he whimpered and fretted. His eyes flickered open. She grazed a soothing hand along his back.

'Mummy?'

'Shh. Whisper.' She indicated Alex sprawled in the bed across the room.

'Mummy, what's happened to Gran?'

'She died, lovey. Remember?'

'So I won't see her again? Never, ever?'

'Not in real life, sweetheart. But you'll see her in your thoughts. I know it's really sad, but Gran would have wanted you and all of us, to remember happy times, and keep being happy ourselves, wouldn't she?'

He nodded and lay thoughtful for a minute before rummaging for his soft brown bear with the chewed ear. She settled the sheet around him and kissed him on the forehead.

'Bear too,' he murmured.

She kissed the bear.

After his eyes closed and his breathing deepened, she sat listening for a while. There was a faint buzzing drone that might have been a mosquito. The tin roof ticked in the cooling night. She looked up to the ceiling, towards the sky or what would be heaven, if she believed in it, at the broken fan with the wide blades that Neal had said he would fix. It was probably the wiring. The whole house needed doing.

I'll try to be happy, Marjorie, she thought. I'll keep trying.

Eventually, she crept out, easing the door closed behind her.

In the dim light, it took her a second to realise Neal was right there, his back against the wall. They stood staring at each other, as though waiting for music to start up before they could dance.

'That was good,' he said at last, in a quiet growl, 'the way you explained it to Billy.'

She tried to smile. She still had to tidy up, do the dishes. The chooks hadn't been fed. She reached out and stroked his arm but as she moved to go past him he grabbed her, held her body to him, tight, the way Billy squeezed his bear, forcing the air out of her. She could not move her arms to comfort him.

2 THE ACCIDENT

At Northam, an hour the other side of Perth, Dom stopped for more coffee before the scatter of shops closed for the day.

The café had plastic tablecloths. The coffee was instant. Behind the counter a pink-faced woman splashed milk into his mug. He asked for an extra spoonful of coffee and added three sachets of sugar from the bowl on the table. He stirred too hard and the coffee spilled over the edge of the mug.

When he got back in the little Nissan — the cheapest hire car at the airport that would cope with the mileage and the roads — he felt awake enough to tackle the long stretch of the Great Eastern Highway through the Wheatbelt to Joondyne.

He drove through four-odd hours of mesmerising sameness, dots of towns and occasional roadhouses, red earth and sheep straggling across flat land. When it got dark, the car's lights speared straight ahead down the corridor of road; he might not have been moving at all.

It was nine before he made it to Joondyne. As he pulled into the Roadhouse a road train, like a giant centipede, rumbled away towards Kalgoorlie.

Inside, the glare of artificial light and buzz of background radio noise felt oddly comforting. The place was empty apart from the man serving. He was young, perhaps in his early twenties. Dom asked for coffee and chose a sausage roll, greasy and limp, from a brightly lit warmer. He wasn't hungry, but he couldn't remember the last time he'd eaten. The man called Dom mate, and asked him if he was from England. He looked pleased when Dom agreed.

'Thought so,' he said. 'I'm pretty sharp on the accents.'

Dom sat down at a clean table with the coffee and sausage roll, flicking through a copy of the *Joondyne and Districts Mercury* someone had left behind. Community volunteers had been presented with certificates by the Shire President. A farmer had found a rare lizard living in a dead tree.

The young man called 'See yu later, mate,' when Dom left.

He headed to the cemetery, a few kilometres away, off the highway on a narrow road; no matter how tired he was, how gritty and heavy his eyes felt, he couldn't diverge from his plan. He had to turn back twice to find the sign.

The cemetery was marked out by a low wooden fence, painted white. He parked and sat for a minute, his stomach churning with the coffee and sausage roll.

In the beam from the car's lights he shuffled around the strange territory of headstones and flat granite slabs, searching, until he found the grave — a mound of freshly turned earth, pinkish, even in the poor light, littered with wilted flowers in cellophane with names on tag cards. She was buried next to his dad. He stood for a while, disorientated, a little frightened by the rustles of wildlife in the surrounding bush. The night air had a dry chill to it.

He didn't stay long.

It took him twenty minutes to get to the Marrup turn-off. The farm was only thirty kilometres away now. The road was narrow and he worried about roos, so he drove slowly. It was past eleven when he finally made it to the Big House. All he could think about was lying down and closing his eyes. He collapsed on the sagging green sofa, the same one he'd curled up on, jumped off and hidden behind as a boy.

Despite his exhaustion it took him a long time to get to sleep, loaded with coffee, surrounded by the strange quiet of the empty house. The cushion he used as a pillow had a musty, complicated smell that reminded him of too many things.

'There was a wild colonial boy, Jack Doolan was his name. Of poor but honest parents, la la la la la la la ...'

Dom had the road to himself. With his elbow poking through the open window, he sang songs ingrained from school days at the top of his voice and let the tepid air clear his head. He was tired after all the travelling yesterday, but looking forward to seeing Marrup again.

The car bounced over a rough patch of tarmac and he brought both hands back to the wheel. Humming the Kookaburra song, he looked around at the bare paddocks and greyish sheep, the stately silver windmills and occasional set-back farmhouses, all stark and clear in the pure light. He breathed in the earthy smell of the land, the sharp tang of eucalyptus, felt a pleasant stir of reassurance at how familiar it all was. The trees' morning shadows stretched over the road, flickering across the car. He couldn't help smiling.

But his mood soon faded. The Marrup sign was pocked with holes. He couldn't tell if they were caused by rust or bullets. In the houses along the road — a few brick, mostly wood or fibro — torn curtains sagged in windows shadowed with pink dust. Letterboxes dangled uselessly from wooden posts, their numbers unreadable. Dom stopped humming. He

21

slowed the car to a crawl, searching for some comfort of recognition. Boards blanked out the doors and windows of the old stone post office. Abandoned shops, charming wooden structures with wide windows and tin roofs, gaped out onto the road, their facia lettering bleached to vague outlines by the sun. Wheat-coloured grasses grew out of cracks in the footpath in front of what used to be the bakery, a seventies building of pale brick, where his mum had bought creamy vanilla slices on Saturday mornings.

Marrup had never been a big town; now it barely existed.

He parked the car at the end of the street and switched off the engine. He shook his head, as if trying to clear the remnants of an unpleasant dream.

He'd come here to get presents for his nephews before going to the cottage — he couldn't turn up empty-handed, not the first time he met them. It was Billy's birthday too, in a couple of days. Usually he sent them books, through his mum. No matter what he thought of his brother, the boys were still his nephews.

There never had been a bookshop here, only a newsagent that sold magazines and a few kids' books and paperbacks. Now, even the newsagent was gone. It was eight years since his last visit to Marrup, when he'd come to say goodbye to his mum before going to London. In that time, the place had withered and collapsed, like some diseased animal.

A crack spread over the window glass of an empty shop across the road. He was pretty sure it had been Brannies, the café and lollie shop. When they were kids the highlight of their week was going to Brannies on Fridays after school to spend their ten or fifteen cents on little white paper packets of lollies. Mrs Brannigan was patient as he and Neal picked out what they wanted from the display under the long glass counter; chocolate freckles and milk bottles, pink sherbet sticks and stretchy snakes. Once, Neal convinced him that the black lollies had gone bad and were no good to eat. Dom trusted his brother, handed over his liquorice and black jacks and hard-boiled humbugs without complaint, as if the older boy was doing him a favour. When he realised the con he was angry with Neal, but furious with himself for being taken in so easily. He felt stupid.

Even now, he was wary of liquorice.

Dom got out of the car. The sound of the door closing echoed down the street. He stepped along the footpath, hesitant and cautious in the surroundings that should have been familiar. A post in front of the old hardware store had crumpled in the middle, chewed away by white ants, giving the tin awning a dangerous lean. He heard the growl of a vehicle. A farmer in a dusty ute stared as he bumped passed.

Strips of guttering hung loose from the Marrup Hotel, an imposing, two-storey Victorian building. Paint flaked off the intricate wrought-iron balcony and faded curtains hung in the windows. Dom was surprised to see a crate of empty bottles at the side of the Hotel and a station wagon parked in the gravel car park. Not everything had closed down then.

Further along the street, multi-coloured fly curtains hung in a shop doorway and a man appeared with an A-frame sign. He set the sign up on the edge of the footpath. As he turned to go back into the shop he noticed Dom and raised a hand in greeting.

OPEN the sign read, Marrup General Store — for ALL your needs!

Inside the Store a ceiling fan clicked lazily. The chiller gave out a low electric buzz. Dom's footsteps on the wooden boards sounded through the shop. Behind the counter, the man was unpacking cigarettes from a box and slotting them into shelves. He called, 'Good morning!'

Dom mumbled a reply.

He wandered past tins of food exposed in half-opened cardboard boxes; beans and chopped tomatoes, frankfurters, mandarin segments and pineapple slices. There were bottles of detergent on the shelves, Glad Wrap and packs of toilet paper. Next to the chiller a chest freezer had its contents hand-written on a piece of paper taped to the lid:

PIZZAS (three cheese, ham and pineapple)

CHIPS

PIES

FISH FINGERS

PETER'S ICE CREAM (vanilla, strawberry swirl)

NOTHING ELSE! PLEASE DECIDE WHAT YOU WANT BEFORE OPENING!

He collected a box of breakfast cereal, milk, some tins of food. He found coloured pencils and colouring books in a neatly arranged stationery corner. A squeaking metal rack displayed bowed cards in plastic covers.

The man turned and smiled as Dom eased his armful of shopping onto the counter. He extended his hand.

24

'Graham Walker. You must be Dom.'

'Wild guess?'

The man put both hands flat on the counter and laughed. 'Aw, look, you know how it is. Small place. Word gets around.' He tilted his head to consider Dom. 'And you're like your brother.'

'Neal? You think so?'

'Yeah. I reckon it's the eyes.' He paused. 'Sorry to hear about Marjorie, Dom.'

'Thank you. Thanks.'

Graham Walker picked up a can of beans and tapped the price into the cash register. 'The wife, Lou — I let her sleep in of a morning — she used to go out to see your mum. Took her the *Women's Weekly*, a few groceries. Played cards with her sometimes.' He shook his head. 'We'll miss her. The place gets smaller by the day.'

'It looks like a ghost town.'

'Yeah. Shocking, isn't it? Me and Lou came out here about five years ago, from Perth. Early retirement. Thought we'd do something different; didn't want to go stale, moulder away, you know? Little business to see us through. Just as the place started to shrivel up. You'll have heard all about the drought, of course. No rain at all, the last couple of years. But we still like it here. Stay as long as we can. Public service really.' He picked a yellow $6.60 sticker off the back of a birthday card. 'For Billy's birthday? Lovely kid. We looked after him and Alex yesterday. Missed the funeral, like you, but Marj would have understood. Good as gold, they were. No grandkids ourselves. Not yet.'

He told Dom the total. Dom thumbed through the still unfamiliar notes in his wallet.

'That's it,' Graham Walker pointed, craning over the counter, 'the red one and the blue — that'll do me, ta.' He gave Dom the change, and packed his shopping into plastic bags.

'Anything we can do to help, Dom, you know where we are. Remind Hester and your brother, too. Be nice for you to be around family, won't it, at a time like this.'

There was a beep when he started the car, and a low fuel warning light flashed. He groaned. Why the hell hadn't he got fuel at Joondyne? He would have to try Johnson's Garage. It wasn't far, just out of town — at least it used to be. He thought about going back and checking with the man at the Store, Graham, that the garage was still open, but didn't feel like getting dragged into conversation. He decided to risk it.

He put the windows up, turned on the air-conditioning and eased the car along in second gear, looking around him. There was the road heading to Dog Rock, the turn-off to the primary school on the opposite side, then farmland again. Long runs of wire fencing topped by a strand of barbed wire marked out empty land. In the paddock on his right the emptiness was broken by a tall windmill and a concrete tank, stained a grey-green down one side from an old water overflow. The stagnant windmill loomed above its own giant shadow stretching across the red ground. Along the backs of the paddocks, trees marked a dark line in the distance. He realised that the paddocks should have been busy, the air full of wheat dust and chaff, the hum of heavy machinery; it was November — harvest time.

Drought. Yes. His mother had written about it in her regular letters, along with average temperatures, yields and price per sheep. He'd become immune over the years, skimmed through the endless details, taken no notice. Drought in Western Australia. It had meant nothing to him. He had not even recognised it when he saw it.

Johnson's Garage looked shabby, but it was open. Dom remembered it being a busy meeting place — the Johnsons had run a farm supplies business, too. As a kid, he'd sometimes sat in the cab of the truck while his dad loaded bags of fertiliser or rolls of wire into the back amidst banter and laughter. Mr Johnson used to lean in with his cheerful red face and ruffle Dom's hair, or squeeze his thigh. It all seemed pleasant and friendly at the time. He wondered about it now.

As he pulled in, a flock of black cockies jostled overhead like a crowd of rowdy teenagers. He'd always loved these big, raucous birds. For a moment they distracted him and made him smile.

He had forgotten which side of the car the fuel tank was on and moved the wheel hesitantly, both ways, before swinging to the correct side of the bowser. There was a dull thump. He felt a shudder of resistance through the steering wheel, a bump, a squealed yelp! He shoved his foot on the brake and pushed the gears into neutral, turned off the ignition and sat, gripping the wheel.

An older man wearing work boots and a battered leather hat appeared in the shop doorway, carrying a large plastic container. He glanced towards Dom, swung the container into the back of a ute parked to one side, and ambled towards the Nissan. The walk seemed familiar — was it Colin Bohan, Andy's dad?

Dom struggled out of the car. He bent down. The dog was under there, near the rear door. It wasn't moving. Blood oozed from its slack mouth. Flies were already gathering on the damp, sticky liquid.

'Shit.'

The man came around behind the car. 'G'day, Dominic. You made it then.' He squatted near the rear door, by the dog's head. The muscles in his thin calves bulged and worked like lumps of kneaded dough.

'Mr Bohan? I ...'

Colin Bohan reached under the car and pulled out the animal in one smooth movement. He tilted his ear towards its nostrils, and stroked its fur with a rough, work-worn hand.

'Not very good circumstances to meet in, Mr Bohan. I'm so sorry. God. I just didn't see it. I'm used to driving in London, it's different, it's ... poor thing.' Dom looked miserably down at the still creature.

The other man stared at the dog in silence. He stood up. 'What?' He tilted his hat back slightly with a finger. 'Our traffic too much for you, mate?'

Dom pulled a brief, tense smile. 'I really am sorry. The cockies were ...' He looked up at the now empty sky.

The dog lay flaccid, rivulets of blood mottling the dusty forecourt. Flies massed around its nostrils and eyes.

'Aw, it's just one of them things, Dom. Can't be helped. She was a beaut worker, but. Understood sheep.' He stared down at the dog, before focusing his attention on Dom again. 'You round for long?'

'Just a few weeks. Mr Bohan, if there's anything I can do to make up for —'

The older man waved a hand. Dom wasn't sure if he was silencing him, or brushing away flies. 'Been a while, hasn't it? Since you were here.'

'Quite a while.'

'The funeral went off smooth yesterday.'

Dom scuffed at the ground with his foot. 'I wish I could have been here, but by the time I got Neal's message, sorted out the flights … and there was a delay in Singapore. Five hours.' It sounded like a list of excuses, and that annoyed him, when Neal was really to blame; his brother had left it a whole day before letting Dom know, in a brief, bland phone message, that their mother had died. And then he'd arranged the funeral so quickly. Neal must have known it would be hard, if not impossible, for Dom to get here with so little notice.

'Not to worry.' Mr Bohan gave him a reassuring nod. 'How's London treating you?'

'Fine. Thanks.'

'You're in, what was it, town planning or something?'

'That's right. Development Control they call it.'

'Good job?'

'Yeah. It's okay.'

At their feet, flies swarmed greedily on the dog's head, creating a droning, black mask. Dom felt his throat tighten.

'Well, good on you, Dom. Your mum was proud, you know.'

Dom glanced down at his feet, embarrassed. 'And yourselves? It can't be easy, with the drought.'

Mr Bohan's shoulders lifted as he drew breath. 'Too dry to even bother planting, the last two seasons. Then there's the bloody salt. Course, when — if — it does rain, it'll bring all the white stuff up. Disaster waiting to happen. But we're a tough lot out here, Dom. You know that. Haven't given up hope yet.'

'Good. I'm pleased to hear it. And what about Andy, Mr Bohan? Is he still in the city? I'd love to catch up with him while I'm over.'

The older man stood, silent, as if Dom hadn't spoken. He squatted and scooped up the dog, sending flies scattering. The animal's head lolled over his arm. 'Andy,' he paused. 'Yep. Still in the city.'

A woman with large, sagging breasts under a faded floral dress lumbered up to them from the shop. 'Bugger,' she shook her head. 'Well, she always was a chaser, wasn't she, Col? Go for anything that moved. You get them, sometimes.' She shuffled towards the fuel pump, still talking. 'I heard Phil Macklay's bitch has got pups on the way. If you need one.'

Colin Bohan nodded to her. He began to leave, then paused. 'Make sure you come up to the farm while you're here, Dom. Lizzie wants to see you.'

Dom watched him lower the body of the dog into the tray of the ute and drive away. The big woman stood by the bowser.

'Sorry about your mum, love,' she boomed.

Everyone was bloody sorry, he thought, irritated. Who was this woman, anyway? A Johnson relative? He didn't remember any kids.

The woman lifted the nozzle and the pump began to whirr. She smiled at him. 'Fill her up?'

As he drove out of town, Dom's hands started shaking. He eased the car to the side of the road next to the Country Women's Association hall. Long grasses lapped at the hall's wooden walls.

He hadn't meant to kill the dog — it was an accident. Still, he felt terrible about it. What must Andy's dad think of him?

He turned off the ignition and leaned his head back on the headrest. The heat in the car built quickly without the air-conditioning. He fumbled for his sunglasses, pushed them on and got out. A ghostly heat haze shimmered over the black tarmac. On the other side of the road were the remains of the Rotary Park. He crossed over.

His footsteps crunched across discarded bark and dry vegetation. The old cement path was barely visible. There'd been a playground here once, where he came after school with Neal and Andy while his mum shopped, or went to the post office. Sometimes she sat on a bench and talked to Lizzie and other mums, while the boys played. The park boasted green grass then; only the tough Buffalo variety with sharp edges that made his skin itch, but it was grass. Now the surrounding bush had taken over, regained control. It was impossible to tell exactly where the playground had been.

A wooden bench, doused with flakes of bark and bird droppings, crouched under a salmon gum. He cleared a space on the seat and sat down. A scurry of black ants came and went from a volcano of dirt near his feet. He brushed a foot over it and watched as the ants speeded up, frantically attending their disaster. He flicked a couple off his shoe before they could crawl up his leg, and moved his feet away.

His mouth felt sticky and dry. He hadn't brought any water with him.

Almost three weeks, he was supposed to be here. Why had he thought he'd need so much time? His new manager at work would be furious at him disappearing for so long with no notice. He'd pushed his last functioning credit card to its limit to pay for the flight and the hire car, and missed the funeral anyway, thanks to Neal. His brother.

If he tried, he could dredge up good memories of Neal. As kids, they built cubbies in trees together, mucked around in the dam, listened to their mother read them stories about bunyips and magic possums at bedtime, when they still shared a bedroom. Later, Neal, the eldest by three years, was left in charge of him when his parents went to a big do at Joondyne, or to the Marrup pub with the Bohans to celebrate a good wool harvest. They played 'scary hidey' in the garden with the torch and ate Milo, crunchy and sweet, straight out of the tin. But Neal would take the torch and leave Dom alone in the dark garden, crouched behind a shrub, listening to the night noises until he cried with fear. He would casually blame Dom for eating all the Milo, as if he hadn't offered him the spoon and encouraged him to dig in.

As they got older, Neal began to spend all his time working on the farm; he was the next in line, the farmer-to-be, the one who was always going to take over from their dad. Neal learnt how to pull a lamb out of an exhausted sheep and to put up fences, when to plant wheat and how much fertiliser to use. Not interested in school, he left the minute he turned fifteen, didn't even stay to finish the year. He was a country boy, through and through. Dom lived in another world — he studied hard, read everything he could get his hands on, oblivious to grain prices and fly strike. Neal made fun of his brother's stupid, useless books. He called him a bludger when he stayed in his room writing essays at harvest time, and a bloody sook when he didn't want to watch a sheep being butchered. Still, the household had a kind of equilibrium, an undercurrent of caring, if rarely displayed. Dom wasn't unhappy. Until everything changed, without warning. It was the year Neal turned seventeen. October, a month after his birthday. A Saturday.

The chain has snapped on Dom's bike and he is waiting impatiently in front of the Big House for his dad to come in for his lunch to help him fix it. He has done his homework and wants to go to Andy's for the rest of the day. He shades his eyes and watches the tractor chug along in the next paddock, his dad casually steering with one hand. Neal is in the far corner of the paddock doing something with the big steel hoe. Clattery sounds of his mum getting lunch ready waft from the kitchen. Dom bends down and spends a minute fiddling with the chain again, though he knows he can't fix it.

When he looks up again he sees the tractor, its engine still echoing its rhythmic chugs across the paddock, heading straight for the fence. He has a glimpse of his dad slumped over the steering wheel before the tractor ploughs into the fence, crashes through it and topples into a ditch, like a shot animal. Neal is running across the paddock and Dom shouts, 'Mum! Mum!' and he is running too.

Neal reaches their dad first, is heaving him out of the cab, breathing so hard he doesn't hear Dom.

'Dad,' Neal moans. He makes a keening sound that makes Dom shake. Neal is crying. It's the first time Dom has ever seen his brother cry. The only time.

A whining hum, like a giant mosquito, flushed a squall of parrots from a nearby stand of trees. The noise rose to a crescendo as a trail bike blasted past on the road, leaving a ticking echo in its wake. Dom stood up and peeled a loose strip of bark off the tree shading the bench.

Since Dom had been in London Neal had got married, had kids. His wife wasn't a local. From the city originally, according to his mum. Dom didn't know how Neal had met her — perhaps she had relatives here. She had taught the kids to swim in the dam apparently, and liked cooking. Hester. An old-fashioned name. Well, no doubt she was a good match for his brother.

He felt a sting on his leg and looked down to see ants swarming on his shoes and around the bottom of his trousers. He swept them off with his hands and picked off the individual stragglers that had made it to his bare flesh. The smell of crushed ants was unpleasant, like hot tar.

He started back towards the car feeling dull and exhausted, each breath of dry air strange and uncomfortable. He needed time to adjust. Neal could wait until tomorrow. There was no rush.

3 CITY LIFE

Andy's eyes flicker open as a sharp sound echoes around him; *click, clack; click, clack.* He struggles to understand the sound, to place himself. He looks at the legs sprawled in front of him on the damp concrete floor. His legs. Yes. He knows that the floor must be cold, that the filthy toilet bowl next to him will stink. His head lolls towards one shoulder. Slashes and scribbles of graffiti show on the walls of the cubicle in the bluish light. He has been trying to cut down, but didn't feel like rationing today. Got greedy. Stupid.

Click, clack. Shoes. Hard soles on the concrete. Then softer footsteps. The rustle of paper. Voices.

'Ten bucks short. Prick. No wonder he pissed off quick.'

'Aw, fuck it, it's only ten bucks —'

'Shh. You hear something?'

The hard-soled footsteps click closer to Andy, like the repeated priming of a gun. He thinks about getting up but he can't. His body is distant and heavy, his breath a bare puff of shallow air. In, out.

Crack! The flimsy lock falls away and the door slams open. A shoe prods him and he dislodges from his place against the wall and slumps to the grey concrete.

A groan oozes around the toilet block. He realises it comes from him.

He manages to heave his eyelids open enough to see white trainers close to his face, a pair of flat black leather shoes next to them. Legs and, further up, faces looking down at him.

'He one of ours?'

'Don't think so.'

The man in the black shoes spits, landing a sticky globule, festooned with tiny bubbles, inches from Andy's face.

'Stupid fucking junkie.'

'Boots look alright. Could get a few bucks for them.'

Andy sees the flash of flame from a cigarette lighter, dark shadows on the man's face. White smoke billows and swirls. He notices the way the cuffs of the man's trousers ruck and crumple where they meet his shoes. The man steps back, shifts his weight onto one leg. The bright tip of the cigarette moves and bobs, drawing patterns of light in the strange blue gloom. One dark leather shoe draws back. Andy could beg the bastard not to hurt him, but he doesn't. He does nothing. He deserves whatever is coming. The shoe swings towards him. He lets his body go loose, his eyelids close.

The nurse with tied-back, glossy hair, who always looked miserable, yanked the needle from his arm and slapped a lump of cotton wool over the puncture wound. She took down the drip from its stand without saying anything. He'd made friends with a couple of the nurses over the week he'd been in here, but some of them still treated him like he was wasting their precious time.

Andy tried to sit up too quickly and winced. He breathed deeply and eased back against the pillows. He knew there was no point asking for something stronger for the pain.

'So does this mean it's time to go?'

The nurse looked at him with disinterest, even disdain, and shrugged.

'You don't know?'

She made notes on a form and ignored him.

'Well, who should I ask?'

'Doctor'll be round tomorrow.' She clicked her pen and slotted it into a pocket in her uniform. 'Oh, and by the way, your girlfriend,' she drew the word out, a sneer picking at the edge of her lip, 'called in while you were out of it. Left you some things.' She nodded towards the bedside cabinet, and strode off on sturdy calves.

'Thanks a fucking million, love,' Andy muttered, half-saluting the nurse's receding back.

There was a plastic Target bag on the cabinet and a scribbled note tucked under the water jug. He carefully levered himself into a sitting position and slid the note out. Water from the jug had smudged some of the writing, but it was easy enough to make out, in Debbie's rough capitals:

ANDY — GOT KICKED OUT OF ROOM. GOING TO KAL WITH MIKE HE GOT A JOB ON THE TRUCKS. SEE YU IN ANOTHER LIFE. D.

He screwed up the bit of paper and dropped it on the floor. He rummaged in the plastic bag. There was his woolly hat, his tattered notebook and lucky stone, his pocket knife and ancient Neil Young T-shirt. All his worldly possessions.

He eased himself back on the pillows and closed his eyes. Tears streamed down his face; he had no control over them. Over the last week he had gone through the agony of detox in a blur of sweat and pain, been left with the ache of his cracked ribs and bruised organs. But it wasn't the physical pain that made him cry — it was feeling. Emotion gushed out of him, years of it, pent-up, pushed aside, ignored. He was not used to feeling. Anything. He'd been numb, for a long time. Now he knew the miserable, soiled reality of being found half dead in a filthy toilet block. A low-life junkie.

Feeling was hard.

It was another three days before they let him out. The doctor, a harassed Indian registrar, told Andy he still needed to rest. He asked, scribbling on the page in front of him, if Andy had someone at home who could look after him for a while.

Andy clutched his plastic bag. 'Home. Yeah. Course.'

It was a warm, late September day. Perfect city weather. In his tatty Neil Young T-shirt and the clothes the hospital had given him to leave in — a pair of worn, thin-soled shoes, too-short tracky pants and a cap — Andy shuffled along amongst the thin wash of office workers and shoppers. Tourists ambled around. Somewhere, a busker played a didgeridoo. With the plastic bag holding his few belongings rolled up and tucked under his arm, and the two dollar bus fare they'd given him safe in his bunched hand, he was glad to be free of the bland, unfriendly hospital.

The light at the pedestrian crossing turned green and he eased himself across the road and headed towards St George's Terrace. As he came down the hill the great swathe of the Swan River confronted him, almost the same blue as the sky. A few white sails dotted the water. King's Park towered, lush and green, to his right. He felt light and happy, overjoyed at existing, despite everything.

He hoped Summie still lived in the house in Inglewood, prayed, to whoever might be listening, that he would be at the solid 1940s place he'd inherited from his Gran. He'd run into Summie in Hay Street a while back — how long would it have been? A year. Maybe less. Time turned confusing and hard to unravel, with the drugs. He did remember that Summie had been looking good; trendy clothes and a nice girl with him. That day in Hay Street, Summie and the girl had stopped to talk to him, even though Andy had been a bit wobbly on his legs. But that was Summie. A top sort.

A herd of cars gathered at the nearby lights rumbled away as the signal changed. An ambulance siren wailed and faded. He knew he could try to hike it over to the squat at Moorlands. It was Saturday — he was pretty sure it was Saturday — Allie and Mick and that lot would be around. He'd be able to get some gear on tick. But he didn't want to. He just didn't. And it was a bloody long way. Summie's was closer, a serious consideration with his insides aching and the pain from his ribs jarring through him when he trod too hard. It would be good to see Summie again.

Summie had got clean. For a while, they'd used together, but pretty soon his mate had stopped. Said he'd rather spend the money on wax for his surfboard. That was back in the days when it was for fun. Casual, on weekends. But Andy wasn't even close to giving up then; he'd only just started. When he finally did stop, it didn't last long. Every time he used again, he thought he could control it, deluded himself over and over.

But something had changed. Lying in the hospital bed, he'd been thinking; it was his birthday soon — in a few months he'd be thirty-three. He was still young! If life began at forty, he would have a head start. Thirty-three. It had a nice ring to it. His girlfriend — on-off girlfriend, admittedly — had left him. He'd overdosed, again. The smack would kill him, sooner rather than later. His body had been smashed up. He was tired of it all. Exhausted. The last eight years had been like a non-stop, sickening rollercoaster ride. It was time, finally, to calm things down. Get his act together. Start a new life. If he didn't do it now, he might not get another chance.

Summie had been good to him when they shared the house in Inglewood, encouraged him to go to detox a couple of times, always let him come back when he got out. But Andy was useless; he turned up late at night, did deals at the house with people who ground their cigarette butts into the carpet. Eventually Summie had told him that he'd better go. Which was fair enough. Andy had nicked Summie's DVD player when he left, but hopefully his mate would have forgiven him for that, by now. It must have been about five years ago. Something like that.

Please be there, please, please, please, he chanted under his breath with each limping step. He slumped against the bus shelter, took off the cap and lifted his arm, gritting his teeth against the pain in his ribs, to wipe the sweat from his forehead. He noticed for the first time that the cap had the word 'Fremantle' emblazoned across the front, as though he were a tourist. It made him laugh out loud. The other people waiting for the bus edged away.

The sight of the familiar house was a momentary relief, but as he came closer he began to worry; the big jacaranda was still there, but the place looked different, neater than he remembered. The front lawn, recently mown, gave out a fresh grass smell. Wooden outdoor chairs and a small round table sat on the front verandah, with healthy-looking plants in huge pots. Did Summie still live here? As Andy limped up the verandah steps it occurred to him what a pitiful sight he must look, scabby and bruised, in his trashy jumble of clothes. His teeth were a mess. He ran a pale hand through his lank, shoulder-length hair.

He pressed the doorbell.

The sounds of soft footsteps washed out to him. A young woman in shorts and a bright, tie-dyed singlet opened the door. Through the grey mesh of the flyscreen he could see she was pretty. Behind her a long, ethnic rug stretched along the stripped wood of the hallway floor.

'What can I do for you?'

'Hi. Hi.' His voice was rough. He hadn't used it much recently. He cleared his throat. 'Sorry, I'm really sorry to bother you. I was just wondering if Summie — Steve, if Steve Summer was here. I'm an old mate of his. I mean, I don't even know if …?'

'Yep, he's here. I'll get him. Who is it?'

'Andy. It's Andy Bohan.'

'Andy Bohan?' She paused for a moment before pulling the screen door open and holding out her hand. Her tanned, bare upper arm was decorated with a complicated Celtic design tattoo. They shook hands. Her grip was firm. 'Jules. Sorry, I didn't recognise you. We've met before, in Perth. It was a while back, you might not remember. Hang on, I'll get Steve.'

He shifted his weight from foot to foot while he waited. Tender blisters had formed on his heels from the shoes he'd been given. His head thumped. The handle of the plastic bag felt slimy in his damp hand.

He heard the lift and run of voices. He waited, wondering if he'd done the right thing. Perhaps he shouldn't have come. Then someone was ambling towards him along the hallway. The flyscreen door swung open again. There was a hint of chubbiness about the man in front of him but it was, unmistakably, Summie. He pushed waves of sandy hair away from his face.

'Summie. Long time no see, eh?'

'Jeez, Andy, where'd you spring from?'

'I'm really sorry to just turn up like this. I've been in hospital, I didn't have — I mean, the thing is, I haven't got anywhere ...' Andy realised he sounded wheedling. He felt suddenly wretched, a pitiful disgrace standing next to his well-fed old mate, on the verandah of his nice house. A baby's cry detonated from somewhere inside. He shook his head, turned and hobbled back down the steps.

'Andy?' Summie let the screen door bang behind him and followed him onto the grass.

Andy stopped. They stood near each other. The sun was high now. Andy was thirsty.

'Bit of a surprise, you just turning up. I don't ... it's just that — Jesus, mate, you look like shit.'

Andy nodded and smiled. 'Feel it too. But I'm not ...' He lowered his voice. 'I'm clean, Summie. I really am. Just so you know.' A car trundled past. The driver beeped the horn and raised a hand. Summie returned the greeting.

'Look,' Andy made a vague gesture towards the house, 'you don't need me around.'

Summie pulled in his lips and dug at the grass with his toes. Andy could feel a dent from the reticulation under the thin sole of his right shoe.

'Yeah, well, there's Jules, and the baby, it's not really ...'

'Course.' Andy nodded. He wondered why the hell he'd come here, how he'd thought even for a second that these people would want him, a fucked-up useless junkie, in their lives. 'I still owe you for the DVD player. I haven't forgotten.'

'Good. Neither have I.' Summie smiled unconvincingly.

The screen door flapped open and Jules stood on the edge of the verandah holding a baby on her hip. 'I'm making smoothies, Andy. You want yours with or without ice?'

Andy shook his head. 'Thanks, but I — I was just leaving.'

'Don't be bloody stupid. They're almost ready.'

'Oh. Well ...'

Summie frowned at Jules. He ducked his head and strode back across the grass and into the house, straight past her and the baby, without a word.

Jules shrugged and jerked her head in Summie's direction. 'I wouldn't worry about him, mate. Come in. We've got something for you.' The baby kicked her legs and burbled incomprehensible sounds.

4 Roo

She had pegged the bathers out to dry and almost finished washing the lunch dishes when a blue car pulled up under the big salmon gum. Hester dried her hands on a tea-towel and watched through the kitchen window. Someone got out of the car. Was it Dom? It had to be.

She stoked the fire and filled the kettle, to be doing something. After a couple of minutes there was a hesitant tap on the wall next to the flyscreen door.

'Hello?'

Hester eased open the squeaky door. 'Hi. Dom, is it?'

'Yes, hi. You must be Hester.' He held a plastic bag in his left hand, and extended his right. They grasped hands, briefly. 'Nice to meet you at last.'

'You too.' She was conscious of her tatty T-shirt and rough-edged nails.

He stood on the threshold of the room until she ushered him in.

'Neal's not here. He should be back in a few hours. About five.'

'Right. Okay. Sorry to — I was going to call, but there's no signal, and the phone at the Big House seems to be cut off.'

'Yeah, I think Neal arranged to have things stopped there. Not sure about the power. Is it still on?'

'Yes.'

'Good. You can forget about your mobile though. Twilight Zone here.' She wiggled her fingers in the air and made a 'wooo' noise, and he smiled, a genuine, relieved smile, as though he needed it, had been waiting a long time for the opportunity.

'I got in late, a couple of nights ago. I should have come up sooner. Been exhausted, to tell the truth.'

She'd seen photos of him at Marjorie's; now there were tired crescents under his eyes, but he was still more attractive in real life. He had the same dark, thick hair as Neal, but his was well-cut. He seemed much younger than his brother, though she knew there were only three years between them.

'It must have been a long trip.'

'Yes. It was.'

'Have a seat. Get you a drink? Tea?' she asked, already spooning leaves into the pot. Tea-bags would have been easier, but Neal wouldn't have them in the house; he insisted on the real thing.

Dom pulled back a chair and laid a pair of sunglasses, sleek and expensive-looking, on the table. He put the plastic bag at his feet. 'I wish I'd made it for the funeral. Went to the cemetery the night I got here. It was a bit — a bit weird.' He smiled again, more nervous this time. Shy.

Hester stopped filling the teapot and held the steaming kettle in mid-air. 'I'm really sorry about your mum.'

'It was a shock.'

'We'll all miss her. The kids are still trying to work it out. They're asleep at the moment. Billy's just about grown out of his afternoon sleep. Unfortunately.' She remembered a small china milk jug that Marjorie had given her and dug it out from the back of a cupboard. She brushed the dust out of it, filled it with milk from the carton in the fridge and put the tea things

46

on the table. 'By the way, the boys have always loved the books you've sent them. Thanks.' It was a relief to be able to say it, finally, to thank him in person.

'My pleasure, Hester. They're my only nephews. Mum always kept me up-to-date with them.'

'She kept me up-to-date with you too.' She turned away as soon as she'd spoken, her face warming, feeling like she'd crossed some line, stumbled into a kind of intimacy.

'I brought an early birthday present for Billy. Only a colouring book this year, I'm afraid — all Marrup had to offer.' He went on, not noticing her embarrassment, or politely pretending not to. 'Got one for Alex too. Didn't want him to feel left out. I went in this morning. Thought I might be able to get books, but the place has completely ... there's nothing there.' He looked bewildered.

She piled biscuits from an old Roses chocolates tin onto a plate. 'I know. There were heaps of shops when I first came here. Now there's only — well, you've seen what's left. In less than six years.'

'Mum said you're from Perth.'

'Yep. That's right.'

'Whereabouts? I used to live in Bayswater.'

'Hey, you've got to try one of these.' She offered him the plate of different shaped biscuits, messily iced. Perhaps he did only know what his mum had told him. 'The boys' creations. They taste better than they look.'

A small voice came from the hall doorway. 'Mummy?' Billy rubbed his eyes and blinked. He stood staring, as though wondering if the stranger in his kitchen was still part of his dream. Hester held out her arms and he padded over and snuggled into her.

'Good sleep? Guess who's here. Uncle Dom! All the way from England. Say hello.'

He murmured hello, curious but gripping his mother firmly.

'Now, let's see … Billy?'

The boy nodded.

'Ah, Billy! We meet at last. Such a big boy. You're — hmmm — almost five now? It must be your birthday soon.'

'Two days!' He flung out an arm with two fingers held up. 'It's my birthday in two days!'

She smiled. Dom was good with kids. He had that in common with his brother.

She told him he was welcome to wait until Neal got back.

Hester strung tough-skinned runner beans at the sink. The boys coloured with their new pencils, while Dom read them a Winnie the Pooh story from a book he'd sent last Christmas. He turned the book around at the end of every page and they leant forward to examine the pictures. She listened to Dom's gentle, expressive voice as he read, and tried not to worry.

When the screen door slapped open she flinched. Neal was there, lumbering across the room with his slight limp — always worse at the end of the day — to his old armchair in the far corner. He dropped into the chair's sagging seat, legs extended, ankles crossed, his white calloused feet angled like strange growths.

Hester emptied the old tea leaves from the pot into the compost bin and began to make Neal fresh tea. The boys clambered on their father's lap, vying for space.

'Uncle Dom's here, Daddy.'

'So I see.'

'Hello Neal.'

'Dom.'

'Uncle Dom knows you. He's your brother!' Billy declared.

'Huh,' Neal grunted. 'My brother? Aw, yeah. So he is.'

'Sorry I didn't make it in time for the funeral. The flight was delayed in Singapore.'

'We managed without you.'

Hester brought over her husband's tea. Under her instruction, the children tidied up their things and put them away in their room.

'It went okay? The funeral.'

'It was a funeral,' Neal shrugged. 'People. Flowers. Said no flowers, but they brought them anyway. Don't know where they got them. Waste of bloody money if you ask me.'

Dom fiddled with the handle of his mug. 'I stayed at the Big House the last two nights. I'll stay there until I go back, if that's alright. I've got a few weeks.'

'Up to you.'

'Look, if there's anything that needs doing, just let me know. I can sort out the stuff in the house. Have you got a headstone arranged yet? If you like, I can —'

'It's done.'

'Right.'

Hester stoked the fire and wiped the table. She picked up Dom's mug and asked if she could get him another drink.

'I'd like some water,' he said quietly, 'if that's okay, Hester.' His face was flushed and damp with sweat. He wasn't used to the heat.

The boys chattered in their bedroom and the stew made a soft, glugging sound on the stove. Hester flicked water on stale bread and slid it into the oven to freshen it. She refilled Dom's glass. 'I told Dom he might as well stay for tea,' she said. 'Since he's here.'

Through the meal, Dom struggled to make conversation with his brother. Neal focused his attention on the boys, clearing up Billy's spilt drink, helping Alex cut a piece of meat. They fidgeted and kicked at the legs of their chairs, overexcited at having a visitor. Wood in the fire fizzed and cracked. She felt sorry for her brother-in-law. She knew Neal didn't like him, but couldn't he at least be polite? The poor bugger had lost his mum too.

She asked Dom about his flight; how long it took, what the food was like. She had never been on a plane herself. Never even been out of the State. Dom seemed grateful for her interest.

'This is lovely, Hester,' he pointed at his plate of food with his fork. 'Just what I needed. What kind of meat is it?'

'It's roo,' Neal cut in, before she had a chance to speak. 'You're eating roo, city boy. Real meat.' He held his knife and fork steady, on either side of his plate, and looked at his brother. 'Shot it myself.'

5 EXPECTATIONS

When Dom got back to the Big House it was dark. He sat in a fraying wicker chair on the front verandah and marvelled at the stars crowding the sky. It had been a long time since he'd seen a sky like that. He sipped a can of gassy Swan Lager from a six-pack he'd bought from the General Store. He and Andy used to drink the stuff when they were teenagers, just cans here and there, taken from a carton Andy's dad kept to restock the fridge.

The outline of the old shearing shed loomed to his left. Hester had told him the shearing teams didn't come anymore — no-one could afford them and there were not enough sheep anyway. Local farmers pitched in to get each other's shearing done. He sensed the solid presence of the tree next to the shed, where his dad had hung sheep from a huge hook to butcher, kept catching sight of it from the corner of his eye, though he knew the tree was gone.

Dom finished the can and got a second from the fridge, trying to avoid looking at the rest of its smelly contents. He settled back on the verandah with the beer and thought about his nephews, the way they'd listened to him read today. He was glad they liked the books he'd sent; he didn't want them to grow up hating books, like his brother. When Dom went away to university he left most of his books behind — he caught the train from Joondyne to the city and couldn't carry everything. The first time he came back for the holidays all his books were gone. Neal had burned them. *To Kill a Mockingbird* and *Catch 22*, his *Penguin Book of Australian Poetry*, *Catcher in the Rye*, all turned to ashes. Neal told Dom the bloody books had been taking up space, bringing white ants into the house. Dom was furious, distraught, but his mother remained silent, baked cakes, washed clothes; she avoided confrontation, kept out of it. Nothing was said. Nothing was ever said.

And perhaps some things were better not spoken of.

Some things.

Dom lifted a hand, heavy with tiredness, to brush away a mosquito. Lights from the cottage at the end of the track cut into the darkness, but there was no sound. It was too far away for him to hear anything.

Sweating and disorientated, he woke on the lumpy mattress he'd dragged into the lounge from one of the dusty, long-uninhabited bedrooms, and remembered. The house was empty. He was on his own.

Morning light cut through the gap in the faded curtains. He lay there and listened to the scutters and sighs from the house, the soothing creak and hum of the windmill, the faint maaaa of sheep. He got up.

The fridge stank. He should have sorted it out the day he arrived. A green mould crept over a bowl of leftovers. There was a block of dried-up cheese in Glad Wrap, a carton of putrid, lumpy milk, a half-used pot of yoghurt. He threw everything except a jar of honey, a jar of jam and a couple of cans of beer into a black plastic bag from a roll he found in the cupboard under the sink. The little rectangular freezer compartment was furred with loose, frosty ice, hiding a single chop, a bag of peas and a plastic container with half a dozen scones. He dropped them into the bag too, and added a few sprouting potatoes and the swampy mess of tea leaves in the pot. He tied the bag tightly and took it out to the verandah.

He walked the length of the verandah, clutching the bag, wondering what to do with it. When he was a kid, they'd thrown their rubbish into a huge hole dug in one of the back paddocks. That was bound to be against some kind of regulation now. But what was the alternative? There couldn't be any rubbish collection out here, could there? In the end, he left the bag at the far end of the verandah. He would find out what to do with it later.

He spent half an hour cleaning the fridge, then made himself a cup of instant coffee in one of his mum's tannin-stained mugs. He wandered around the house. The long hallway was cool and dim, cloistered from the heat, the outside world. He clicked open doors and peered into empty, musty rooms. He'd grown up here, at the Big House, with its high ceilings and big bay windows. His great-grandparents had built the place, nearly a hundred years ago — they'd managed a good living out of wheat and sheep. But even when he'd lived here the house had suffered from neglect; now it was falling apart. In the long disused formal dining room the ceiling had crumbled in places, leaving chunks of white plaster like splattered cake on the rich, dark wood of the floor. A crack sliced across the glass in the window of his childhood bedroom and mouse droppings littered the floor. There was no furniture in the room — Dom wondered if Neal had taken it up to the cottage for his boys.

He ran a finger along a dusty table in the hallway, leaving a shiny trail.

The only room that had been in regular use in this part of the house was the one at the end of the hallway, on the right, where his mother had slept on her own for the past twenty years and, before that, for about the same amount of time with Dom's father.

He glanced in, caught a cloying, confined smell and shut the door quickly. He had to go in there, but not now. He needed time to think, to work out what to do. Should he just throw away all his mum's things, take everything to the nearest charity shop? Was there one in Joondyne? He wondered if Neal wanted to keep anything. His mum had left the contents of the Big House to Dom. The farm, with the house and the cottage, had been passed over to Neal years ago. He thought that was fair enough, though it riled him that Neal had let the house fall into such a terrible state. Maybe his brother would fix it up now his mum was gone, move in with his family. He wouldn't put it past the self-serving bastard.

There didn't seem to be anything valuable in the house — some of the old bits of handmade wooden furniture might be worth something, and they'd be clamouring for the 1950s Formica kitchen table at Spitalfields Market, no doubt. But that wasn't much use to him here. Dom admitted the hope of his mum leaving him something had tingled at the back of his mind on the trip over. He could certainly do with some help; the garden flat in Primrose Hill had never been realistic, financially. Why the hell had he done it? Because he wanted that life, he'd been tired of the years of grime in Turnpike

Lane, the scrum and noise of Hackney. And he did it to please Claire, who grew up in Hampstead, with a country house in Devon. But he didn't belong there — not only did he have the wrong accent, he spoke the wrong language; he was Australian. Just a sheep farmer's kid from the back-of-beyond.

Claire was gone within a year anyway. Then he found Sara, who loved the flat more than she loved him. They'd argued when he told her he was going to sell the place. In the end, the housing market bottomed out and he was stuck with it and his huge mortgage. There were no more weekends in Berlin and Paris, no opening-night seats, just walks on the common and demands for payment. Sara didn't stay around long after that. He hadn't met anyone important in the two years since. He was lonely but had become wary, and lost confidence in his choices. The only thing he knew for sure was that he wanted to be with someone different; a woman who cared about him and didn't give a shit about the gorgeous damn flat.

Back in the lounge, he pulled the curtains and let an onslaught of light into the shabby room. Cheap ornaments lined the shelves. Stacks of *Women's Weekly*s, crammed under the sideboard, spilled out onto the thin carpet. He picked up a flimsy grey ceramic owl. A stamp on its flat base read 'Made in China'.

Why was he left to tackle clearing the house on his own, when Neal and Hester were just up the road? It didn't look like either of them had set foot in the place since his mum had gone. Hester had not offered to help yesterday. She had plenty to do up at the cottage of course, but he suspected there was more to it. Had Neal forbidden her? He'd thought, last night,

55

that there was something not right between them, the way his brother expected her to run around after him like he was bloody royalty. Why did she put up with it?

She had been a surprise, Hester. He had expected a frumpy, dull farmer's wife, but she was funny and bright and kind — the opposite of his brother. There was something unkempt about her, but measured too. She had a kind of subdued self-assurance, an attractive way of moving; fluid, but precise. Sexy, he supposed.

She was not what he had expected at all.

6 SANCTUARY

She took the boys swimming the next morning, wanting to get back to the normal rhythm of their days. Both were remarkable in the water for their ages. She had started teaching them while they were babies. Once, she'd overheard Neal telling Jack Bryson that his boys could float before they could walk, with an uncharacteristic edge of bragging in his voice. When she'd first come here, Hester had listened to the stories of farm children drowned in creeks and dams and flash floods, tragic tales told and retold until they took on a sad inevitability. Even before getting pregnant with Billy she had been prepared. It was a fear she could confront, take control of; her boys would know water as well as they knew land. She gave them lessons every morning, before the sun was too fierce, and let them muck around for a while afterwards.

The boys played on the huge tractor tyre inner tube and with the old surf board Neal had found by the side of the road, left behind by some adventurous tourist making a quick escape back to the coast. She watched Billy balance on the board, his little limbs brown and strong. Alex sat astride the tube, kicking his legs.

She settled into a float close by. With her ears submerged, the sound of the boys playing became distant and hollow. She smelled sheep and hard-baked soil, dry grass and the spicy sap of the swamp mallet along the windbreak. She belonged here, on the farm, and the dam was her special place. Neal had given it to her, this big slab of water surrounded by dusty paddocks, like a gift. He had put up a fence to keep the sheep and the roos and rabbits out. To keep it clean. For her.

When she came here it was a revelation to swim again, after so many years. She'd panicked when the water level had started to lower at the end of that first summer. Neal had explained that it was normal — it was a run-off dam, and wouldn't fill up again until the next rain. But it upset her so much to see the water inching downwards, sinking into the ground, being sucked away by the heat of the sun, that Neal had rigged up a pipe into the dam from the big windmill that pumped artesian water for the sheep troughs around the farm. Since then it had always been full enough to swim in, even when the rain didn't come and all the other dams sat bone dry, the land around parched and desolate. The dam was always there. Her sanctuary. The locals allowed Neal this odd extravagance with tolerant good humour. With anyone other than Neal Connor, she suspected, the attitude would more likely have been derision and scorn.

She made her eyes into slits and stared up at the sky, a vast blanket of perfect blue reaching to the edges of the land, clear and precise and effortless. When she was a girl she had floated like this in the sea, looking up at another huge sky, listening to the squawk of the gulls, people's shouts and laughter muffled by the stir and crash of the waves, tasted the salt in her mouth, felt its gritty crust on her skin.

She swam every day in the summer, and after school and weekends the rest of the year when it wasn't too cold. She took her lifesaving exam at twelve. Her knee-boarding skills made tourists on the beach stop and watch. A true-blue water-baby, her dad called her. His clever girl. He always said he was proud of her. Still, it didn't stop him leaving.

Her body lay, buoyed, weightless in the water. Since Neal's brother had turned up, fleeting memories of the past, thoughts long buried, had startled her at odd times. Yet meeting Dom had lifted her mood. She admitted to herself that she was looking forward to seeing him again.

One of the boys popped up next to her, spouting water. She dived under, smooth and quick, slipped away to come up in the middle of the inner tube. She waved her arms in the air and teased her boys that they couldn't catch her. They splashed towards her, laughing.

It had shocked her to realise, seeing Dom and Neal together, how difficult her husband had become, how tight and gloomy and inward. He had treated his brother badly last night. She had been embarrassed.

They walked back along the track to the cottage, still damp and fresh from the water, the boys kicking at gravel, collecting sticks, chattering. The swimming wore them out; they would have lunch, then sleep for a little while — at least Alex would. Billy was probably too old for an afternoon nap, but she encouraged him to have a lie down, to rest. She craved that time, a little gap in the day, to herself.

A dull, rhythmic sound carried across to her, growing louder as they moved along the track. She could see Neal, digging, on the far edge of the paddock.

'There's Daddy!' the boys called. They stood at the fence and waved but he was turned away and didn't notice them. She watched his shoulders dip and swing, dip and swing as he wielded the shovel. A couple of sheep carcasses were sprawled nearby. He dipped and swung again, then flung the shovel away and leaned over with his hands on his thighs, his head lowered. He didn't move. She thought, for a moment, that the sound she could hear was a bird. The boys watched and said nothing.

'Come on you two, let's get some lunch. Daddy's busy.' She shooed them on towards the house.

7 LETTERS

Andy was a liability, a pain in the arse, not to be trusted. That's how Summie saw it and who could blame him? Summie was a family man now; the bloke had a little kid for God's sake, and a girlfriend he was trying to protect. But it was her, Jules, who stuck up for him. He could hear them in the next room, their voices starting as low hisses, matching each other as they rose.

'I gave him loads of chances before, Jules.'

'Yeah, well now he needs another chance.'

'He's managed all this time without us. What are we, the Y bloody M C A?'

'No. You're meant to be his friend. You don't just abandon people when it suits you. I thought you were better than that Steve, I really did.'

Andy looked at the froth in the bottom of his glass and wiped his mouth with the back of his hand. His tongue tingled from the ice and the tang of raspberries. He hated to be the cause of this conflict. He thought about leaving, just getting up and going quietly, but didn't move. Weariness closed in on him. He needed a bit of time to summon his strength, to gather himself.

He brushed his hand across the wood of the big pine table. The kitchen was painted a lemony colour, with bright yellow and blue tiles around the sturdy cooker. Pans hung from hooks on a wooden rail and herbs in pots lined the sill. A stained-glass bird hung in the window. It looked so different from when he had lived here, it might have been another house.

The baby began a whimpering cry and the door of the next room swung open. Summie stalked away down the hall and Jules came into the kitchen jiggling the baby on one hip, murmuring soothing noises. The baby calmed quickly and sucked at the ear of a toy elephant she was clutching.

Jules smiled at Andy. 'How was the smoothie?'

'Great. Really good. Thanks.'

The baby stared at Andy. He managed to raise a hand and give her a gentle wave. 'She's wondering what the hell the cat dragged in. What's her name?'

'Callie. She's almost one and a half.'

'Ah, one and a half. Those were the days.'

Jules laughed. She slipped Callie into her high chair. The baby kept her eyes on Andy.

He looked away. 'I'm sorry for causing all this grief, Jules. I should go.'

She frowned and tilted her head as if the idea was absurd. 'Don't be silly. Summie's just doing some macho protective shit. Underneath all that, he is pleased to see you.' She handed Callie a plastic baby beaker. 'The back room's empty, Andy. You've got no excuse not to stay.'

Callie whacked the beaker on the tray of her high chair and kicked her legs.

Jules picked up an apple and a small knife from the kitchen counter and sat down at the table near Callie. 'Summie'll come round. Don't worry.'

He stared into his glass, swirled the now-watery dregs of his smoothie. He had appeared in these people's lives out of nowhere. What right did he have to expect anything from them? He didn't deserve this woman's thoughtful generosity. 'Thanks,' he said quietly. 'I appreciate the offer, Jules, but I think I'd better —'

Summie thumped into the room and stood opposite him. He handed Andy a bundle of papers across the table. 'These are for you.'

It was a clutch of long, white envelopes held together with an elastic band. Letters. After a confused moment, Andy recognised his mother's neat, loopy handwriting. He felt so tired he thought he might slump over onto the table. He blinked, working to keep his eyes open.

'From your mum. She phoned me after you did a runner from the farm that time. Asked if she could write to you here, in case I ever saw you.'

'Thanks. Thanks, Summie.'

'No skin off my nose, mate.' Summie shrugged. 'You not been in touch with your oldies all this time?'

'No. No.'

At the other end of the table, Jules cut the skin off a slice of apple and put down the knife. She handed Callie the fruit but looked at Summie. There was no plea in her look, no challenge or threat. Her face was open; perhaps it was a look of trust.

Summie lowered his head and gripped the back of the chair in front of him with both hands. After a few seconds, he sat down. 'She's written a few times a year, your mum. We told you the letters were here when we saw you last year, in Hay Street.'

'I remember seeing you. I don't remember anything about letters though.'

'You were a bit messy.'

'Yeah. I probably was.' Andy smiled wearily.

Summie chuckled and looked down at his intertwined fingers on the table. He rubbed his thumbs together. 'Listen, the back room's empty. Hardly been used since we had those parties.' He made a huh sound in his throat and shook his head. 'Every weekend back then. Remember? Half of bloody Perth used to turn up. Never knew who you'd find in that room in the morning. God, they were mad days, eh?'

'Mad,' Andy murmured.

Callie cried, 'Da-da, da-da,' and stretched up her arms in her high chair.

Summie got up and lifted her out. 'You won't be having wild parties like that will you, my girl?' He pressed his face into her tummy and blew. She screeched with delight.

Andy's tears came without warning, streaking down his face. There was no noise, just the gush of liquid from his eyes. He felt disconnected from himself, distant and strange. Summie stared, his mouth half-open.

Jules' hand was on his shoulder. Her voice came from down a long tunnel. 'Think you could do with a lie down, eh?'

For a few days Andy existed in a blur of sleep and confused, foggy exhaustion. Jules appeared with food, like a vision. He must have eaten.

On the morning he woke with his mind clearer, his thoughts more settled, he lay in the narrow single bed with the sun squeezing through the slatted cane blinds of the back room, listening to the muffled sounds of the house: Summie looking for car keys, making Callie laugh with a goodbye tickle, Jules asking him what he wanted for tea. He heard the clatter of dishes and hum of the radio, took in the cluttered bookshelves in the room, the piles of surf magazines stacked on the floor. A surfboard with a broken fin stood propped against the wall, next to a big wooden chest and a pair of old biker boots. On the bedside table a cheap alarm clock gave off a faint brrrr as the seconds moved by.

Jules was hanging out washing in the garden with Callie in a sling on her back when he finally emerged into the sun, blinking as though it were his first view of the world.

He got up just after Summie left for work. After breakfast he washed the dishes and swept the floor. He hung out washing and worked in the garden, began to settle into the routines and rhythms of the house. He did not want to be a burden.

He ate lunch with Jules and Callie on a plastic table in the shade of the back patio. Callie smiled back when he smiled at her. Sometimes he spoon-fed her and cleaned up her sticky spills. They sat in the sandpit together and poured sand from plastic containers, over and over. He made himself stop swearing.

In the evenings, Jules produced vast, colourful meals — she had given up her job as a chef in a wholefood restaurant to look after Callie — and loaded Andy's plate with more salad each day than he'd eaten altogether in the last five years. When he flagged, she called him a lightweight, with a chiding smile.

'It's lovely, Jules,' he assured her, sitting back in his chair, a hand on his full stomach, 'but sometimes you can get too much of a good thing, you know?'

'Yeah, well, homemade lemon mousse is a good thing too, and you won't get any if you don't eat your salad.'

Sometimes Jules seemed more like his long-time mate than Summie. It was hard to miss the way Summie grabbed his wallet and slipped it in the back pocket of his jeans when Andy came into the room, or slid the car keys off the table and clutched them in his hand. It made him feel like shit. But Summie thawed a bit more every day. When he relaxed and forgot his stance against having an ex-junkie waster in the house, he was almost like the old Summie, wolf-whistling Andy wearing his own too-small cast-offs, almost pissing himself laughing when he cajoled him onto Callie's tiny plastic slide.

Summie had worked in the same sports shop for six years and practically ran the place, Jules told Andy. They'd met surfing, but rarely got their boards out now. There were other things to do, she explained without regret.

Andy and Summie had surfed together too, starting on the small waves up the coast, graduating to the killer ones down south at Mallin. After Dom, his best mate from home, went to London, he and Summie spent weeks at a time down south, sleeping — when they did — in an old station wagon in the car park at the beach. Andy liked to surf, but preferred the company of people to communion with the sea; he spent more time in the Mallin tavern than in the water, drinking and smoking joints, sorting out where to score something a bit

66

more serious later. There wasn't much the hedonistic little hippy town couldn't provide. Looking back at that time, he remembered a feeling of sad loneliness, an overwhelming emptiness. Sometimes he'd sat in the station wagon looking out to sea, tired and bleary, scribbling long letters to Dom — far away, living some other life — on whatever scraps of paper he could find. Occasionally he even posted them. He wondered if that time was the beginning of his downward spiral, or if it had really started earlier. Like from birth.

Jules offered to tidy up his long, straggly hair. She told him she always did Summie's. She'd learnt to cut hair on her three younger brothers. They all grew up with a fear of scissors, she said, opening and closing the pair in her hand with her eyes wide.

'Spare me!' Andy crossed his fingers and turned his head, as if warding off evil. She laughed and threw a towel at him.

He wore an old pair of Summie's board shorts, pulling the tie as tight as it would go to get them to stay on. Jules sat him down in a plastic chair in the shade of the tall lemon gum at the back of the garden, with the baby alarm on another chair on the patio, in case Callie woke from her afternoon sleep.

Andy closed his eyes as cool water from the hose drenched him in a luxurious stream. White shampoo foam streamed down his body onto the grass at his feet. He felt fingers splay across his scalp, massaging, soothing, allowed himself to relax into the unfamiliar pleasure of a simple act of touch, the feel of human caring. Hester had cut his hair a few times too. He remembered the way she had stood in front of him when she had finished, her head tilted to one side. Hester. He had wanted to give her so much and believed he could do it, for a while. How had he got it so badly wrong? He felt like crying, but he didn't. He was taking control of his tears.

Through the veil of water Andy heard Jules' voice, softened, distant.

'My youngest brother had hair like yours — thick, with just a bit of a curl. Easy to cut.'

She draped a towel over his head and pulled it tight across his damp hair. 'Can't do much about the grey, I'm afraid. You'll have to learn to live with that.'

'Distinguished?' he suggested.

'Yeah. Too right. Distinguished.'

Sometimes, he half-woke in the night to Callie's shimmering cries and heard the lull of a parent's voice soothing her back to sleep.

Andy watched Summie push his daughter on the swing from the shade of the patio, with a John Le Carré paperback spread-eagled on his lap. He'd found it on the shelf in the back room amongst the books on surfing, babies and old collections of Gary Larson cartoons. He'd discovered that reading stopped him worrying too much. It was a kind of company. He'd never had much patience to read before, or the necessary concentration.

Summie lifted his daughter out of the swing, whizzed her through the air and lowered her into the sandpit next to Jules. The little girl flung sand in an ecstasy of excitement.

'Woah! Calm yourself, Cal.' Jules shielded her eyes.

'Abandon ship!' Summie bounded to the patio. He swung a plastic chair next to Andy and dropped into it. 'Friday at bloody last! Your week been busy?'

'God yeah. Non-stop.'

'Don't know how you do it.'

'It's tough.'

Jules had been right — despite his initial reluctance, Summie had come round. There was a familiar easiness between them now. They were mates again. But no matter how welcome Andy felt, he didn't like imposing on his friends. It had been over a month since he'd turned up on their doorstep. He'd thanked them so often that Jules had threatened to throw him out if she heard another word of gratitude. He was still waiting, after endless form filling and two interviews at Centrelink, for a benefit payment.

The day was cooling off. Late afternoon shadows draped across the grass. Magpies hopped at the back of the garden where scrub huddled against the fence. The hum of end-of-week suburban noises — kids calling and laughing, the splash of bodies in a swimming pool, cars pulling in and out of driveways — fluttered around them like a soft quilt.

In the sandpit, Jules sang, 'Row, row, row your boat, gently down the stream,' with actions that Callie tried to copy.

Summie got himself a beer, slightly bemused, as ever, by Andy's polite refusal. He slumped in his chair with his legs stretched straight out and took a long draught, then frowned towards the back of the garden. 'That branch on the gum — see, up there?' He lifted his glass of beer to indicate. 'Isn't it a bit black? Could be dangerous, couldn't it? I heard they can fall off, just like that, those branches. No warning.' He snapped his fingers. 'You're a country boy Andy, what do you reckon?'

Andy peered at the gum. He didn't know anything about lemon gums. They didn't grow where he came from. It was too dry there. 'Hard to tell,' he said. 'I'd get a tree surgeon to check it out, if I was you. Just to be on the safe side.'

Summie nodded. 'You're right. Good thinking. I'll call someone tomorrow.' He slugged at his beer and surveyed his garden. 'Listen,' he said without looking at Andy. 'I'm sorry if I was a bit, you know, before …'

'No Summie, I don't blame you at all. You're a bloody star for putting up with me for so long.'

Summie waved a hand in the air. 'Aw, not a problem. Stay as long as you like.' He glanced over at the sandpit, leaned in towards Andy and lowered his voice. 'To tell the truth, it's done Jules good having you around. Think she was starting to get a bit stir crazy being alone so much with Callie.' He paused. 'And — she say anything about her brother?'

'Her brother? No, I don't think so.'

'Nasty story. Od'd. Smack. Only eighteen. No-one found him for days. She's got a soft spot for hopeless cases because of him.' Summie paused and slapped Andy's thigh. 'Like you, eh?' He tipped his head back and laughed. 'Seriously though,' Summie said when he'd stopped laughing. 'I'm glad you turned up, Andy. I was a bit surprised at first. But now I'm really glad you came.'

A good feeling trickled through Andy, as though he'd downed a double shot of whisky.

Merrily merrily merrily merrily life is but a dream.

Row row row your boat …

That night, when the house was quiet, Andy sat up in his bed and eased open the drawer of the bedside cabinet. He took out the bundle of letters, pulled off the elastic band and flicked through them. He noticed the Marrup postmarks and could make out most of the postal dates. Years had passed since his mother had sent some of these. Years.

He closed the drawer and picked up the John Le Carré book.

He wasn't ready to read the letters. He couldn't. Not yet.

8 RUBBISH

His flight was still more than two weeks away. Dom flicked through the pages of his diary and wondered how he would get through so many days here. He saw he should have been meeting Carole, a friend he used to work with, that night at the South Bank to see the new David Hare play and felt guilty, imagining her standing there, checking her watch, trying his dead mobile. He would have to send her a nice card to apologise when he got back.

It was disorientating, thinking about his London life from this distance, in this place. He imagined himself moving around in the course of his days; work, home, meeting friends for dinner or a movie, an exhibition on the weekend. Sitting at the kitchen table with the Saturday Guardian and a pot of coffee. It was like life on another planet, compared to here. A comfortable life.

He dropped the diary back into his open suitcase and went outside. Flies were congregating around the smelly bag of rubbish he'd left at the end of the verandah that morning. An animal of some sort — a rat, or maybe a fox — had got into the bag, made a jagged hole where rubbish had spilled out. He hadn't heard anything.

Holding his breath, he lowered the damaged bag into a fresh one, creating a small storm of flies. A few alighted on his face and he shook his head and blew air out of the corners of his mouth to get rid of them. He used a dustpan and brush to clear up the mess that was left on the verandah.

Where had the rubbish hole been? He paced down to the back of the house with the bag and scanned the empty paddocks. He tried the wooden gate at the end of the path leading from the back door, but the catch was broken and the gate was secured to the post with a thick piece of twine. Clutching the bag, he stepped over a pile of tangled wire between two collapsed fence posts and set off towards a lone clump of mallee trees. He wore a baseball cap he'd picked up from the General Store, a grey thing already faded when he bought it.

The day was the same as the one before it — quiet and still. He marched over the red earth, hard under a thin layer of powdery dust, scattered with tufty bunches of pale grass. He felt oddly anxious being out on the open land, conspicuous and exposed. Halfway across the paddock he turned his head as if to make sure there was nobody there, though he knew he was alone. Behind him the house sat, ramshackle and sad.

He wondered if it had been the Big House that had inspired his idea of becoming an architect. Not that it mattered now; his dream was so faded he hardly recognised it. After his first degree in Perth he had stopped studying, when he could have carried on to become properly qualified. An architect. A creator of structures that would last, spaces that people would use, long after he was gone. He'd panicked, lost his focus, unable to tell if the life he was living — and heading for — was what he wanted. It seemed to Dom, grinding through his own ordinary days of essays and lectures, coming back to his tiny campus room, that his best friend Andy lived a far freer, more exciting and worthwhile life.

While he thought about what to do, he took a minor job with Bayswater Council. After two years he'd saved a bit of money and made a decision. He wanted something different, needed to do things his own way. He set his horizons wider.

Dom noticed a movement on the ground and stopped still. Only feet away a brown snake navigated, silent and unhurried, through its territory. He watched the creature's effortless movement, fascinated, and had an urge to stroke it, run his hand along its glistening skin. He'd done that once, as a kid. His dad killed a snake near the shearing shed and Neal brought it to the house to show him. His brother held the snake up next to him, its head in line with Dom's, its tail reaching his feet. They laughed because it was exactly as long as he was. Its body had felt firm and cool when he touched it.

Now the brown snake moved out of sight and Dom carried on towards the trees, lugging the bag of rubbish.

London had been a shock at first, the chaos of it, the cost of everything. He struggled, working in a warehouse packing videos into boxes during the week, in a bar on weekends. It wasn't much of a life, but he had no desire to return. What did he have to go back to? Besides, there were the buildings; old, ornate, full of history or new and fascinating, like nothing he'd ever seen. What little money he managed to save he spent on short trips to Europe — Amsterdam, Barcelona, Vienna, Paris. He stayed in cheap hostels and revelled in the architecture, the busy variety of these new places.

Finally he landed a job at the planning department of Islington Council. He was so relieved to be released from the purgatory of the warehouse and the bar that he worked with ferocious enthusiasm. He moved up the ranks fast. But he wasn't an architect. He wasn't that.

By the time he reached the mallees he was hot and sweating. The bag felt heavy. He put it down and squatted in the shade, as though he was hiding, looking back at the Big House. A waft of stinking rubbish overpowered the rich smell of earth and bark, and he moved further away from the bag.

Eight years. He had always been too busy to make the trip home, found other things to spend his money on. There was never a right time. He picked up a twig and brushed the dirt with it. Why had he stayed away so long? He wondered if he might have put off returning because he felt a failure, could not present himself to his mum as a success, as the person he felt he should have become. He'd never considered the possibility before.

He stood up and walked around to the other side of the trees, surveying the paddocks around him. There was nothing that looked like a rubbish hole — only an endless expanse of flat ground spread thinly with scrubby grass, interrupted occasionally by wire fences. For a moment he thought about leaving the bag of rubbish out there, under the trees, but dismissed the idea. It didn't seem right.

Flies scattered when he picked up the bag. He trudged back towards the house.

He'd invited his mum to London once, when he bought the flat, even offered to pay for her flight. She laughed off the idea as though he'd suggested a trip to Mars. Perhaps she was happier not to know the details of his life, to let go of responsibility for him, in a way. And, he admitted, it was probably the same for him.

He never asked her to visit again, but they spoke on the phone a few times a year, on birthdays and at Christmas. He wrote too. All the time when he first left, every week at least. Then less often as e-mail took over from letters. His mum never had a computer.

For a few moments he put the bag on the ground and rested, shaking his arm to get the circulation going again before trudging on. He remembered that he'd even written to Neal for a while — made an effort, tried to do the right thing. It was a chance to forge a new link with his brother. To start again. The notes he wrote were simple and friendly, asking how Neal was, about the farm. He tried postcards too. He never had a reply. Nothing. Neal ignored his overtures, remained belligerently silent, and Dom gave up.

What more could he have done?

A sudden change in the ground caught Dom by surprise and he lost his footing, felt himself let go of the bag as he lurched and sprawled. Spitting dust from his mouth, he sat up and brushed at his clothes, settled the cap back on his head. Around him the ground was spongy and insubstantial; his foot had sunk into the earth.

He eased his foot out. The thin, rusted metal of a tin can was visible and a corner of white — a plastic bag. He'd found the old rubbish hole.

He got up and tested his weight on his foot. It didn't hurt. He picked up the bag of rubbish and studied the ground around him, trying to gauge a safe path, but there was no way of telling. The hole had been perfectly disguised.

With cautious steps he walked back to the house and dumped the bag in the corner of the old garden. He didn't know what else to do with it.

9 DEBRIS

Hester found the mauve toilet bag squashed at the back of the bathroom cupboard, behind spare rolls of toilet paper, a bag of cotton wool and half a dozen cakes of cheap pink soap.

Squatting on the bathroom floor, she pulled the bag out, unzipped it and looked inside. There were two bottles of nail polish, one a vibrant pink, the other a deep red. When she dug her hand in and rifled through the bag, the bottles of polish clunked against the other make-up — a thin stick of black eye liner, a tube of lipstick, a bottle of foundation and a small powder compact. Debris from her past life. She sat down on the cool cement floor. She didn't know why she had kept all this stuff. She hadn't touched any of it in six years, had almost forgotten it existed.

The compact clicked neatly open. The powder inside was worn away in the middle, its edges rising. In the small magnifying mirror she looked at her face, the fine lines around her eyes, the pale down above her lip. She closed the compact, dropped it back into the toilet bag and picked out the red nail polish. She pushed the toilet bag to the back of the cupboard again.

That night, Neal put the boys to bed while she washed the dishes. She heard them messing around, the boys squealing as their dad tickled them. They'd be hyped-up and take longer to settle. She might have to read them two stories. Reading was the one thing Neal refused to do with them. The boys used to pester him about it, but now they didn't bother asking.

He came into the kitchen and stoked the fire as she was finishing the dishes. She told him she would go and read to the boys.

They must have been tired; even with Neal's bedtime play they fell asleep before the end of the first story. She crept out of the room without even kissing them goodnight, in case she woke them, and hurried down the corridor to get the bottle of nail polish from her underwear drawer where she'd hidden it.

In the bathroom, she filled the sink with warm water and washed her feet. She rubbed moisturiser into her cracked heels and trimmed her toenails. The lid of the polish was stuck tight and she struggled to get it open. When it finally twisted loose, scraps of dried colour cracked off from around the lid, leaving bright red flecks on the washbasin and the floor. She cleaned it up, then applied the polish with careful, upward strokes of the tiny black brush, holding her breath against the sharp, astringent smell. While the polish dried, she sat on the toilet seat, looking at her toes. They glittered when she turned them to the light.

Back in the bedroom, she pushed the bottle under a pile of underwear. She paused and began searching the drawer for a pair of knickers with lace around the edge and a white bra which she rarely wore because it was cut too low. She found them and changed quickly, putting her normal clothes back on over the fresh underwear.

The colour on her toes flashed as she trod barefoot down the hallway, smiling to herself, happy with her plan. She wanted to make Neal feel better, to show him they had something good together, remind him that, while the farm might not be doing well, they still had each other.

To give her lips colour, she pulled at them with her teeth.

She opened the door to the kitchen.

Neal was in his chair, legs extended, ankles crossed. His eyes were closed. Even in sleep, his face somehow looked fixed and stern. She hovered in the doorway for a few seconds before turning to go back; already she had lost her nerve. She began to worry about how to get the nail polish off and wondered if kero would do it.

After only a few steps she heard his voice.

'Hes?'

She stopped, held her breath, let it out. It would be alright. She went back and stood in front of him. She smiled. 'You fell asleep.'

'Hmm.' He yawned and propped himself up straight in the chair. She moved forward, lowered herself onto his lap, leaned against his warm body.

She undid the buttons of her shirt, in a deliberate, lingering way, took Neal's hand and placed it under the soft material of her bra, his rough fingers splaying out across her skin. She slid his hand down across her belly to rest between her legs.

'What's that?'

He was looking at her feet. She brought one foot up to rest flat on her other thigh, creating an arch.

She tilted her head, a little coquettish. 'I wanted to look nice for you. You've been working so hard, you deserve —'

He stood up, pushing her off him so that she tumbled to the floor in an awkward heap. She eased herself up and sat back on her heels, her head lowered.

He was standing over her, looking down, breathing fast. 'Where did you get it?'

'The nail polish? I found it, in the bathroom. It's been there for years. I just thought … I wanted to …'

He stood unmoving for a few seconds before stomping to the sink. She heard a glass filling, Neal drinking. The crack of the glass being put down, too hard. He thumped towards her. Her body tensed and quivered with fear but he didn't stop. The uneven fall of his footsteps receded. The bedroom door opened, closed. She pulled her unbuttoned shirt around her and stayed where she was until the tops of her feet, pressed onto the floor, began to hurt.

Easing herself up, she stretched her ankles, letting the blood flow back to her feet. She looked through the kitchen drawer and found the knife she wanted, the one with the wooden handle and the sharp, thin blade that she used for testing cakes to see if they were ready. In the harsh fluorescent light, she sat with her foot propped on the edge of a chair and scraped the bright colour off her nails.

10 NEVER LOOK BACK!

The day Andy's first Newstart payment finally came through, he took the bus to the shopping centre in Morley. In Target, he bought himself a pair of trainers, a T-shirt and a pair of jeans. The shop assistant cut off the tags and let him go back into the changing rooms. He bought a plastic bag to carry Summie's cast-offs that he'd been wearing.

On the way back, he got off the bus near a small Italian café with tables on the footpath, shaded by a striped awning. Inglewood had a café strip now — in just a few years the place had gone from nondescript to trendy. He sat outside sipping an espresso, watching people pass by: men in suits, a woman carrying a bunch of flowers, a bloke with tied-back dreadlocks pushing a child in a four-wheel drive of a pusher. A couple sat at the table next to him, chatting.

He felt good sitting there on a warm day amongst people going about their lives, with a bit of money in his pocket. He wasn't desperate to be onto the next thing, didn't crave anything else. He was happy to be right where he was. He signalled to the waiter for another coffee.

After his second coffee he paid and strolled down the street. He was close enough to walk the rest of the way back to the house. On the way, he looked in at the shop windows; handmade jewellery, a surf shop, music and health food. At a deli he stopped and bought a tub of plump stuffed olives as a treat for Jules and Summie.

Towards the end of the street he came to a book shop with a big window display of fiction, cookery and children's books

— he liked one with a picture of a pig with floppy ears on the front. In the far corner of the window a book with a shiny silver cover and purple lettering caught his eye.

Never Look Back! the title shouted, *Number 1 Bestseller!* He moved closer. The subtitle read: *How To Be Happy In The Here And Now — Guaranteed!*

'Yeah, right,' he smirked.

Inside, the shop was cool and hushed. He browsed through the kids' section, marvelling at the variety of books on offer. He remembered his mum reading to him from a book of fairytales, when he was little. Little Red Riding Hood, Jack and the Beanstalk, Hansel and Gretel. Strange and unsettling stories that had made him glad his sister was sleeping in the same room. Maybe there'd been other books but he didn't remember them. His parents were never big on reading.

He considered getting a book of fairytales for Callie, but in the end chose the book with the cute pig he'd seen in the window.

Another customer, a grey-haired woman with glasses, nodded at him and smiled as they passed each other in the quiet shop. He found himself in front of a section headed 'Self Help/Personal Awareness' with *Never Look Back!* as the main display. He glanced through some of the other titles: *Drive Your Own Life Train; Spirit Guides And How to Find Them; 10 Easy Steps To Inner Peace (Free CD).* Andy picked up a copy of *Never Look Back!* by Dr. Joanne B. Philmore, MBBS MRCPsych, MA, and flicked through it. He looked at the price on the back and counted how much money he had left. He weighed the book in his hand. It was about the same price as a bag of smack and could hardly do him as much harm. He headed for the till.

That night, Jules and Summie savoured their olives with cold cans of beer and Callie cooed with delight over the pig book. Andy stayed up until three in the morning reading *Never Look Back!*

He couldn't put the book down. It was trite and ridiculous and full of so many sentences that ended in exclamation marks it made him feel out of breath. *No-one can live your life but you! ... Self-belief is the fire that drives your soul, you must never allow it to go out! ... Now means now — not tomorrow or next week — NOW!*

Yet he was compelled to read on. It was outrageous and stupid and he should have hated it, but he didn't. He loved it. And at the end he felt better; a light, easy feeling had come over him. He closed the book and placed his hands on its glittering cover. A car on a nearby street revved its engine. The clock on his bedside table brrred quietly. Thousands of people all over the world must have got their lives into a total fucking mess like he had, if this book was a bestseller. And not only this book — there was a whole section of books devoted to helping people sort their lives out! He felt reassured, legitimate — it was okay to be a hopeless case. It might not have been the greatest club to be part of, but the knowledge made him feel connected to the world somehow, linked to others. Human.

He knew that when he left here, moved away from the comfort and security of his friends, he had found something to help him feel less alone.

He put the book on the bedside cabinet, turned off the light and fell asleep smiling.

Andy went back to the bookshop the next day. He spent an hour in the Self Help section looking at the titles and flicking through the books. It was a deep disappointment to him that he could not afford them. He would have to wait nearly a fortnight until his next payment, before he could choose a new one. The idea of slipping a book or two into his backpack came to him, but he quickly banished it.

He scuffed up a side street to a cavernous Salvation Army Op Shop Jules had told him about and flipped through the racks of out-of-shape T-shirts, discarded shorts and oddly sized trousers. The place gave off a musty smell. He was about to leave when he noticed the books in a back corner of the shop.

Westerns spilled out of plastic washing baskets next to shelves of thin romances. Stacks of sci-fi novels and cookery books were piled on the floor. A slip of paper on a low shelf, held in place with yellowing sticky tape, said 'Self Help' in faded handwriting. He squatted down and scanned the titles: *Reading Rainbow Auras; Banish Bingeing; Love, Money, Happiness — How To Get It All AND Keep It!*

The dusty paperbacks from the 1970s with oddly stained covers were priced at ten cents, recent hardbacks no more than a couple of dollars. He felt like he'd discovered treasure.

Taking buses as far as Subi and Freo, he scoured the Op Shops, bringing back bags full of dusty titles which he stacked against the walls of the spare room. His book collection grew. Summie joked that he didn't have planning permission to open a bookshop.

Andy had an enthusiasm for life, sober and drug free, he hadn't come close to since he was a teenager. When he wasn't searching for books or reading them, he was happy helping Jules in the house, playing with Callie, or sitting quietly in the garden, letting his thoughts wander.

But his friends' hospitality was a burden to him. It was getting towards the end of November — he'd been with them for over six weeks. It would be Christmas soon. He felt guilty, and he wanted to move on, get going properly on his new life. The problem was, he had nowhere else to go. He studied *The West Australian* and shop windows for rooms to rent, but they all specified professional, or at least working, people. He searched for jobs too, but he had no qualifications, no tidy CV. His last legitimate job, working as a bed salesman, was years ago, and he'd screwed that up. He would never get a reference. He knew he was not physically capable of doing any of the jobs he might conceivably get — digging, lifting, labouring. Driving work was out too. He'd lost his licence years back, driving drunk, then been caught behind the wheel again. Twice. He wondered why he hadn't gone to jail. Or maybe he had.

He might eventually go and study, get a degree or something, but he wasn't ready for that. He didn't have the confidence yet. When he'd left school he hadn't even considered studying — he was too excited by the prospect of all the life to be lived, the fun to be had. It was Dom, his best mate from home, who did the sensible thing and went on to university. Dom. It was a long time since they'd been in touch. He missed his old friend.

When Jules came in from collecting the post, Andy was sitting at the kitchen table glancing through *Potential And Possibility; Unlock Your Inner Winner!*

Callie sat in her high chair, sucking from her cup and banging a plastic spoon on the tray. 'Addie,' she said. 'Addie, Addie, Addie.'

He smiled at her.

Jules tilted her head to read the title of his book. '*Your Inner Winner*? Jeez. Sounds like an ABBA song.'

Andy lay the book face down on the table. 'Yeah, it was. Don't you remember? *Inn-er Winn-er, here we go again, my my, da da da da da da.*' Andy sang and moved his head in time to an Abba beat.

Callie jiggled in her high chair. Jules smiled and shook her head as she flicked through the post. 'Hey, Andy. There's one for you.' She stood with the letter in her hand for a moment before passing it to him. It was another thin, white envelope. A shock of recognition jolted him.

Jules took a container from the fridge and spooned the contents into a plastic bowl with a pattern of teddies around the rim. 'From your mum?'

'Looks like it.'

She nodded and left him a space to speak, but he was silent.

He tucked the letter inside his book. 'I can feed her, if you like.'

'Okay. Thanks. I'll put the washing out.' She paused and looked at him. She blinked a few times. 'I don't know how we'll manage without you, Andy.'

That evening, instead of reading a book, Andy took out the letters from his mother.

It was time.

He started with what seemed, from the blurred post-mark, to be the earliest letter. It was short — a plea for him to get in touch and to keep safe. He would, she said, always be her son, no matter what. The others were more newsy and rambling, like diary entries, with mention of the drought, the salinity, his sister's second baby, his dad's bad back.

The last letter, the letter that had come that day, the ink still fresh, the glue on the envelope barely set, was the one that finally made him cry.

Dear Andy

It's been a long time I know, but I hope and believe that you are safe and well and will get this letter one day.

Things are changing here again. Marjorie Connor died. You know, Dom and Neal's Mum. She was my best friend I suppose. We knew each other for fifty years. Dom has come over from London. I haven't seen him yet.

It's still dry here. People are leaving the place like rats off a sinking ship. The Carmodys went in July, the Scotts not long after. Just left everything. Poor Bill McSwain did himself in a while back. Too old to change, to go anywhere else. Massive debts, I heard.

One of these days me and your dad will go too, decamp to our little place by the sea, near Gillian. Not just yet, but soon. I'll miss the farm. And the town — well, I miss that already. It's not what it used to be. Gillian is pregnant again, by the way. Her and Gary are well, and the two kids.

Please get in touch Andy. Come and see us. Don't let all this doom and gloom put you off. I miss my only boy very much. You know you will ALWAYS be welcome. Don't worry about Dad — it was a long time ago now.

From your loving Mum.

Andy leant back against the pillows and ran a hand over his chest, feeling the ridges of his sturdy, healed ribs.

This was what he had been waiting for.

It was late, but he began to sort his meagre possessions. He picked out a few choice books from his collection to take with him. The rest he stacked neatly against the wall and under the bed — he was sure Summie and Jules wouldn't mind hanging onto them for him.

He knew what he had to do.

It was time to go back.

11 Dead or Alive

Dom got up early the next morning, when the birds woke him. He made himself a strong coffee and started sorting through his mum's things. He rifled through packed cupboards and emptied drawers bursting with neatly ordered receipts, ancient clothes patterns, minutes of CWA meetings and yellowing ledger books, creating an unruly sea of paper on the lounge floor.

He made a space amongst it all, the accumulated detritus of his mother's life, and sat down. Did any of this mean anything now she was gone?

He flicked through a ledger book from 1982. She'd been careful, frugal, had liked to keep things in order. It was a good way to be — if he'd been more like that, he might not be in the financial mess he was in now. She had wanted to make sure she did the best for her children; that was what it was all for.

He picked up a blue ring binder marked 'Salads' in his mum's neat, faded printing. Some of the recipes cut from magazines and taped to A4 sheets of paper were still crisp and clean, others well-thumbed and grubby. The Curried Rice Salad recipe from the *Women's Weekly* was dotted with greasy, translucent flecks. He was sure it gave off a faint smell of curry powder. Had she made it recently? The bright yellow mass full of raisins had been her exotic dish. People had liked it.

He closed the recipe file.

It hadn't been a bad life, had it? She had brought up one son who took over the farm, another who achieved something — apparently — out in the world. She had friends. Was she lonely? His dad died so young. Neal was around of course, then the grandkids. But had Neal looked after her? Was he good to her?

He stood up and stretched his arms in the air. In the kitchen, he rinsed out his mug and put the kettle on for another coffee. He took the milk out of the fridge. The carton was nearly empty — he would have to go to the Store later. He stood waiting for the kettle to boil. His mum must have been worried about the future of the farm, but she'd never said anything to him. Not that he remembered.

One side of the tall cupboard with the smooth wooden doors was filled with more dusty-smelling paperwork. On the other side he found neat bundles of letters, stored in plastic bags. He spent an hour going through them, but apart from the odd dull missive from distant relatives over East, the letters all seemed to be from him. Like a punishment, he made himself read pages of the inadequate, superficial rubbish he'd sent her over the years.

On the shelves above the letters were half a dozen photo albums. It was the place the photos had always been kept. He pulled an album from the pile and took it, with his coffee, to a clear patch of floor by the window. Sitting cross-legged with the album in his lap, he opened it randomly. The first photo he saw made him smile — a slightly overexposed shot of him and Andy standing in front of the Big House, next to the dirt bike Andy's dad had built for him. They had their arms around each other's shoulders, grinning. Andy's hair was tousled with pale, sun-bleached streaks. Dom had a straight-across fringe. His mum must have taken the photo. Or Neal — could it have been Neal? He sipped his coffee and stared at the photo. It was Andy's birthday. He had brought the bike over to show Dom and afterwards they took turns on it around the dirt track at the back of Andy's farm. They egged each other on to go faster, try more treacherous jumps and corners, until Andy came a cropper. He lay still while Dom ran over, swearing and panicked, then laughed as soon as Dom touched him. But when Andy tried to stand up he collapsed; he really had hurt his ankle. Dom wheeled the bike back to Andy's house with his friend hopping next to him, a hand on his shoulder for balance. It was a bad sprain. Mrs Bohan had strapped it up.

Dom pulled back the plastic film, carefully picked the photo out of the album and slid it into an old envelope. He had an urge to show it to someone, to talk about those days. The first person he thought of was Hester, but he didn't want to make a nuisance of himself. He would see her tomorrow, anyway; she was putting on a little birthday party for Billy, and going to Dog Rock afterwards. Billy's request. Neal did not look happy the other night, when Billy begged his Uncle Dom to come.

He surveyed the mess around him and puffed a lungful of air through his lips. He couldn't go through all this right now. He couldn't stay here on his own all day either. A jittery anxiety tingled around his body. Too much cheap coffee.

He pushed the envelope with the photo of him and Andy into his shirt pocket. Why not go up to the Bohans' place? Colin had invited him, even after what had happened to the poor dog. He still felt terrible about that. The right thing to do would be to apologise properly. He could get Andy's phone number too, give him a call later and arrange to meet up in Perth.

But first, he had to get one thing over with.

The 1950s dressing table in his mother's bedroom was dominated by a large, adjustable mirror, tilted slightly back. An open bag of cotton wool lay next to a bottle of antiseptic. Wiry grey hairs sprouted from the teeth of a comb and a cut-glass jewellery box sat, not quite centred, on a hand-crocheted doily. The smell of antiseptic tinged the clinging, fusty odour of the room. Dom felt sick. Was it in here it had happened? Did she have the stroke while she was in bed or later, while putting on her shoes, or cooking her tea? Something else to ask Neal, if his brother would ever speak to him.

A jumble of bits and pieces filled the jewellery box; hair clips, a pair of silver cufflinks, old make-up. Dom fished out a tube of lipstick, pulled off its top and twisted the tube until a waxy, red stub peeked out, rounded and smooth. He caught his reflection in the dresser mirror and dropped the lipstick back, like a startled thief.

The top drawer was packed with neat, colourless underwear. Without opening the other drawers, he slunk over to the wardrobe, past the bed with its worn candlewick bedspread pulled up roughly on one side.

When he yanked open the double doors of the wardrobe, a loose line of hanging clothes swayed lightly, like dancers at the end of a long night. He ran his hand along them, feeling the brush of fabrics on his fingers; rough cotton, gritty nylon and, at the end, something smooth and silky. He bunched the cool material in his hand and let it go.

He stood on the dresser stool to look on the shelf at the top of the wardrobe, pushed aside linen, old blankets, a patchwork quilt. There was a biscuit-tin full of buttons and a bag of material scraps. A shoebox. He tried to pick up the shoebox with one hand, as though it might contain leftover thread or old zips, but it was heavy. He needed both hands to lift it.

He put the box on the dresser. His fingers left prints in the film of dust on the lid. His nose itched and he rubbed at it with his arm.

The jewellery flashed at him when he lifted the lid, bright stones and gold on a bed of deep red velvet. He stared, not daring to touch, alarmed at first by such unexpected glories.

He took the box into the kitchen and opened it again on the table.

The jewellery lay solid and stark on the layers of roughly cut red velvet. He explored his haul slowly; necklaces set with tiny clear stones, some with red jewels, others that he took to be pearls. Delicate earrings, bracelets and brooches, often matching sets. Was this stuff real? He didn't know much about jewellery, but it looked authentic to him. Where had it come from? His mother had seemed such a plain, even austere person — it was difficult to associate her with this stunning treasure.

He weighed a jewel encrusted necklace in his hand. This was meant for him. His mum would not have left him empty-handed. She'd made sure he had his share. It must be worth a small fortune, he thought.

He fitted the lid back on the box with care, gulped a drink of water and found the car keys.

The Bohan farm was a few kilometres away, off the main road towards Marrup. It was a route Dom remembered well.

In front of the house a tiny section of garden clung to life. A dark green climber festooned one side of the verandah. The blades of a windmill between the house and the shed shifted smoothly, though he couldn't feel any wind, and flashed when they caught the sun.

As Dom climbed out of the car, the screen door opened and a rounded woman with short grey hair came out onto the verandah, wiping her hands on her apron.

'Mrs Bohan? Hi. Hope you're not too busy, I — it's Dominic.'

'I know who it bloody is, Dom. My sight's not that far gone! I'd know you anywhere. And please, it's Lizzie.' Dom smiled shyly, as though he were fifteen again and being questioned about who he was taking to the school social.

'I'm sorry, Lizzie, about ... at the garage. I must have been jet-lagged, I didn't even see the poor thing.'

'You mean the dog? Oh, Dom, don't worry about it. She was a crotchety old thing anyway. Useless. Come in, come in, I've just made scones.'

He trod up the verandah steps with the shoebox tucked under one arm.

'It's good to see you, Dom.' Her face was comfortingly familiar despite the scrunch and sag of her wrinkles. She opened her arms and pulled him to her. 'So sorry about your mum.'

He gripped the box under one arm and curved his other arm around her back lightly. Uncomfortable with this intimacy, he patted the warm cotton of her dress a couple of times. She smelt of baking and soap.

Inside, she put the kettle on the gas stove and rinsed out the teapot. Dom set the shoebox on the table.

'Have a seat, Dom.'

It was the same wooden table he'd sat at twenty years ago, the same hard-seated chairs, though now they were padded with square, flattened cushions.

Mrs Bohan bustled about making tea. 'When did you get here?'

'It must be about five days ago, I think. Yes. Thursday night. Too late for the funeral, unfortunately.'

'It was nice. Big turn out. Everyone in their finest.' She slid a cup, with a saucer and a teaspoon, in front of Dom. She paused and looked at the shoebox, then at him. 'What, you've bought me a pair of shoes? Is that an English custom or something?'

He smiled. 'No, it's — I wanted to ask you about it. I found it this morning.'

'Ask away.' She rested a fist, trailing a tea-towel, on one round hip.

'Okay.' Dom pulled the box to him, eased off the tape and lifted the lid.

'Ah! Well. Haven't seen this for a while. God, look at it. It's bloody beautiful.' She held up a diamond-studded necklace, let it dangle and glitter.

'You knew Mum had it?'

'Oh, yes,' she smiled. 'We used to pick out a piece or two to wear to dances at Marrup Hall, in the old days. Said she didn't like to be the only one in the place pretending to be posh. Thought we were the bee's bloody knees. She snared your dad at one of those dances, you know. A new face, all the way from over East, for the shearing.' She peeled back a couple of layers of velvet. 'Oh, this brooch! She wore it with that red taffeta dress.'

'I don't remember her ever wearing any of this.'

'Well, you wouldn't,' she said. 'We both practically stopped going out once you kids came along. And then the dances finished anyway. Don't really know why. Just went out of fashion I suppose.'

'So it's genuine? I mean, this is gold, these are real diamonds?'

'They're real alright, Dom. Fair and square. Came from — wait a minute.' She bunched her lips, thinking. 'Your Great-Grandmother. On your mum's side. Yes. That's it. You know, the rich, adventurous Germans. She didn't tell you about it?'

'I knew about the Germans, but not the jewellery. I wonder why she kept it in a shoebox? And in the wardrobe of all places.'

'Oh, she would have had her reasons. Anyway, you know our generation; we like to do things our own way.' She patted him on the shoulder.

'You should keep something, Lizzie.'

'No. God, no. Thanks, but this is an heirloom Dom. It's yours. For your family.'

Lizzie made tea and put a dish of butter, shiny from the heat, on the table, with a small china bowl of apricot jam and a plate of steaming scones.

She sat down, rested her chin on her lumpy knuckles and smiled at him. 'Well, look at you. You've done well for yourself, my boy. You made your mum so happy. She mentioned you a lot. Talked about how hard you worked over there, how you'd bought your own place. Your travels.'

Dom tried to smile and averted his eyes, which she might have taken as modesty. He buttered another scone. 'These are perfect, Lizzie. Never found scones as good as yours anywhere. Nice to know some things don't change.'

She smiled a weary smile and shook her head. She clutched her cup with both worn hands. 'Lots of things have changed, but, Dom. Too right. A lot has changed. Not least your wonderful mother passing away, God rest her.' She was quiet for a few seconds.

He could hear the lightly laboured whistle of her breath.

'I'll bloody miss her. We were friends for a long time you know. But maybe it's best she won't be around to see this place finally give up the ghost.'

Dom put down the scone he was eating and licked sweet jam from his lips. 'It's that bad?'

'Dead as a bloody dodo, I'm afraid. There's nothing more to be done. It was never meant to be farmed round here, the way it has been. The land can't cope anymore. Salt's taken

98

hold. Then there's the drought. Government's propped things up over the years, tried out schemes here and there, but it's too late. We're alright, me and Colin. Bought a little place years back near Gillian, up the coast at Malyburn. Got a bit put by from before, when things were good. But lots of people have been left with nothing. Or worse.' She paused. 'Neal's managed to keep your place going, so far. He's a damn good farmer, but I don't know if …' She shrugged and shook her head.

The scone felt gluey in Dom's mouth. He gulped his tea to wash it down. 'I haven't got a clue what's going on.'

Lizzie patted Dom's hand with her own warm, rough one. 'It's been hard for your brother. Remember that, Dom.' She stared down into her cup and seemed about to say more. The house was quiet. Lizzie lifted her head, as if she had come up for air, and smiled at Dom. 'Anyway, what about you? Life's good in the Old Country, eh? Not married yet?'

'No. Not yet.' He wanted to unburden himself, tell the truth about his hopeless relationships, his boring job, the financial mess, to admit he was a failure, a fraud. But he couldn't. How could he explain? It was not the time, and too much to expect of her. Instead he changed the subject. 'While I remember, Lizzie, I wonder if I could get Andy's phone number off you? I wouldn't want to miss the chance to see him while I'm here.'

He pulled the envelope from his shirt pocket, took out the photo and handed it to her. 'Look, I found this while I was going through Mum's stuff. Don't know if you've seen it before.'

She peered at the photo, pulled it away from her face, then scraped back her chair and went to get her glasses from a shelf in the corner. She sat back down, perched the glasses on her nose and turned her attention to the photo. She stared and stared, without saying anything.

Dom shifted in his seat. 'It's the day he got the bike Mr Bohan built for him — his birthday. We had a brilliant time with that bike. Do you remember we took it to the track up the back and Andy —' He stopped, aghast, when he realised Lizzie was crying.

She pulled off her glasses and wiped her face with the back of her hand. 'Oh dear. Sorry Dom. Sorry.'

He shook his head, not knowing what to say.

She fished out a tissue from a pocket and patted her eyes. 'It's a while since you've seen Andy, isn't it?'

'Eight years I've been gone. We wrote for ages, but it sort of fizzled out somehow.'

She dragged a breath in and huffed it out again. 'Look Dom, I wasn't sure if you already knew, but it seems like you don't. So I'll tell you now, before Col gets back. Andy ... he's had a lot of problems. We don't know where he is. Haven't seen or heard of him in four years. Last we knew he was in Perth.' She took a sip of her tea. 'Andy got into drugs. Heroin. We tried to help him. Managed to track him down, in the city, and get him into detox, brought him back here afterwards. A few times. The last time he stayed two days, then nicked off in the middle of the night with his dad's wallet. Haven't seen him since. Colin refused to try again after that. Says he's washed his hands of him for good. I could never feel like that. He's my son.' She looked so weary, so elderly, all of a sudden. So sad.

Dom did not know what to say. Andy a junkie? The idea wouldn't stick — it seemed strange and wrong. He realised how much he had been looking forward to seeing his old friend. He rubbed his hand across the back of his head.

The tick tick tick of a trail bike sounded outside.

Lizzie pushed the photo back to Dom. 'Put it away,' she whispered.

He slipped the photo back into the envelope and into his pocket. He heard the scuffle of boots being taken off on the verandah and Colin Bohan came into the kitchen.

'Dominic. We meet again.' He shook Dom's hand.

'Hi, Mr Bohan. How are you?'

'Can't complain. I leave that to Lizzie. She's better at it than me.'

'Ha bloody ha.' Lizzie got up to put the kettle on again. Colin Bohan eased himself into a chair and took a scone, slavering it with butter and jam.

'I wanted to say how sorry I am about the dog. If there's anything I can do, anything at all, just —'

The older man held up a palm. 'Accidents happen, Dom. Forget it.'

They talked for a while. Colin Bohan asked Dom where he'd got his hire car from and how many miles it did to the gallon — though the country had worked in kilometres and litres for over thirty years. They discussed Dom's job, and the cost of living in London. He offered to take Dom for a ride around the farm on the motorbike, later in the week. There was still a bit of decent bush he said, down the back paddock. It was nice at dusk, when the roos came out. He'd learnt to accept the feed-munching buggers more as he got older.

Before he went back to the Big House, Dom drove into Marrup. He needed milk and breakfast cereal and something to eat that night. He wanted some beer.

As he drove he looked at the bare paddocks and slack-wired fences. He tried to concentrate on what Lizzie had said about the farm, about the whole place being finished but, instead, kept coming back to the picture of her sad face, wondering if her son was dead or alive.

Andy was his oldest friend — Dom had few memories of his childhood and teenage years that didn't feature Andy. He had been like a brother to him, much more than Neal ever had. Dom resolved to go back to Perth early, stay in a cheap hostel, spend a week or so before he left looking for his old mate.

He should have tried harder to keep in touch. Even though he was busy and tired when he first went to London, he always found time to write to Andy. But he moved a lot, from one cheap room to another, slightly quieter, or larger, and didn't always remember to give Andy his new address. And as time went on, he found it harder to know what to say; they were living different lives, their points of reference were no longer the same. When Dom bought the flat, he sent a brief card to the last address he had for Andy, but he heard nothing back.

His mum had not told him anything about Andy's heroin problem, though she must have known — Lizzie was her best friend after all. He presumed she had been trying to protect him and the thought angered him; she'd had no right to keep something as important as that from him.

A tractor rumbled along the road, going the other way. Dom pulled off onto the gravel verge as far as he could, to let it past. The driver raised a finger in greeting. He nodded back.

After the tractor had disappeared he stayed where he was, letting the car idle quietly. No, he couldn't blame anyone else — it was he who had fixed the past in his head, as if it were static, imagined his mum would always be there, the farm and Marrup remain the places of his childhood, Andy forever his gangly mate, brimming with a passion for life. But his past had slipped and shifted. Nothing was the same anymore.

12 Hitching

A wide-shouldered mine worker driving a Land Cruiser picked him up just outside of Meckering, on the outer edge of the Wheatbelt. Andy spent half an hour listening to the man's problems; his wife had been having an affair while he was working in Kalgoorlie and had left him for the other bloke. Heartbroken, the miner was heading back to Kal for another tough, if profitable, stint. Andy tutted, shook his head and agreed that you just never knew what life would throw at you next. He thought he had a lift set up all the way to Joondyne, another three-odd hours drive, until the man's mobile rang. He could hear the tinny seep of a woman crying. The man breathed soothing endearments. He left Andy by the side of the road, turned the Land Cruiser around and headed back to Perth to make up with his wife.

Andy stood in front of the bloodless remains of a snake, embedded into the rough tarmac by the repeated pressure of heavy vehicles. He kicked at the roadside gravel. He liked the part of hitching that involved talking and listening, finding out about people's lives, giving what advice he could. The thing that really got to him was the waiting, being passed over again and again, watching the cars and trucks with no-one but the driver behind the wheel hurtle on without even a glance in his direction. It was dispiriting. Degrading. He brushed away pestering flies and tried not to think about Jules and Summie's cool garden. They had made him stay another day, to make sure he was properly prepared and well fed.

He walked for a while. In a spot where the gravel verge widened out, he sat on his pack, as far off the road as he could, and ate the hummus and salad sandwiches Jules had made for him. It wasn't much fun waiting for a lift but his determination, his feeling of rightness about going back home was still strong. He would see his mum, apologise to his dad. He suspected his old man might not be too pleased to see him, at least to start with. When his parents had picked him up from the detox clinic in Perth four years ago, his dad had made it clear it was his last chance.

'I won't be doing this again, Andy. Never again,' he'd told him in a grim undertone, while his mum was out of earshot, getting a cup of tea. His dad always chose his words carefully; Andy knew he was serious. They'd brought him back to the farm but, despite his dad's warning, it hadn't gone well. Andy would have to think carefully about how to approach him now. He had to get it right — it was important. He was starting afresh, beginning his new life with a clean slate.

Then there was his old mate, his best buddy, Dom. He hoped he would still be around — the letter from Andy's mum was only a few days old. Mrs Connor had died. Poor Dom.

He could hardly believe so much time had gone by — eight years! — since they'd last set eyes on each other. Dom, the one who had done all the right things, taken the straight course. Andy had felt a bit sorry for him, living such a tedious, predictable life — degree, safe job with the council. While Dom had studied, then gone to work five days a week, Andy had lived in squats or cheap communal houses, worked in bars and helped up-and-coming bands find venues. He'd protested against the logging of native forest and for Aboriginal land rights, learned to juggle fire sticks and brew his own beer. He'd grown weed and eaten fresh fish he'd caught himself. But even with their different lifestyles, they had stayed close, him and Dom, going to the beach together, eating at the markets once a week. They'd talked on the phone. Dom had introduced him to a girl on his course who Andy had gone out with for a while. They'd driven home to see their parents now and then in Dom's car — a vehicle was a luxury Andy could never afford — sharing the driving. Once they had a holiday together in Exmouth, camping on the beach, fishing and swimming, their skin turning dark and tight in the sun. They were constants in each other's lives, stable points, connections to a line that went right back to their first memories.

When they were both twenty-five, Dom had suddenly gone to England, leaving Andy shocked and confused. Dom could take risks after all; he wasn't afraid of change. Andy had been left behind, trying to squash the nagging feeling that he'd got it all wrong, that it was him who had taken the easy route, him who might have been wasting his life.

He'd thought that Dom wouldn't last long over there but he had. He had.

Andy stood up as a truck rumbled by, flicking debris from the road in its wake. With everyone going on about saving energy, didn't it occur to these people that he was doing the planet a favour by not driving? People should be made to pick up hitchhikers, he thought, by law. He started walking, head slightly lowered, arm lifted, thumb out. His hair still reached his shoulders; with any luck he might be mistaken for a woman.

Andy's life had disintegrated into a chaotic, drug-fuelled mess after Dom had moved to London. Had he relied on Dom somehow? Andy had certainly felt hurt when Dom had left; his friend had not even talked about it, had given no clue about his intentions. Would things have turned out as they had for Andy if Dom had stayed around? Not that he would ever blame his friend for his own shitty life; he knew his decisions had been made by him alone, his problems were no-one else's responsibility. It was probably his own fault too, that he and Dom had fallen out of touch. But what could he have said about his life these past years? He'd survived. It was something to be proud of, he supposed, when there was nothing else.

He came to a stand of white gums and stopped in their shade. The road was empty apart from a couple of crows further up picking at the exposed pink guts of a small animal. It might have been a rabbit.

A thin expanse of wheat straggled in the paddock opposite. He could make out a harvester, trailed by a cloud of dust, in the distance. The faint drone of its engine carried across to him. There must have been a bit of rain here. A few weeks ago when he had been watching the TV news with Summie and Jules, there'd been a story about the salt problems and the drought in the Eastern Wheatbelt and pictures of the desiccated land had flashed up on the screen. Andy had got up and left the room, stood on the back patio listening to the spray of a hose on the garden next door, the splash of another neighbour washing their car, whistling. People in the city complained about their water restrictions.

Strips of dry, tea-coloured bark littered the base of the white gums. Andy crunched across the bark and pressed his hand to the pale trunk of one of the trees. He leaned against its cool, solid strength for a minute, drank from the water bottle he'd filled at Meckering, and trudged on. He preferred to be walking than standing still, moving towards his parents and Dom, people he'd neglected for too long. And Hester. There was Hester too.

13 PARTY

On the potholed track near the turn-off that led to the dam, a scraggy sheep stood, unmoving. Dom beeped the horn and it shot away at a startled trot. He knew he could have walked to the cottage in ten minutes or so, but the heat was getting to him and the flies drove him mad. Besides, if they were going to Dog Rock after Billy's birthday party they would need his car; Neal only had the ute. And a tractor. Dom had no idea how the whole family usually got around. Perhaps they never went anywhere.

As he approached the wide, blank circle of space in front of the cottage and tin shed a red dog rushed the car, barking. Dom inched the Nissan into the shade of the salmon gum.

Snarls of wire, old tyres and rusting machinery loitered in scattered clumps around the open-fronted shed. Scrawny chickens fluttered from a hole in a corrugated water tank rolled on its side. The cottage, built for a farm manager in the more prosperous past, sprouted awkward, shambolic additions. It had been abandoned for years until Neal moved up from the Big House when he got married. There was something odd and old-fashioned, Dom thought, about a man living with his mother until he was thirty.

In Dom's memory the farm was a place of vaguely genteel order, of industry and subdued prosperity — not like this. Had Lizzie been trying to tell him, yesterday, that the farm was going under? It seemed impossible that it could simply cease to be. *I have to go home for a few weeks*, was the message he'd left for his boss. After all this time. Home.

Neal appeared at the threshold of the shed, wiping his hands on a rag. He shouted the dog with a sharp 'Oi!' and the dog slunk away to the shade of a wheel-less car on blocks at the side of the shed. He made his way over to the Nissan. Dom wondered if his brother's limp had become more pronounced. He had ended up with it after an accident in his early twenties — something to do with a hay baler, as far as he could remember.

Dom got out of the car and waited. A shiny spot on the windmill shot back a dazzle of sunlight. Neal stopped in front of the car, pulling at each greasy finger in turn, with the rag.

'Hi.'

Neal nodded, but didn't speak.

'Billy excited about his big day out?'

His brother shrugged.

Dom's teeth clamped together in annoyance. Neal took a step back from the car, then came in closer, bending down to inspect the front bumper. 'Looks like you hit something.'

'Yeah. I did.' Dom hesitated. 'Colin Bohan's dog. At Johnson's Garage. It practically ran under the wheels.'

Neal straightened and folded his arms across his chest. 'Paintwork's scratched. They'll charge you for that. Better be more careful, eh?' He looked at Dom, his face set in an inscrutable sun-squint, then turned and began to walk away. The skin at the back of his brother's neck, Dom noticed, was dark, with folds like worn, soft leather.

'Neal! We've got things to sort out — Mum's stuff, the house. Can we meet up later today, after Dog Rock? Or tomorrow? Whenever. Just say.'

'I'm busy,' Neal threw back, lifting one hand in a dismissive wave.

Dom could not let it go, refused to be ignored. 'Well, why don't you give me something to do, if you're busy? I might as well help out, while I'm here.'

Neal stopped and turned around. Dom thought he was smiling and began to smile back, until he realised his brother's lip was lifted in a sneer.

'You? You want to help on the farm. Huh! Probably bloody kill you, a bit of real work.' He shook his head, and carried on to the shed.

Dom drew deep breaths to control his fury and the powerful urge to chase after his brother, grab him by the shoulders and shake him, to scream in his face: What makes you so fucking superior? I saw you! I bloody saw what you did, you bastard!

They eat their tea without speaking. It's just the two of them that night; their mum is at a CWA meeting, for the Joondyne Show. She has left them a casserole in the slow cooker.

Neal eats fast and jiggles his leg under the table. He has already downed a few tinnies before tea and as soon as he finishes eating he gets up and takes another one from the fridge. He pushes open the flyscreen door and goes out, while Dom is still eating. His brother likes a beer now and then, but he doesn't usually drink this much.

When Dom has finished, he scrapes the plates and does the dishes. The shed light is on — it's getting dark. He can see one side of the tractor lit up, Neal moving around. He never sits still, Neal, doesn't know how to relax. Dom thinks it's a stupid idea his brother messing around out in the shed when he's been drinking.

He shakes Neal's empties and necks the dregs from a couple but the beer is flat and bitter and he gets himself a drink of cordial to take the taste away. He goes to his room to finish off his geography essay on the movement of the earth's crust and changes to the continents. It doesn't take him long. He puts down his pen and stretches his arms up. A faint clanging comes from the shed.

In the lounge, he turns on the TV and catches the end of A Big Country, about some footballer. When it's over he wanders back into the kitchen and gets the vanilla ice cream out of the freezer. He pours chocolate topping on it from a bottle. As he puts the bottle away, the flyscreen door swooshes open and Neal comes back in. He stops short when he sees Dom at the fridge, stands waiting for him to get out of the way.

Dom leans against the cupboard and licks ice cream and topping from his spoon. He watches Neal take out another tinnie.

'Want some ice cream?'

'Nuh.' His brother cracks open the can. It froths a bit and he sucks at it.

'Sure? There's chocolate topping.'

Neal doesn't answer. He walks out, tipping back his head to drink the beer.

'Your loss,' Dom calls after him.

Dom takes his ice cream into his room and sits on the bed. He starts reading *Of Mice and Men*, one of the books on their

Lit reading list from the school library. After a while Neal comes back in. Dom hears the suck of the fridge door opening, a clunk when it closes. The TV goes on. Dom gets up to shut his bedroom door. He thinks about Janine at school, who Andy reckons fancies him, and starts to get a hard-on, but he doesn't do anything about it and it passes. He keeps reading.

Later, he sees car lights come down the track and checks his clock. It's nearly 9.30. He finishes the page of the book he's on and puts in a bookmark. He's tired and has to go to school tomorrow. It's over an hour bus ride each way to the High School in Joondyne.

He gets up to take his ice cream bowl into the kitchen and clean his teeth. As he walks into the lounge he hears his mum and Neal talking, and realises that the voices don't sound quite normal. He stops halfway across the room, where he can't be seen, and listens.

'There's no need to get het up, Neal,' his mum says. 'I just said there were a lot of empty cans, that's all.'

'What you going to do, make me go to bed early, like I'm a kid?' There's an unusual, confrontational edge to his brother's voice. Dom hesitates, then creeps to the kitchen doorway and peers into the room. He can't see Neal's face — his brother has his back to him — but his fists are clenching and unclenching.

'Well, you're acting like one,' his mum snaps. She begins to drop the empty cans into a plastic bag. 'You know I sometimes wonder if it isn't really Dom who's the eldest out of you two, the way you —'

As she reaches for a crumpled can lying near the sink Neal lunges forward, propelling his mum backwards, his wide hands

113

gripping her shoulders. Her arms flail out and the bag drops from her hand and clatters to the floor. The cans spill out. Her back slams against the wall and her head makes a clear *thunk* sound as it hits the hard surface.

Dom holds his breath. The ice cream and chocolate sauce feel like they're curdling in his stomach. He stands, mesmerised. He can see the fingers of Neal's left hand wrapped like tentacles around his mum's throat. Her eyes are fixed on Neal's face, shoved inches from her own. Dom watches as his mum's face turns red. A whispered plea escapes from her lips. He knows he should go to her, do something, but his body refuses to move, as if his mind cannot translate the reality of what he is seeing. His brother's other hand comes up, slowly, in a fist, and settles against his mum's jaw. Dom feels fury rise up in him and his body quivers; finally he is ready to act, to save his mum. He is just about to step into the kitchen when the scene changes in an instant; Neal's fist has turned into a flat hand and is stroking his mum's hair. His other hand is gone from her throat — she draws in air with a rasping gulp. Both Neal's arms are wrapped around her, his body pushed up close against hers, his head on her shoulder. A quiet crying, a miserable whimper, comes from his brother. After a while, his mum pats Neal's back in a soothing way, though Dom can see her hand trembling.

Dom doesn't know what to do. He feels sick. He scurries back to his room, his sticky ice cream bowl still in his hand, and closes the door.

Eventually, he hears Neal come down the hall and go into his own room, next to Dom's. There are soft tidying-up sounds

114

from the kitchen. He puts the pillow over his head to try to drown out the sounds of Neal's crying, but even when there is silence he lies awake.

The next day, it's as if nothing happened. His mum makes him and Neal porridge in the morning, as usual. She asks Dom if he got his homework done, and Neal and her talk about the possible case of foot and mouth disease they've heard about. Dom feels confused and disconnected, as though he's made up the whole thing, or dreamt it. But he hasn't. There are vague marks on his mum's neck. Neal's eyes are red. The kitchen smells of beer.

Dom never sees his brother drink again.

Chickens scattered in Dom's wake as he barged up to the cottage. A clump of brightly coloured balloons tied to the verandah post at the top of the steps wobbled and bounced as he brushed past. He stood for a few seconds, trying to calm down. He could hear the boys' chatter and giggles inside, the chink and scrape of a spoon on a bowl. He clutched Billy's birthday card and tapped on the wall next to the screen door. Scraps of peeling paint flecked off and scattered on the verandah boards. He pushed the door open.

There was no colourful tablecloth. There were no hats or whistles or party bags. No other guests.

Hester smiled at him and wiped a flour-dusted hand across her damp forehead. She hooked a stray length of straw-coloured hair from her mouth with a little finger. Her face was pink, under the smudge of her freckles. He felt the churn of his frustration and anger ease away.

'Just a quiet one this year,' she said.

Billy tore open his card and, grinning, thanked his uncle. While Hester spooned cake mix into delicate patty cases, Dom played with Alex and Billy on the far side of the room. He blew up a green balloon and tapped it to the excited boys. They stretched and clamoured for it, tangled themselves together on the worn lino in a writhing heap at Dom's feet.

'Not many kids left around here now, anyway.' Hester spoke above the children's noise. 'The school closed last year.'

'The school closed?'

'Yep. I'm going to teach the boys myself. Joondyne's too far on the bus every day. They're too young for that.'

He wondered how Hester could be expected to teach the kids at home without a TV or a computer. Was it even legal? She told him they'd decided it was best for the boys not to have things like that, but he wasn't convinced it was Hester's choice. It had to be Neal. His brother was trying to contain them all, himself, Hester and the boys, in his own tiny world. Dom couldn't help thinking Hester didn't quite fit. What was she doing here?

He got down on his knees and tickled the boys. His glance flicked to Hester again and again. He saw her rub at an itch on her face with the back of her hand, tilt her head slightly to one side as she filled a water jug from the filter barrel. He settled the boys and helped them put smiley faces on balloons with a squeaky marker. Hester made them all green cordial with ice blocks, in plastic mugs. The fake-tasting sweetness clung to Dom's tongue.

'Sorry I can't offer you a beer or something,' she said. 'Neal doesn't drink, and I only have a few at Christmas.'

He reassured her the cordial was perfect.

She slid a tray of fairy cakes out of the oven and stirred chocolate icing in a clear bowl. He saw her wince, as if she was in pain, when she turned to put the bowl in the sink.

14 DOG ROCK

The sunglasses were red plastic. She'd brought them from the General Store years ago, for a few dollars, but never worn them. She did her hair in a braid at the back, slipped on the sunglasses and stared at her reflection in the rust-speckled bathroom mirror. Her face seemed odd and unfamiliar with the glasses on; she didn't recognise herself. The stranger in the mirror smiled, frowned, pouted. She turned away.

The leftover sausage rolls and cake were packed into the Esky for their afternoon tea at Dog Rock, with plastic bottles of frozen cordial pushed up close to the Esky bricks. She put the boys' bathers and towels into a bag for their swim later and made a thermos of tea for Neal.

At the kitchen window, she smoothed sunburn cream into her face as she watched Neal unload farm gear from the back of the ute. He lifted out a toolbox with one hand. Even from this distance she could see the movement of muscle and sinew in his arm. He handed Billy a coil of rope. Her oldest son struggled with it, half dragging it across the ground. Neal leant down and gave Alex something small to hold, a box of nails perhaps, and he scampered away with it towards the shed.

She saw Dom shuffle around near the ute. He gestured towards the blue car and Neal shook his head. Dom must have been offering to take the boys in his car, so they wouldn't have to go in the back of the ute. The Corolla, her perfect little car, the car that Neal had taught her to drive in, had broken down six months ago and Neal had said it couldn't be fixed. They would have to manage with just the ute, he'd said. They did.

They managed. It was safe enough. There was not much traffic. No police around anymore. They had old tractor seats to sit on.

She watched Dom shove his hands into his pockets and walk towards the house. It would do them all good to go out, to have a change of scene. She settled the sunglasses onto her head and smiled, without meaning to. It was her own. A real smile.

At Dog Rock, Neal parked the ute in the shade of the trees, near a dusty but smart-looking camper van, the only other vehicle there.

Hester jumped down from the back of the ute and lifted out the children. Her ears rang from the road noise and her mouth felt clotted with dust. She wanted to spit, but couldn't in front of Dom — she would feel stupid. It was not a good example for the boys, either. When she swallowed, grit caught in her throat and she coughed, once.

Dom clambered over the side of the ute and brushed dust from his hair. He stood with his hands on his hips, gazing at the rock. 'Wow. I'd forgotten how amazing this place is.'

Hester pushed the boys' hats on firmly and straightened her sunglasses. It thrilled her, the scale of the rock, the surprise of it in this uneventful landscape. The rock's huge presence dwarfed its surroundings, made everything else insignificant.

About sixty feet high, double that in length, the rock was mostly flat, but with a round lump creating the dog's head and two jutting slabs on the ground, like paws laid flat. Tiny caves dotted the base of the rock. For a while, the place had been promoted as a tourist site; Neal had brought her here not long after they were married. There were still a few ragged wooden picnic tables and a children's play area with a rickety seesaw and a couple of swings. An information panel explaining the geology of the rock, giving its Aboriginal name and history, was faded and unreadable, but the warning on a metal sign was still clear enough: Climb at your own risk!

The boys ran around, hyperactive with excitement. Alex chased Billy to where Neal stood in front of the ute with his arms folded, awkward and out of place.

'Daddy! Look at the big rock! It's a doggie!' Billy held up his hands and panted and Alex tried to copy him, before he turned his face up to his father and patted his leg urgently. 'Can I go on the swing, Daddy?' Sensing he would not get the right answer, he bolted to his mother. 'Mummy? Swing?'

'We'll go to the rock first,' Neal pronounced. 'Swings later.'

Hester dug a bottle of cordial from the Esky and gave it to Billy. 'That's to share with Alex, right?'

He managed the bottle with one hand and tugged Neal towards the rock with the other. 'Come on, Mummy!' he called.

Hester waved them on. 'In a minute. I just have to put on some sunburn cream.' She needed a moment to herself, a bit of time to savour the rock.

Neal hesitated and turned to her, but she was already lugging the Esky over to one of the shaded picnic tables and pretended not to notice. He moved off, with the boys flitting around him like pestering birds.

'Here. Let me.' Halfway to the table, Dom was there.

He put the Esky on the hard ground next to the table and stood looking at the rock. She sat down. The children's voices grew slowly fainter as they skipped away, around Neal's lumbering form. Neal paused, bent down and let Alex clamber onto his back.

'Ever climbed it?' Dom had turned to her.

'The rock? No. Never.' She took off her sunglasses and wiped her face where the sweat had accumulated in hot patches around the plastic frame. They weren't much use really. Dom pulled a water bottle out of his backpack and offered it to her.

She shook her head and patted the Esky. 'I've got some, ta.'

Two people, a couple — the camper van owners, Hester assumed — appeared from behind the rock. They walked around the front, where the dog's paws jutted out, admiring. The taller one, the man, pointed, then stood with his hands on his hips. The woman lifted a camera and ushered the man into her sights. He stood posing in front of the rock as Neal and the boys approached. Hester watched the distant scenes: the strangers greeting Neal and the boys; Neal lifting the boys onto one of the paws; the strangers, animated, gesturing, taking photos.

'You want to?' Dom's voice invaded the silence. 'You want to climb it? There's a kind of lookout, with a railing, on the dog's back. You can just see it, there.' He pointed. 'Me and my friend used to come here when we were teenagers. We climbed it loads of times.'

He must mean Andy, Hester thought. Dom must have found out about Andy by now, if he hadn't already known. She had a sudden urge to talk to this placid, attentive man, to pull away the layers of silence and open up to him.

She slid the sunglasses back on and said nothing.

'Amazing we didn't fall off and break our necks the way we used to carry on.' Dom shook his head. 'But I'm sure it's safe if you're not a mad teenager. And it's a great view. Come on. Neal'll be okay with the kids for a bit.'

Hester wanted to climb the rock. She desperately wanted to. Could she? Neal would already be unhappy about her sitting here now. It wasn't worth it. 'Nah, don't worry. Too hot. You go. Wave to me from the top.'

'You sure?'

She nodded.

Dom retied his shoelaces. He drank from his water bottle and returned it to his backpack. He shuffled the pack to get it comfortable. He was walking away.

'Hang on!' It came out louder than she had intended. 'I might as well come, eh? As long as we're quick.'

The way up was easy to follow. It had been worn and moulded over many years along the natural flow of the rock. Mostly, the climb was steady and gradual. Footholds had been hacked into the rock and a loose chain strung from ugly, cemented-in metal poles in the steeper, more difficult spots. Hester strode up. The dark surface pulsed with absorbed heat. She felt her calves clench and pull, her thighs stretch and tighten as she climbed. A tiny lizard darted out of her way.

By the time she got to the wide, flat plateau she was damp with sweat and breathing hard.

Dom came lumbering up behind her. 'Bloody hell,' he panted. 'I'm sure it was a lot easier when I was fifteen.'

The bottle of water he shared with her was warm and not refreshing. In her rush, she had forgotten to bring a drink. She recovered her breath and looked around.

Dom stood next to her. 'Told you it was a good view.'

A panorama of flat land lay below them. Parrots flashed from the trees where the two vehicles nestled, like toys. She could hear snatches of the boys' voices as they played on the rock below somewhere. Hidden.

'Everything seems so neat and tidy from up here.' Dom said, his voice slightly hushed. 'The roads look like ant trails.'

Hester shaded her eyes and gazed out. 'Makes you feel different, doesn't it? Tiny. Puts you in your place.'

'Yes. I know what you mean.'

'You could lose yourself out here. Just disappear. Get swallowed up.'

They stood side by side in silence for a minute, the sun's blaze pressing down on them.

'Look,' Dom pointed. 'That's Marrup. The farm's over there.'

She nodded. 'Joondyne must be that way.' She waved a hand. 'And over there would be the coast, wouldn't it? Perth.'

'That's right. And Sydney,' he turned, 'is in that direction, I think. If you kept going long enough. London's probably out there, somewhere —' He stopped. 'Hester?'

She covered her eyes with her hand. She had started to cry, without warning. She should not have let it happen now, in front of Dom. His comforting arm lay across her shoulders. He pulled her to him. 'Hey,' his voice was gentle. 'You okay?'

'Sorry. I don't know why … I'm alright. I'm fine.'

'You sure?' He gave her shoulder another gentle squeeze. She let her head fall against his chest for a moment.

'Hester, I don't want to interfere, but — well, if there's anything you want to talk about, anything I can do to help. It can't be easy, Neal's not the most —'

'Thanks.' She cut him off and pulled away. 'Thanks, Dom.' She wiped her face on one long sleeve of her cotton top. 'I'm tired, that's all. Just tired.'

She drank the dregs of the water he offered her and turned away, staring out towards distant places.

Later, she took the kids exploring in the caves around the base of the rock and pushed them on the squeaky swing. She laid the afternoon tea out nicely on the table and kept the ants away.

The couple, enthusiastic retirees from Melbourne touring the country off the beaten track, joined them at the picnic table and shared their food; orange juice from the fridge in their camper van, cold grapes, nectarines and sweet biscuits. They took photos of the boys with their digital camera; the boys were intrigued to see instant pictures of themselves on the little screen. The retirees couldn't quite believe the family had no computer to send the photos to. They tried to talk about the drought and the salinity, but Dom eased the conversation towards their travels and grandkids. Hester was busy with the boys and preoccupied with Neal. Her husband did not touch the food the older couple offered. He ate only what Hester had provided. He drank his tea in silence then sat in the ute, waiting.

She packed up as quickly as she could.

The long slab of dam water was the colour of dark clay. It looked so dense it was a surprise to see bodies penetrate it so effortlessly.

Hester sat on the low bank in the shade of the windbreak trees with her knees up, watching Neal and Dom and the boys in the water. The swim was Billy's last treat for the day. She'd said she had a headache.

Dom dived from the rickety wooden platform that jutted over the water and swam up and down neatly, alternating overarm and backstroke. The boys squealed and shrieked with pleasure. Neal let them jump from his shoulders, pulled them along, submerged himself and came up again in unexpected places, making faces and blowing bubbles. The only time he seemed to really relax now was with the children.

The sounds of the moving water tormented her. She longed to plunge in, to feel the cool liquid on her skin, the soothing, weightless freedom of it. But she couldn't. Not today. She could not swim in her own dam. There were marks on her body that would show when she put on her bathers. She was used to wearing the right clothes, keeping herself hidden from everyone except Neal and the kids. Perhaps the boys would ask more questions when they were older; for now, they accepted what they saw. But Dom — she could not let Dom see. How would she explain? What would he think of her? And Neal. Neal would need her to stay covered up, in front of his brother.

As Dom backstroked across the dam, Billy swam up and splashed him, and they started mucking around together. Dom turned towards Neal and said something but she didn't hear a reply. He seemed a good man, Dom, gentle and kind. She liked that he had confidence, yet was not quite sure of himself. He didn't act like he was better than other people, even with his education and travel and busy London life. He listened to her properly, and looked at her when he spoke, as though he was interested in her, in what she had to say. When he'd put his arm around her today on the rock she'd felt safe. She could have kissed him. It would have seemed natural.

Perhaps Andy had not told him about her.

She lay back, using the boys' towels as pillows, and closed her eyes. She imagined herself in a different life. Life in London. With Dom. She was striding down a busy street, wearing good, well-cut clothes. Perhaps she worked in an office. Yes. A smart office. She met Dom at lunch times. They sipped coffee and laughed together. Her hair was long and loose and she flicked it back over her shoulders. In the mornings the boys bounded off to school wearing blazers and ties and sturdy shoes. On weekends they all went to a big green park to play, coming home to snuggle up in front of a fire, with hot chocolate. When the boys were asleep Dom and her went to bed. He held her face and looked into her eyes and — one of the boys squealed and she sat up with a start. She shielded her eyes and looked over the dam. They were playing. Just playing.

It was stupid of her to let her thoughts wander like that. She was married to Neal. He was her husband, this was the choice she'd made, and she was grateful for what she had. She'd been happy with Neal — still was, in lots of ways. It would come right again. She had endured worse. It was just a bad patch; she had to weather the storm. Strange saying, she thought.

She lay back and looked up at the flecks of sky showing through the scrappy canopy of leaves. There hadn't been a real storm here in years. Last August a clump of cloud had blown in suddenly on fierce winds. They'd lost a section off the shed roof, but there hadn't been any rain. Not a drop.

15 PILGRIMAGE

Andreas and Stephan, two young German tourists, dropped Andy off at the roadhouse on the edge of Joondyne, still laughing about the fact that they'd thought he was a woman. They called out, 'Goodbye, Miss Andy!' as they drove off, heading for the Nullabor Plain. He smiled, and raised a weary hand in farewell. It was more than seven hours since he'd left Perth.

In the roadhouse shop, the chill of efficient air-conditioning prickled his skin. He bought a pastie and a bottle of cold water. The last time he was here he'd nicked the same things, on his way back to the city. This time he took his change and thanked the woman behind the counter.

He would go to the small park in the town and eat his pastie while he thought about what to do. His idea of hanging around the roadhouse until he found someone to give him a lift to Marrup had seemed reasonable in Perth; now he wasn't so sure. It had taken him this long to get here on the Great Eastern Highway, a major route — Marrap was a good sixty kilometres away, on a tiny road that went nowhere much. He might get a lift to the turn-off, about twenty kilometres away, but then what? He hadn't thought it through.

Andy meandered into the town. The heat of the day was starting to ease off, but the excessive light still glared. A rich red pulsed from an old brick building and black tarmac seared the ground. He felt dizzy and drank some water. The feeling passed.

A scattering of cars and utes were parked diagonally in front of a row of set-back shops and along the edges of the wide street. The Joondyne Newsagency advertised the *Countryman* and *The West Australian* on its carefully painted facia. A few shops were boarded up, neatly. There was no graffiti.

Low houses crouched on wide blocks behind hardy grevillea and wattle. A man on the opposite footpath in shorts and work boots nodded a greeting. Andy nodded back. There was always a chance he would see someone who remembered him; plenty of the kids he went to school with wouldn't have made it any further than here.

On the walls of the public toilets at the edge of the Rotary Park, school kids had painted a colourful mural featuring sheep and dogs, wheat and windmills and smiling faces. Country life.

He found a shaded spot on a bench in the empty park and ate his pastie. Across the road at the Shire offices, a squat building made of dark brick, a couple of people came and went. He considered, briefly, getting a room in town for the night — there were a couple of hotels and at least one motel — but such an extravagance would put a huge dent in his meagre finances. Now he'd made it this far he might as well keep going, he thought. There must be a few hours of reasonable light left; he could still get a lift, if he was lucky. If not, he'd be in for a long walk.

Back at the roadhouse Andy refilled his water bottle from a tap in the forecourt and considered prospective lifts. A burly truckie swung down from the yellow cab of a road train parked across the road and lumbered towards the shop. Andy smiled at him as he passed. The big man frowned, spat noisily and muttered, 'fucking hippies'.

Andy felt very tired suddenly. His energy drained away. He looked around him, uncertain and anxious. An edgy panic threatened him. Scuttling across to the toilet cubicles at the side of the main building he waited until he saw the truckie come out and hurried back into the shop. He stood in front of the shelves of wine and beer and spirits; VB, Fosters and Swan Lager, vodka and gin. His mouth was dry. He tapped his hands against his legs and circled the shop a few times. The man behind the counter was watching him. Finally, he strode up to the counter and bought a pack of twenty Winfield Red cigarettes and a plastic lighter.

He rushed back to the park, sat on the same bench and smoked one cigarette after another, grinding each generous stub into the cement paving with his foot. It had been a long time since he'd had a cigarette. As he lit the tenth one he began to cough and cough, until his stomach heaved. In the doorway of the Shire offices, a woman with a bunch of papers in her hand paused to stare.

Andy wiped his mouth and sat quietly until his breathing was even. He guzzled most of the water then picked up the stubs at his feet and dropped them into an empty bin nearby. He almost threw the whole packet in, but instead shook out all the unsmoked cigarettes except one and put the packet with the single cigarette into his backpack.

It could have been worse, he thought. It could have been much worse.

He lay along the bench with his head resting on his backpack and closed his eyes.

By the time he woke up, it was getting dark.

After he'd been walking for about an hour a young couple, barely teenagers he guessed, stopped to give him a lift. They were driving an old Holden station wagon. Both had jobs lined up in Kalgoorlie.

'Look out, Kal, here we come!' they whooped at regular intervals. Their positive mood buoyed him. He politely declined the joint they offered and tried not to breathe in any of the smoke. The couple were concerned about dropping him in the middle of nowhere, but Andy reassured them; he didn't have far to go, he said, and there was plenty of moonlight. He had a torch.

When they had driven off, Andy stood on the gravelly edge of the tarmac, alone in the night, letting his eyes adjust. A shiver tingled through him. In a tree nearby a mopoke called a soft welcome. The moon was fat and the sky crammed with stars. He felt enlivened, wide awake. He'd made it! Of course, the place would not be the same as he'd left it — he knew the land was a mess, that things were bad. But he was almost there. Home.

He pulled on a jumper against the chill of the night, crossed the empty highway and started to walk. Lights glowed in scattered farmhouses. He sang Neil Young songs — Heart of Gold, Old Man, Helpless — not caring how out of tune he was.

It was too late to turn up at his mum and dad's. He wanted to be fresh for that meeting, to do it properly. No, his first stop would be Dom — presumably at the Big House, if Neal hadn't taken over the place. He couldn't imagine Dom staying with Neal; those two had never got on.

Andy hoped to God his old mate was still around.

Marching along in the middle of the road he started to sing Southern Man, but he couldn't remember the words and it petered out into a hum. It occurred to him for the first time that Dom might have brought a girlfriend or wife with him — maybe even children. Eight years was a long time. He stopped humming.

He stumbled on a chunk of tree branch lying on the road. When he righted himself he walked more carefully.

He would have to make sure he kept clear of Neal, but he might have a chance of seeing Hester.

Hester.

They had been perfect together, Hester and him. He had never loved anyone that way before; perhaps he never would again. But he ruined everything. Fucked it all up. When they met, he was trying to sort himself out, to get clean. He had pulled himself from a mire of days and weeks that had no beginning or end, no meaning, shocked into trying to change by his first serious overdose. He was twenty-six. Hester was three years younger.

They rented a flat together and Andy found work as a salesman in SleepTite, wearing a suite and tie. It was a good job. He enjoyed talking to people. The manager told him he was the best salesman they'd ever had. Even when he found

Andy asleep on one of the beds after a long, liquid lunch — preceded by a drug-fuelled night — he kept him on. Until it happened again the next week. And the one after. Andy threw a chair through the office window when he was told it was time to go. His kind manager didn't press charges but Andy forfeited his last two weeks wages.

Hester had deserved better. So much better.

He stopped. A fox, sleek and golden in the evening light, followed by two small cubs, trotted across the road ahead. He smiled at the sight. Life went on, he thought, beginning to recover his earlier mood. There was no point dwelling on the past; it could not be changed. He was looking to the future now.

Soon his shoulders began to hurt, no matter how he repositioned his pack. His ribs ached and he had a blister on his heel. But these physical inconveniences didn't bother him. He enjoyed them, in a way; there was something cathartic about coming home like this. The weary pilgrim. Yes. A pilgrimage. He liked that idea.

Of course, if a car turned up he wouldn't say no to a lift.

16 REUNIONS

On the floor next to the mattress his tiny travel clock glowed 22:05. Dom scratched at itches on his legs, twisted and turned, rearranged the blanket and sheet. He was tired after the climb up Dog Rock and the swimming, but still couldn't sleep.

He flung off the bedclothes, felt his way across the room to the standard lamp with the tasseled shade and clicked it on, blinking in its thin light. Back on the mattress he tugged the sheet and scratchy blanket up to his chin. The blanket smelt of dust. The sheet was worn and thin, washed too many times, pegged up, over and over, by his mum's dry hands.

Shadows from the lamp crawled across the walls and ceiling. The old building sighed and creaked around him. He heard a rustle, a faint scratching sound. Every noise seemed to resonate through the hollow house. Outside, an animal called. It could have been a dog. Another replied, a lingering echo.

His thoughts meandered; he wondered how Neal could be such a bastard but still a good dad, how Hester, even covered in sweat, managed to smell so good. He remembered the feeling of her body pressed against him on Dog Rock, her head on his chest, and —

He sat up. No. He wouldn't think about Hester.

A small black bug had landed in his mug of water. He fished it out with a finger and drank. He touched the lid of the shoebox. It was still there, safe, behind his pillow at the end of the mattress.

When he'd first found the jewellery he was excited by the idea of what it could do for him. He'd thought of it in terms of instant benefit, useful cash. But it wasn't that simple. *It's for your family,* Lizzie Bohan had said. The jewellery was an heirloom, passed down and down, until he was its keeper. Would he be wrong to sell it? He had the feeling it might be a betrayal of his mother and of the generations before her.

He lay down again. Rivers of cracks — some wide, others tiny tributaries — flowed across the once-white ceiling. He stared up at them, followed their meandering trail through the shadows, right to each cobwebbed corner of the room.

Didn't there come a time when someone in the family needed what had been passed down, a moment in history when the inheritor was justified in converting the precious items into ready cash? Wasn't that the whole idea of it? He could fix his financial mess, perhaps get rid of the burden of his mortgage once and for all, give himself a breather, a chance to make some choices. Or maybe that was just selfishness. Greed. Refugees used their family heirlooms to flee, to escape death or torture. They sewed bracelets and earrings and silver spoons into the hems of their clothes. All he was escaping was a bit of financial difficulty.

But if he were to be the keeper of the jewellery who was he keeping it for? Not Neal. Why should that bastard get it? He hardly even felt like family. Besides, he'd had his chances, been given the farm and the houses. There were the boys of course, his nephews. But they were only boys. Would he even know them, when they were grown? Hester? Did she count as family?

A burden of hopelessness began to settle on his chest like a weighty ghost. Even if he sorted out his money problems, he would still be stuck in his pointless job, slogging it out in the impersonal rush and hassle of London. He would always be a middle-ranking council hack. He was tired of churning on, alone. There was nothing substantial, nothing of consequence in his life. Even his brother had two great kids and a lovely wife. Somehow, Neal had Hester.

A tapping sound, a faint noise that could have been his name disturbed his thoughts. He held his breath and lay still, listening. It was probably possums in the roof. He remembered the havoc they used to cause, scrabbling about in the ceiling, chewing wires and peeing on everything. Giant bloody rats, his dad had called them.

The sound came again, louder, definite. Was it a knock? Someone was calling his name. It was real. He threw off the sheet and jabbed his limbs into a T-shirt and jeans. Who the hell would be here at this time of night?

The light from the lamp spilled through into the kitchen. Dom stepped across the lino, the soles of his bare feet catching on its sticky surface. He switched on the main kitchen light. The fluorescent tube flickered then settled. Black cockroaches scuttled away and vanished into cracks and gaps. The knocking came again, more insistent.

'Hello?' It was a male voice he didn't recognise.

He felt the coolness of the brass handle on the kitchen door, smooth and black from generations of sweaty hands. The catch clicked. He eased the door open. There was nothing but the flimsy flyscreen door between him and the figure on the other side. He gripped the edge of the open door, and wondered if he should have picked up something he could use

136

as a weapon. A buzz of night-time insects dashed around the bare bulb of the verandah light as soon as he turned it on.

'Dom? Is that you?'

Dom pushed open the screen door. The man stepped back. He was thin and lanky and slightly hunched, like an awkward teenager. An Army Surplus backpack sat propped against the wall. He smiled, showing a gap in his teeth at the top. His hair was almost shoulder length and streaked with grey.

'It can't — Andy? Jesus. Andy!'

'Did I wake you up? Sorry, mate. I saw the light on.'

'But I thought ... I mean, I was going to look for you, in Perth ...'

'Saved you the trouble, eh? Sorry about the time, mate. Ended up walking half the way from the Marrup turn-off. Luckily the woman from Johnson's garage turned up, gave me a lift, just before my legs gave out. Great accent you've got there, by the way.'

'But — how did you know I was here?'

'Got a letter from Mum. Long story. Thought about heading straight home but I chickened out. Me and the Old Man ... well, let's say I don't like my chances of a good reception there straight off the bat. So,' he spread his arms, presenting himself, 'here I am. Hope you don't mind. Listen, you haven't got anything to eat by any chance? I'm bloody starving. And how about a hug, eh? Or are you too English for that now?'

The two men sat on the sagging green sofa in the living room with a midnight feast — cheese sandwiches, salted nuts, Granita biscuits — laid out on side tables.

Andy rubbed his hands together and surveyed the food as though it was the most delectable spread he'd ever seen. 'Jeez, this is great. Thanks Dom. Bloody brilliant.'

It was the same Andy — he took life up a notch, made the most mundane thing seem exciting. It was easy to feel good in Andy's company. Appreciated. He politely refused the Swan Lager Dom offered him, but the cup of tea was 'perfect, just what I needed, best tea I've had in ages'. He sat hunched over his sandwich. He looked well, Dom thought; clear skin, steady hands when he poured the tea. His right wrist was stained by a few small, blue-black tattoos, indistinguishable shapes. Andy was a bit worse for wear, but he seemed fine. Normal.

'Got used to my friend's right-on salads the last couple of months, but you can't beat a good old white bread cheese sarny.' Using his tongue, Andy cleared sticky lumps of bread from his teeth, sat back and sipped his tea. After a moment, he looked thoughtful. 'You're here because of your mum, aren't you? Sorry, mate. Really sorry.'

'Thanks. It's so strange her not being here. I just wish I'd seen her, or talked to her, before she … I hadn't written in ages, or phoned. I'd been meaning to. Got so busy. God, that sounds lame, doesn't it?' It felt good to speak about it, to start to air his guilt.

Andy leaned towards him, clasping his mug of tea. 'Mate, people get caught up with things that stop them seeing what's really important. Everyone does it. Just think on it, let it go, and move on. Try to remember the positives, the good things. She was a lovely woman, your mum. She wanted the best for you. And she sure as hell did the greatest roast lamb I've ever had in my life.'

Dom smiled. 'The roast lamb. That's right.' He tipped back a mouthful of frothy beer. 'This is really weird, isn't it? I'd been thinking about you, then you just … turn up.'

Andy nodded, a knowing smile on his face. 'Dom, the universe works in mysterious ways.'

It crossed Dom's mind that Andy had turned religious — it was common in addicts, wasn't it? Ex-addicts. 'Your mum's worried, you know. Really worried.'

Andy pulled his lips together and let his face contract for a second or two of regret, but no more. 'I should have got in touch with her. But things weren't too good, for a while there, Dom. Fell into a bit of a hole. You know about the drugs?'

Dom nodded.

'Yeah, well, whatever terrible things you've heard about me — they're probably all true. I've wasted a lot of years. Spent a lot of years wasted even. Ha! Been bloody stupid. But everything's different now. Like I said, let it go,' he waved a hand expansively, '… and move on.'

'Well, she'll be pleased to see you, that's for sure.'

'Can't say the same for my pa.'

'He'll come round. I ran over his dog the day after I got here. Accidentally, of course. He doesn't seem to have held it against me.'

'Yeah, well, you're not his son. Is he okay, the old fella?'

'Seems to be.'

Andy rummaged in his backpack and brought out a crumpled cigarette packet. He shook out a lone cigarette. 'I've given up really. Just had a sudden urge at Joondyne. Might as well enjoy the last one. Unless you...?' He offered the cigarette to Dom.

Dom shook his head. 'It's all yours.'

'You never smoked?'

'No. Couldn't get the hang of it.'

Andy tapped the end of the cigarette against the packet and smiled. 'Yeah, that's right. We used to nick fags off my dad, didn't we? Or your mum sometimes, before she gave up. Smoked them in the bush. You coughed like shit every time you tried to inhale.'

Dom tipped his head back, embarrassed but pleased too, at the memory of him and Andy sitting on a log in the bush holding a match to a stolen cigarette. It wasn't just the smoking that got their teenage hearts going; the very act of lighting a match in the dry bush was as much of an exciting transgression. But by fifteen, while his brother drenched sheep and ploughed paddocks, Dom had stopped bothering with the cigarettes. Instead, he snuck off to the bush to compose emotion-laden poetry in his notebook. Andy wrote poems too, but always with a cigarette smouldering away in his hand. Sometimes they wrote them together. They read poetry out loud — other people's and their own — Andy blowing out a stream of smoke during dramatic pauses. It was their secret. If they'd been found out, they would have been called *poofters*. Around here there'd been no leeway in deciding manliness, and he doubted things had changed much. Andy would have sloughed it off more easily than Dom. He had cared less what others thought.

An acrid whiff of tobacco smoke trailed Andy when he came in from the verandah. Dom offered his friend the mattress to sleep on, but Andy insisted on taking the sofa. He had his own sleeping bag.

It was late. Dom switched off the lamp and stumbled back to the mattress. He fought his exhaustion like an excited teenager. His old mate was there with him. Their years apart had fallen away easily and they were left with their young, essential selves again. Perhaps none of his friendships since had been as real, or true.

'You still write poetry, Andy?'

'Poetry? No. Did I ever write poetry?'

He'd forgotten. Andy had forgotten about their poems. How could he forget? Dom was too tired to remind him.

'You not married, Dom?'

'No.' Dom yawned.

'Any kids?'

'No kids.'

'Me neither. Hey,' Andy's voice was soft in the darkness, muffled by tiredness. 'It's good to see you, mate. If you need to talk about your mum, or anything, I'm here.'

'Okay. Thanks Andy.' Dom closed his eyes.

'Dom?'

'Yeah?'

There was a long pause and Dom began to drift into sleep.

'You never told me you were going to London. You never said anything until the night before you left.'

Dom opened his eyes and stared into the dim light of the room. 'I'm sorry. I suppose I was worried that … I didn't want to be persuaded to stay.'

Dom heard Andy's deep, slow intake of breath. 'Yeah. Course. I can understand that.' There was another silence before Andy spoke again. 'And Dom?'

'Hmmm?'

'I should just say too, that I need to avoid your brother. Neal said he'd kill me if he ever saw me around here again.'

The next morning, Dom drove to the Bohans' farm to get Andy's mum. After a few seconds of disbelief and confusion, Lizzie swung into action. Dom watched as she made sandwiches at a speed only fifty years daily practice could provide, put them on a plate, covered them with Glad Wrap, and wrote a tidy note:

Dom needs some help going through Marj's stuff. Back before tea.

Sandwich in fridge. Cake in tin.

Liz x

She washed her hands, took off her apron and was ready to go.

On the way to the Big House, Lizzie touched his arm. 'Thanks for coming to get me. It's good of you to think of us, Dom.'

It was a happy moment, but in the close-up confines of the car, her sun-spotted, sagging face and watery eyes caused a drift of melancholy to wash over him.

There was a feeling of occasion as Lizzie followed Dom up the verandah steps at the Big House. She tugged at the hem of her loose cotton shirt and brushed off non-existent crumbs.

The flyscreen door yawned open when he pushed it. Andy appeared from the lounge with his huge, gap-toothed smile, and opened his arms wide. 'Hey, Ma!'

Lizzie was crying and laughing, wiping at her eyes. Dom turned away and put the kettle on. He rinsed out the teapot. Andy and Lizzie moved into the lounge to sit down. He put out two cups and called to say he was going up to the dam. This time was theirs. He did not want to intrude.

He kicked at hardened black pellets of sheep droppings along the track. Perhaps a swim would make him feel better. Clear his head. He thought of Andy standing there with his arms open, ready to embrace Lizzie. To him, there was something embarrassingly intimate about the scene. Dom and his mother had never been like that. They had not been a family comfortable with shows of physical affection. Should he have tried harder to be more affectionate, before he went away? She probably would have been shocked and hated it. It was not what she was used to.

He began to relax as he walked, enjoying the peace of the stark surroundings, feeling the heat, for the first time since he'd been back, as a comfort, a familiarity, something he knew, had always known. Pale tufts of hardy grasses and low scrub bristled across the paddocks either side of the track. Sheep grazed or milled at the occasional water trough. A part of him eased and softened.

He wondered what it would be like to come back, start a new life. Live simply, on the land. Not here of course — even if the place was thriving, instead of shrivelling up, it would be too close to his brother. He would go the other side of Joondyne, or even down south where it was green and rained every year without fail. He could learn to farm; it was not alien to him — he'd grown up here, hadn't he? It might not be an easy life, but it would mean something; he would be carrying on the family tradition, bringing prosperity back to the Connor name. He would need someone to help him though, to share it with — a real woman, practical and straightforward. Someone who didn't waste half their life putting on make up and craving designer clothes. A woman like Hester.

She was obviously unhappy with his bastard of a brother. Neal didn't deserve her, couldn't possibly appreciate what he had. Or maybe he did — was that why he tried to keep his wife isolated, as cut off from the outside world as possible? He remembered then, that Andy had said something about Neal last night. What was it? Yes — Neal had threatened to kill him! He'd forgotten about it this morning, with all the busyness and excitement. What on earth could Andy have done to warrant a threat like that? Knowing Neal, it would be some ridiculous over-reaction; his brother was bound to hold some archaic prejudice against drug users. Idiot.

Bursts of noise reached him when he was close to the dam. Someone was already there. He stood and listened, then tramped up the slight incline of the bank. It was Hester and the boys. He smiled. They swam as though they were born to it, the boys. Hester had done an amazing job teaching them. Amazing.

The boys were playing around the inner tube with an inflatable ball. They seemed small and fragile in the expanse of flat water. Hester had one arm draped over the inner tube and tapped the ball back to the boys with the other. He noticed a blur of a mark on her upper arm.

He waved to them.

Billy shouted, pointing, 'Mummy, there's Uncle Dom!' Both boys waved frantically. Hester turned, startled. The ball dropped next to her, sending tiny ripples across the water. She didn't wave. Perhaps he was interrupting a lesson. He stood for a minute, indecisive, but the boys called and gestured for him to come in. He stripped to his boxer shorts.

He stepped along the rickety platform that jutted over the water. The platform looked like a strange jigsaw, with sections of different sized wood slotted in to replace rotten boards, but it was still the same platform he and Neal had learnt to dive off. They had competed to see who could dive in and swim the furthest under water. It was usually too close to call, and they bickered about it.

Dom stretched out his body and launched himself into the water. When he came up, he overarmed to Hester and the boys. He tasted dam water in his mouth, muddy and strong.

'Look what I can do, Uncle Dom!' The boys clambered onto the inner tube, vying for his attention, before he had his breath back properly. They tried one-legged balances and little dances until they toppled off and heaved themselves up again.

Hester trod water with only her head out. Her wet hair sat flat against her skull. Her face looked small and delicate and beautiful.

'Hope I'm not in the way.'

'No, they've had their lesson. Can't stay in much longer, but. Getting late to be out in the sun.'

Dom hooked an arm over the wide curve of the tube and pushed wet hair from his eyes. 'You've done a great job teaching the boys. They're incredible swimmers, for their age.'

'Well, it helps that they love the water. They're naturals.'

They both turned to watch as Alex toppled deliberately into the water, backwards.

'I enjoyed going to Dog Rock, Hester. Did Billy have a good time?'

'Yep. Sure did. Could hardly get him up this morning.'

She paused and looked away for a few seconds, before turning back to Dom. She lifted one arm onto the tube, then the other, hoisted herself up so that her torso rested on the warm rubber. Her breasts were small and flattened in her Speedo bathers. He could see now, that the dark mark on her right upper arm was a tattoo. There were more on her other arm, a blurry cluster; a heart, some initials. Half her back was decorated with intricate designs crashing messily into each other. A dragon's tail disappeared into the scoop of her bathers at her buttocks. There was something else too. Bruises. They looked like bruises on her back, splashes of marked flesh, dark blue, yellow-green. On her arms too.

She slid off the tube and dropped under the water, coming up in the centre. She hoisted herself up so she was sitting on

146

the tube with her legs dangling in the middle. He saw a scatter of scars across her brown thighs, mostly small and circular and slightly puckered, like burns. She stretched out her legs, pointed her toes to reach the other side of the tube, as if laying out her secrets before him.

Billy called, 'Count, Uncle Dom, count!'

His nephew showed him how long he could hold his breath under water. The boy came up sputtering and grinning.

'Fifteen. Fantastic!'

Hester swung her legs around and dropped into the water like a seal. 'Watch them for me?'

She glided the length of the dam and back, muscles tight, tattoos flashing. He played with the boys, then swam two lengths himself while she herded them to the platform and out of the dam.

He got out, brushed the gritty dirt from his feet and pulled his shorts on over his wet boxers. He would be dry in minutes.

The boys were inspecting a bleached sheep's skull they had found, just outside the fence.

'Out already?' Hester pushed her fingers through her damp hair. The marks on her body were covered by a loose cotton shirt now, and a pair of jeans cut-off at the knee. But he knew they were there. Bruises. He'd wondered, but now there was no doubt. His brother had turned out to be that kind of man. He felt dull with shock and confusion.

'I'd better get back. I'm kind of presiding over a family reunion. Andy Bohan's turned up — you know, Lizzie and Colin's son? My old school mate.'

She stopped with her fingers burrowed in her hair and slowly lowered her arms. 'Andy's here?'

'You know him?'

'Yeah. Yeah, I know him. Is he okay?'

Dom nodded. 'He seems well. But how —?'

'It's a long story, Dom. I'll tell you sometime.' Without giving him a chance to speak she pulled a bottle of water out of a plastic carrier bag and called, 'Boys! Come here, please!'

There were so many questions. He didn't want her to go. 'Look, Hester, if you need any help, I want you to know that —'

'I don't need anything.' It sounded sharp, and her shoulders sagged a little, as though she regretted this. She reached out and brushed his arm with her damp fingers. 'You wouldn't just go and see if you can drag the boys away from their trophy, would you? And when they ask you if they can bring it home, please say no. They've already got a collection of the horrible damn things.'

Later, Dom drove Lizzie back. When he pulled up outside the farmhouse she turned to him, her face still blotched with emotion.

'It might sound naive, Dom, but Andy —' She paused, her mouth moving slightly, as though she was having an inner conversation, grappling with herself, '— he really does seem changed, this time. More like the old Andy, don't you think?' Her face was anxious and eager.

Dom agreed that Andy certainly seemed to be doing well.

'Colin'll come round.' She patted his hand, as if she needed to reassure him, instead of herself.

The sun was going down fast. Muddy purple, the colour of a child's dirty paint water, streaked the sky. Andy had cooked lamb chops, mashed potatoes and fat broad beans, all provided by Lizzie, but Dom hadn't been able to eat much. On the verandah, a plate of sliced-up fruit cake sat untouched between them. Andy's book — *The Search: Finding Inner Peace* — was spreadeagled on his lap. It wasn't religion Andy had found, Dom realised, just some mishmash of new-agey ideas.

'Amazing sky, isn't it?' Andy said. 'Look at that colour. You don't get a sky like that in the city.'

Dom swigged at his second-last can of Swan Lager. He'd bought half a dozen in Marrup after dropping Lizzie off. He wished he'd got more. Questions clattered in his head. He tried to settle them, to order his thinking. 'I'm glad you got to see your mum today.'

'Yeah. Good plan. I shouldn't have left her to worry like that for so long. But regret's a useless emotion. I'm just pleased it's happened. Thanks mate. And thanks for letting me stay. As soon as Mum's got Dad on side I'll get out of your hair.'

'Don't worry. Stay as long as you like.' Flies danced around the fruitcake. 'I meant to tell you, I saw Hester today when I was at the dam. Neal's wife. She was there with the boys.'

'Hester.' Andy said the name slowly, like a special code. 'How is she, Dom?'

'As well as you'd expect, I suppose, being married to my brother.' Dom felt a kick of resentment. How did they know each other? Secrets and bloody silences. What the hell was going on? He took another swig from the can and wiped away a dribble of beer from the corner of his mouth.

'But she seems — you know, happy enough?'

'Andy, for Christ's sake!' Dom gripped the can in frustration. The thin metal popped and creaked. 'Give me a clue — how is it that my old school mate knows my sister-in-law?' He knew he sounded belligerent but he couldn't let it go. He thought he might be drunk. 'How the poor bloody woman even became my sister-in-law in the first place is a mystery to me, for that matter.'

Andy seemed about to speak, then stopped. Finally, in a quiet voice, he said, 'I wrote to you about her.'

'Hester?'

'A few times, I think — I'm not sure; it was a long time ago.'

'I — sometimes my mail went missing. I moved a lot back then.'

'It doesn't matter. I can't remember what I said, but it wouldn't have been the truth anyway.' He looked straight ahead. 'Not the whole truth. I didn't want you to know about the drugs, for a start. Thought it was just a blip, a passing phase. Huh!'

Dom didn't know what to say. He traced a bead of condensation down the beer can with his finger.

'Hester and I, we — mixed in the same circles, you might say. It's old stuff. History.' Andy waved a hand dismissively. 'Mate, you know, it's not really up to me to tell you about —'

'Andy, I saw her. She's got tattoos — and not just cute little butterflies. Scars too. And bruises.'

'Bruises? You mean …?

Dom nodded. 'Looks like it.'

'Jesus.' Andy leaned forward in his chair and his book clattered to the ground. 'Fucking bastard. He was meant to look after her. That was all she wanted.' He picked up the book and placed it, closed, on his lap. He looked down at a spot on the verandah, his thin forearms resting on his thighs.

After a while, he spoke again. 'She worked the streets around where I used to go to score. She had a rough time, Dom — some nasty bloody wankers out there. We talked a bit. Made each other laugh. She seemed different to the other girls; more vulnerable, but kind of tougher at the same time. After I went into detox — the first of many — I didn't see her for weeks. But I couldn't get her out of my head. When I went back to find her she was gone, so I asked around — Perth's not a very big place, there's nowhere to really hide. She was staying in a hostel. Trying to get clean, sort herself out, like I was. She smiled at me when I went to see her, like she'd been waiting for me to show up.' His voice trailed off. He rubbed his hands together slowly. 'We shared a flat together, but it didn't work out. My complete uselessness could have had something to do with it.' He tried to sound light-hearted, but he couldn't disguise the pain in his voice.

Dom felt sorry now, for pressing him. It wasn't fair.

Andy gave Dom a tight smile. He sat back. 'And as for your brother, well, he came to the city — I don't know why exactly; something to do with the farm. Mum and Dad had asked him to drop off a package for me. Homemade cake, jam, socks. You know, the kind of packages they used to send soldiers in the war.' He gave a brief, dry laugh. 'That's what I called them — Mum's War Supplies. God, I used to be so pleased when one of those packages turned up.'

The gassy beer fizzed in Dom's stomach. Neal in the city? He didn't even know his brother had ever been to Perth.

Andy scratched at his head. 'Neal was bowled over by Hester. It was a total obsession, right from the start. I knew he was coming to see her, taking her out. God knows where he got the nerve. But she encouraged it and I didn't blame her, I really didn't. I was a mess. I wanted what was best for her, Dom. She saw a way out. A new life for herself, totally away from the old shit. Legitimate married woman. Wholesome farm life.'

Despite the beer, Dom's throat felt dry. 'Wholesome.'

The word hung around in the stillness.

Andy wiped a hand over the cover of the book on his lap. It was dark enough now to see flecks of stars and lights from the cottage, up the track.

Dom drained the warm dregs from the can in his hand and clattered into the kitchen for the last beer. Even though he'd cleaned it, the fridge spat a sour, musty smell. He took out the last can and clicked the ring-pull. After a few foamy mouthfuls, he shuffled back outside and dropped into his chair. A metallic taste lingered on his tongue.

Andy was eating a slice of the fruit cake. 'So Neal's jealous of me,' he said, between chews of cake. 'And doesn't like being reminded of Hester's past, I reckon.' He wiped crumbs from around his mouth. 'Cake's good. You should try some. Listen, the mozzies are getting bad. I'm going to go in and read for a while. Tomorrow you can tell me all about London, eh?'

'London. Sure.'

'And Dom, I've just remembered. The poems. There was one you wrote. I loved it. How did it go now?

Fire in the heavens, and fire along the hills,
and fire made solid in the flinty stone …'

'Andy, please.'

'What?'

'I didn't write that.'

'No?'

'It's by Christopher Brennan. A famous poet. He died seventy-five years ago.'

'Christopher …? Oh, right. I remember you reading it. You read it really well, Dom. That's why it's stuck in my head. You read it so well.'

17 MAIL

The ute swooped across the open space in front of the cottage and lurched to a halt near the shed. Neal didn't even bother to park in the shade of the salmon gum, she noticed, watching through the kitchen window. He'd stopped caring about other things he used to think were important too — making sure there was kindling chopped ready for the fire, his quick but thorough shower every night. Some nights he sunk into bed and closed his eyes with his hands still grimy, his body stinking of exhaustion, unable to manage the simple effort of cleaning himself. She didn't know from one day to the next whether he would be ravenous at tea time, or hardly touch his food, ignore her or be angry for something he hadn't cared about the day before, like her wasting water on her few struggling tomato plants, or his clean socks being too stiff.

At the table, Alex traced the lines of the big and small letters F with a pencil. He was working his way through the alphabet. She had written the word 'fruit' and drawn pictures of an orange, an apple and a banana for him to colour in. Billy copied a simple sentence: 'Ernie helps his friend Ellie eat eggs', and was supposed to draw his own pictures to go with the sentence. He was due to start Year One in January and Alex could go to kindy, but she was not going to send them. She couldn't bear the thought of them travelling all the way to Joondyne and back each day, being away from her for so long. Neal thought they should go, had argued that he didn't want them to miss out, that their education was important. She'd reminded him that she had taught them to swim and promised they would go next year. Eventually, he'd agreed.

The ute's door slammed.

The boys stirred, distracted from their tasks. 'Daddy,' Alex murmured, looking up.

Hester nodded towards his paper. 'Keep going — you're doing a great job.'

With a pen in one hand and a slip of paper that was the beginnings of her shopping list in the other, she squatted down in front of an open cupboard and continued with her list-making. The self-raising flour was getting low. She took the lid off the tin and bent her head to smell the flour, bland and clean, without any suggestion of the aromas it could give off once it was mixed and baked. She pushed the lid back on; it had to be tight, or the flour would end up full of weevils. Sometimes they got in anyway. She didn't understand how.

Neal launched into the house, past the boys and down the hallway, without a word. The study door slammed shut. She stood up. Both the boys sat still, unsure, looking at her. They had their father's increasingly unpredictable behaviour to deal with, on top of Marjorie's death. She tried to smooth things for them, to keep it as easy as possible.

She forced a smile. 'Come on then, you're nearly finished. Daddy's busy at the moment, but he'll want to see what you've been doing later.' She hoped to God it was true. He was still good with the boys, his beloved sons, so far. He was never angry with them.

She opened the fridge to take stock of what else she needed to get at the General Store. It was Thursday — shopping day.

155

She stared into the fridge, trying to concentrate. Milk. Butter. Eggs. She hadn't been shopping last Thursday, because of the funeral. They were short of everything.

Hester closed her eyes and felt the wash of cool air from the fridge on her face, listened to the gentle hum of its motor.

She gave the boys a cold drink of cordial. As she put their plastic cups on the table she spotted something on the floor near the door. A letter. She picked it up. She used to collect the mail once a week when she went shopping, from the post office until it shut down, then from the General Store. About six months ago Neal had told her that he would collect the mail himself. He'd said it would be easier, that he could deal with urgent things straight away. It didn't make any difference to her — no-one ever wrote to Hester Connor. In six years she'd never had a letter.

The envelope in her hand was white with a clear window. The return address on the back was The Western Bank, in Perth. She stroked her finger across the edge of the envelope, glanced at the boys, and ducked down the hallway to the study.

For a few seconds she stood in front of the door and listened. There was no sound. She rubbed her thumb back and forth on the smooth white paper, raised her arm, hesitated, knocked.

As she was about to turn away the door shot open and Neal was there, his face tight, furious. Her husband looked at her like she was some strange invader. His body filled the doorway.

She handed him the letter. 'You dropped this. Back there, in the kitchen. Neal, I —'

He grabbed the envelope and slammed the door shut so quickly and with so much force she stumbled back, reaching out a hand to steady herself on the wall. She brushed her hands down her clothes, as if recovering from a fall. The boys were bickering now.

She could not even think what it was she had been going to say to him.

In the kitchen she settled the boys again, giving them a biscuit each, hardly registering their chatter and minor complaints. She went out to the verandah and sat down.

Andy was back, Dom had said.

Andy.

He is passed out on the sofa, wasted. His shallow breath charges the stingy rented living room with alcohol fumes. On the side table next to him a dribble of pale beer empties from a tipped-over can and oozes towards scattered debris: a red plastic lighter, a scrunch of silver foil, a small plastic bag, dusted white. No needles at least.

She tiptoes around the featureless flat, even though she knows a truckload of cops bashing at the door won't wake him. In the kitchen she eats cereal leaning against a cupboard, listening to the *tink tink* of her spoon against the chipped bowl. The milk tastes like it might be off.

For a while, she poises over a piece of paper with a pen gripped in her hand, as if the act itself will be enough to inspire the right words. Nothing comes. She can hardly explain to herself what she is doing, though she is sure it is the right thing.

She flicks the pen between her fingers with the restless tick of the clock. They bought the clock in Woolies when they moved in here, along with a bath mat and an Indian print throw for the sofa. The throw is already dotted with tiny burn holes and stained from spilt drinks.

A damp patch on the kitchen counter darkens the paper. She screws up the blank page and drops it in the bin.

At the door, she grips her bag and puts on the new sandals Neal bought her just a few days ago. They are sturdy and comfortable.

She pauses, without meaning to, and turns. She puts down her bag and steps across the room to the sofa. She brushes Andy's hair off his face. His skin is hot. Dark veins show through his thin eyelids. She kisses him on the forehead. He doesn't stir.

She picks up her bag, clicks open the flimsy door lock and steps out.

18 IMAGINE

Note: Refrain from the use of any stimulants at least two hours before your Practice.

Andy looked into his mug of coffee. He took a last sip and put the cup down.

Lie somewhere comfortable and quiet with your arms by yours sides and your palms facing upwards. Close your eyes.

He tugged the faded curtains across the wide bay window, leaving a gap in the middle; dust particles flurried in the gash of sunlight. He stretched his too-long body along the sofa, pushed a cushion under his head and held up the tattered paperback. He closed one eye and peered at the page with the other.

Now, you must regulate your breathing. Use whichever method you prefer to achieve this (see Section 2). It is vital to settle your body so your mind may be allowed the energy and freedom it needs.

He cleared his throat and took deep, regular breaths.

Your job now, is to look inside yourself. Your imagination is the only tool you need to achieve this. Imagine. Imagine you are standing on top of a hill. The breeze ruffles your hair. You stand, strong, proud and peaceful. Imagine. Imagine the words themselves: Strong. Proud. Peaceful. Let the words infuse your body. They are you and you are them.

'Andy? Hey, Andy.'

'Hmmm?'

'Wake up.'

He opened his eyes.

'What? Shit — I was … Hester?' He wondered, for a few confused seconds, if she was a vision, a dream, something he'd conjured with his mind. He sat up. The book resting on his stomach slid to the floor with a soft bump. He watched Hester as she stepped forward, picked up the book, moved back again towards the light from the window.

'*Imagine!*' she read. '*The Concept and Practice of Inner Visionary Healing for the Spirit.*' She raised her eyebrows. 'Wow.'

Andy sat blinking at her, still not quite taking in the truth of her presence. 'Hester.'

'Yep. It's me alright.' Her tone was light, bluff. 'So how's your spirit feeling, Andy?'

'My —? Oh — huh, pretty good, really. Yeah. Good.' He nodded and rubbed his hands together. 'All the better for seeing you, Hes. It's been a while, eh?'

Hester ducked her head and held the book with both hands. 'It has,' she said, her voice softer. 'A long while.'

She rifled the pages of the book with her thumb and looked around the room as though trying to memorise everything in it. Even in her baggy clothes she seemed thin and there were grey crescents under her eyes. But he'd seen her in worse shape. Much worse. Her hair was longer than before and paler. Bleached from the sun. She was still beautiful.

'Marjorie's gone. And now you're here. It's so ….' She shook her head.

He nodded. 'It must be.' He watched her. She looked away.

'Dom's at the cemetery. He missed the funeral, poor bugger.'

160

'I know.'

He made room on the sofa and patted the cushion next to him. 'Come and sit down. You want a drink?'

'No. Thanks.' She tapped the book against her thigh. 'Look, I can't stay. Neal watches the boys for an hour or so while I go shopping on a Thursday. If you can call going to the General Store shopping.' She came forward and dropped the book onto a side table next to the sofa.

For a panicked moment he thought she was going to leave, but she took another step forward and lowered herself onto the worn green velour. It was hard to believe she was right there, next to him again. He felt the pull of the past bond between them. God, he'd missed her. 'So. How are you, Hes?'

'I'm good. Fine.'

'Are you?'

There was a silence. Her face was controlled, almost stern. 'I can handle it, Andy.'

'Really?'

She nodded, once. 'I love it here. Take the boys swimming every day, in the dam. They're brilliant in the water. You should see them, they're like little fish.' She wove her flat palm vertically through the air.

Andy smiled. 'It'd be great to see them. Your boys.'

'Andy —'

'I know I can't. It's okay. I don't want to make things hard for you. Don't particularly want to get my head shot off either.' He paused and rubbed his temple with a stubby-nailed forefinger. 'Did you know I tried to come and see you last time I was around? Four years ago. Neal got to me before I got to you. I was at the start of the track, near the road. I wanted to see you, that's all. Make sure you were okay. Neal waved his rifle, said he'd use it next time he set eyes on me.'

She winced and tilted back her head. 'Shit.'

Andy held up both hands as if in compliant surrender. 'I said, "I'm hearing you buddy".'

'You did not.'

'Something like that.'

They laughed then, both of them.

'Jesus.' Hester's face was pink under the freckles that he used to trace with his finger. 'It's not funny.'

'No.'

'He might just do it, Andy.'

'That's what I thought.'

'Keep your head down while you're here, eh?'

'I will.'

She nodded slowly. 'How long are you around for anyway?'

'Not long. Spend a bit of time with Mum. Hopefully the old man too. He won't see me at the moment. Mum's working on it. After the thing with Neal last time, I nicked Dad's wallet and pissed off back to Perth.'

'I heard that bit.'

'My head wasn't in a good place then. Not that I'm trying to make excuses.'

'Your dad'll forgive you.'

'I hope so. He's put up with a lot, I suppose. But I'd like things to be good between us now. I want him to know that all the shit's in the past.'

She tilted her head, considering him. 'You seem well.'

'I am. I really am, Hes. Things have changed for me, at last. I'm a new man.' He noticed the fine lines at the corners of her eyes when she smiled.

'Good. I'm pleased for you, Andy. I might even forgive you for getting into that new-agey shit.'

'I know it's ridiculous, but it's fun, you know. And there are good bits. It's about hope, I suppose. You've got to have hope, Hes.'

'Well, if it makes you happy, mate. If it makes you happy.' She twisted at the plain gold ring on her finger. 'Look, I'd better —' She began to get up.

'Hes!' He blurted, terrified that she was going, leaving him, disappearing again before he'd had a chance to say what he needed to. She blinked and didn't move.

'I have to —' He'd thought endlessly about the right words, but now it was all lost, obliterated in a flood of emotion. He bent his head onto his hand. 'I'm so sorry, Hes,' he managed at last, without looking at her. 'I wish things had been different. I didn't give you what you deserved. I couldn't manage to put you before the drugs and the booze. I know it's too late now, but I want you to know I'm sorry.' He lifted his head to look up at her.

'We both made our choices, Andy,' she said quietly. 'I didn't want to hurt you either. I never wanted that.'

'You've got nothing to apologise for. Nothing.'

'I tried to leave a note, but …'

'I know.' He hesitated, looked down at this hands, back to her. 'I felt like I'd been left for dead at a car crash after you

163

went. I hung onto blaming you for a long time. For everything. Bad drivers, the state of the economy. Everything.'

Hester gave him a sad smile. 'It had to end.'

'Yes. I just want to know you're alright.'

'Like I said, I can handle it. Don't worry.'

'Hes —'

'I've got to go now, Andy.' She stood up. 'It's been good to see you. Take care, eh?'

He rose stiffly from the sofa, like an old man. 'You too, Hes. You too. Maybe I'll see you again, while I'm around.'

'Yeah. Maybe.'

He wanted to grab her, enfold her, protect her in a way he should have years before but had never quite managed. His arms stayed by his sides. He watched from the verandah as she drove off in the ute, speeding down the track in a flurry of dust.

After Hester had gone he sat on the sofa listening to the tick of the ugly wood-burl clock above the mantelpiece. He didn't know why he hadn't noticed the sound before. He remembered making the burl clocks at High School, in woodwork. This one must have been Dom's or Neal's. He wondered what had happened to his. Perhaps it had been on the wall at his parents' house all along, and he had never noticed.

He picked up his half-drunk mug of coffee, now cold, then sat still again, as if that small movement had tired him out. Hester had not found real contentment and happiness with Neal and her life here after all. It was not the brand-new start she had been expecting. There was no fairy-tale ending.

After a while he put down the coffee mug, got up and whipped back the curtains. He blinked at the onslaught of sun into the room. Where would he go next? What would he do? He hadn't thought that far ahead. A flash of panic threatened him. Were there ever any happy endings?

He picked up *Imagine!* and flicked through the pages.

19 HISTORY

Dom sat in the Nissan parked across the road from the Marrup Hotel and watched a mangy dog scratch itself on the verandah. He imagined how it once would have been; men tipping their hats as they passed acquaintances in the shade of the curved verandah roof, sulkies and traps vying for space, horses drinking from troughs.

He remembered going to the pub on his last day of High School. He must have been almost seventeen. They'd had their final exam and weren't wearing school uniform. He'd allowed himself to be cajoled by Andy into having a celebratory drink. Inside, it was cool and gloomy. The publican, Willy McFadden, said, 'Good afternoon, gentlemen,' and pulled them each a beer. Andy paid. Dom was anxious, but Andy was in his element, lighting a cigarette and leaning back in his chair, talking about all the places they could go now they were free of school; Sydney, Melbourne, maybe Darwin — get on a boat from there, drive across Asia! He'd seen something about a trip like that on TV. Dom nodded, but he already knew his foreseeable future. He was going to the city, to university. That was enough for him, then. A contained, manageable goal. Their glasses were still half full when they heard Willy McFadden talking loudly on the phone at the bar: 'That's right, Bob. Two under-agers, if you're quick.'

The boys made a rapid escape, ran halfway down the main street and hid behind the bank, giggling with the excitement of a close call. But Dom spent the whole of the holiday, before he went away to Perth, half-expecting to see Bob Swan's police car bumping down their track to find him.

The pub was still gloomy. Dom stood close to the heavy double doors for a few seconds, waiting for his eyes to adjust. The air was heavy with a yeasty smell, the floor dull and scratched. Fans clicked around on the high, yellowed ceiling, stirring a thin stream of cigarette smoke. ABC radio voices hummed. It was a strange, subterranean world.

A middle-aged farmer in a scruffy checked shirt, stretched taut by his beer gut, perched on a stool at the bar. As Dom approached, the red-faced man behind the bar squashed out his cigarette and leaned across with his arm outstretched.

'It's Dominic Connor, am I right?'

They shook hands. Jamie McFadden, Willy's son, had been in Dom's year at school. He'd worked in the pub alongside his dad even before he was legally old enough. Dom could smell alcohol on the man's breath. He was jowly, with thin, receding hair. Dom wouldn't have recognised him.

Jamie said he was sorry to hear about his mum. He called him Dommie and insisted he have a shot of whisky and a beer chaser on the house. The other man's name was Charlie. Apparently, he'd gone to school with Dom too. Dom pretended to remember him. Charlie added his sympathy and bought him another whisky. Dom had only come in for a quiet beer; he hadn't felt like going straight back to the Big House, after being at the cemetery. He didn't even like whisky much.

Jamie took the shot measurer out of the whisky bottle and splashed the golden liquid into Dom's glass, until it was almost half full.

'What the hell, eh? Not often we have foreign visitors,' he winked. 'Got to use it all up, anyway. Last of the Marrup Pub's stock you're drinking. You're part of history now, Dommie.'

He pulled more beers for all three of them, and told Dom that his mum and dad had moved away last year, over East, to the Gold Coast, where his sister lived.

'The missus is out there too. That's Debs — Debbie Oldfield, remember? The best looker in our class.' He winked again and made a clicking sound of appreciation from the side of his mouth. Dom winked back. It might have been the first time he'd ever winked at anybody.

'She's been there a month or so, with the kids. Got three of the little blighters. I'll go over in a few weeks myself. Only stayed back because I thought we might have a buyer for this place, but it fell through. Knew it was too good to be true. Some big corporate chain, hadn't quite realised where Marrup was. Now I'm meant to be finishing up. Just have to walk away. Gold bloody Coast. Can't see myself there, to tell the truth. But what can you do?'

'Be a damn shame to lose this, Jamie.' The whisky eased through Dom's gut, warm and comforting. 'I just don't get it. It's wrong.' He thunked his fist onto the sodden bar mat.

Jamie put both hands flat on the bar and leaned towards Dom. 'You could probably buy the place, couldn't you, Dommie? Buy up the whole bloody town if you wanted, I reckon. Got your big job over there in London, your nice house. Must be rolling in it.'

'No no no,' Dom shook his head emphatically. 'It's not like that. Whatever you've heard, it's —'

'Yeah, well,' Jamie stepped back and picked up his beer. 'What would you do in a dead shit-hole like this, anyway? You're better off out of it.'

'Too bloody right,' Charlie agreed. 'Bugger-all left to save now. It's a disgrace. Fucking pollies. Places like this're the backbone of the country, but they're bending us till we break.' He pulled both hands down, fast, as if snapping a stick. Dom flinched. 'They want to get all of us into the cities, that's what it is. Round us up, like bloody animals. To control us better.'

Dom looked at the red-faced man and nodded. Just now, he was inclined to agree with this logic.

'I dunno,' Jamie scratched at his protruding beer gut. 'Whatever the reason, it's happening, and we all gotta do what we gotta do. Every man for himself it is now.'

Dom tipped back his head and drained his beer. Jamie picked up the glass as soon as it touched the bar and refilled it. He chose coins and notes from the handful of money Dom dug from his pocket.

'You can pay if it makes you feel better,' he shrugged.

Dom stared into the frothy head of his beer. 'I suppose it's a blessing that Mum went when she did,' he mused, 'if things are really that bad.'

'You're not wrong there, Dom my boy. Real tough on the oldies, all this change. Bet she hated being stuck in that hospital too. So far away.'

'Hospital?'

'Yeah,' Charlie put in. 'Fucking hospitals. Death traps. Never know what —'

'To Marjorie.' Jamie lifted his glass. The three men raised a toast to Dom's mum. Their glasses clinked together.

'Marjorie,' Dom murmured.

A hand was on his shoulder.

'Dom! What're you doing? Look, give me those.' The voice was familiar. He leaned against the car and blinked, trying to focus in the brilliant daylight. The keys were out of his hand.

'Hester? Hi, hello. What're you doing here?' He smiled at her. Hester. God, it was good to see her. So good.

'I've been to the Store. Shopping. Come on, hop in, I'll give you a lift back. You're not going to get far. Except up a tree.'

'Oh, no, you don't have to, it's …' He found himself being led by the arm. She opened the door of the ute and steered him in.

'Hes.' He tried to concentrate, to speak clearly. 'I don't want to put you to any trouble.'

'No trouble. But I'm late, so let's go.'

His legs gave way suddenly and Hester was there again, holding him up, shoving him into the ute. She leaned across him and clipped in the seatbelt.

He tried closing his eyes on the drive back, but that made him feel sick.

'Thanks for the lift, Hes. Appreciate it.'

'No worries.'

'You know, I never thought I liked whisky.'

'Bloody Jamie McFadden, letting you go in that state. He's a cruel bastard.'

'Went to the cemetery. Felt so sad.'

'I know, mate.'

He frowned, trying to hold onto his fuzzy thoughts. 'You alright, Hes?'

'Yeah.'

'Must be hard for you with my brother. I don't know why —'

'Dom. Don't. You're pissed.'

'Maybe. A bit. But this is the truth, Hes; I think you're the most special, most beautiful woman I've ever met.'

Hester shook her head, but she was smiling.

'You know what? I had this idea. About coming back. Having my own farm.'

'Is that right.'

'Yep. And that's not all. Listen, Hes.' He held his breath. She glanced at him. 'I thought that we could do it together. You and me. I know it might seem a bit — well, we hardly know each other really, but we'd be happy, I —'

'For God's sake leave it, will you?'

'Hes, I think you should —'

'Dom! I swear I'll stop and leave you by the side of the bloody road if you don't shut up.'

At her raised voice, he held up his hands in defeat and shrunk back into his seat. He sat quietly for a minute. Damn. He'd said too much. Offended her.

His stomach lurched. 'Oh, shit —'

She pulled onto the gravel verge just in time.

171

He slept for the rest of the day, woke groggy and dry-mouthed on the mattress at the Big House in the early evening. Apparently Lizzie had been there.

'God, how embarrassing,' he groaned, when Andy told him. 'She's always thought of me as a good boy.'

'Oh, you know Mum. She's not the judgemental sort. By the way, there's ham and potato salad and fruit scones, in case you're feeling peckish. And she said she'd come back in the morning, give you a lift into Marrup to pick up your car.'

Dom sat up and took the mug of tea Andy offered him. 'Think I might have been a bit out of order with Hester too. Bloody hell.'

'She'll forgive you. We've all been there, mate.'

As his friend spoke, Dom saw the way his thin face caved in along his cheek bones. He'd hardly noticed how discoloured Andy's teeth were before. There was the awful gap where one — or was it two? — of them were missing. The tattoos on his wrist were harsh and ugly. This was a man who had lived most of his adult life dictated by urges, cravings and base desperation. He was not like Dom. Not at all.

Dom put down the tea. He fell back on the mattress and closed his eyes.

He felt ashamed of how he had behaved today, getting drunk, mouthing off to Hester. Ashamed too, of his financial problems, his failures in life. Unlike Andy, he valued hard work, thought success of some kind was important. What did Andy know of the real world? Even now, he might not be using drugs, but he was living in some fantasy land, with his half-baked self-help bollocks. He was nothing but a wasted, worn-out junkie. How could Dom explain his feelings, his hopes and fears to this man? Andy would understand nothing.

A memory nagged at the edge of his thoughts as Andy wittered on about his dad still being stubborn. What was it? Hospital. Yes. In the pub, they'd said his mum had been in hospital. Neal had never mentioned anything about that. Another secret. More silence.

The blue car was still there the next day, late in the morning, waiting outside the pub for him, bright and incongruous in the faded street. He thanked Lizzie for the lift and she squeezed his hand. He could have asked her about his mum being in hospital but it didn't seem fair; she'd already had the job, today, of telling Andy that his dad would not see him. She had tried everything. Colin refused to budge. He would not speak to Andy, or allow him to come to the house. As she drove, she revealed to Dom what she could not say to Andy — that Colin would not even acknowledge him as his son anymore.

She seemed sadly resigned. 'At least I've seen him now. I know he's alright.'

Dom felt sad for Lizzie, and knew that Andy would be devastated by his dad's rejection. But he could understand Colin's stance too; he was sticking to his guns. Enough was enough.

He drove back to the Big House slowly, thinking about his mum being in hospital and his visit to the cemetery yesterday that had unsettled him so much he'd let himself get embarrassingly drunk. His grandparents on both sides were there, as well as his mum, freshly buried next to his dad in a spot that had been kept for her all this time. There was still space nearby. Would Neal end up there too? Dom wondered if he would bother to come back for his brother's funeral, or visit his grave. He could not imagine it. Perhaps Dom would be there himself one day, tucked into the ground, surrounded by his family. No — he wouldn't die here. He'd be buried somewhere else. Would there be anyone to mourn at his graveside, wherever it was? His nephews? His own children?

Soon he would be gone from here. This is where it ends, he thought. It's finished. His family, the farm, the town. Everything. It was as though his past was being wiped away. How could anyone have a future without a past? He laughed out loud at such a strange concept and wondered if he might be going a bit mad.

He parked the car haphazardly in front of the Big House, grabbed his day pack from the back seat and half-jogged all the way to the dam. He needed to be alone. He had to get into the water.

The dam was empty. Quiet. It was well past the time that Hester and the boys would be there. Insects caused ripples on the water's smooth surface. In the next paddock a couple of crows hopped and fluttered over a dead sheep.

He stripped to his boxer shorts, curled his toes over the edge of the rickety platform and plunged in, stretching his body, making himself long and tight. He churned from one side of the dam to the other, arms pulling, flat hands cutting through, moving fast like a wind-up toy let loose, not thinking, feeling his muscles work over and over, heaving air into his lungs, pushing it out, in and out, thrashing every thought and feeling from his mind. When he felt he couldn't take anymore he floated on his back for a while, looking up at the vast, pure sky, before starting again.

Later, he lay his body along the wooden platform, exposed to the press of the sun. He felt its power, the uncompromising, relentless heat that stripped everything back to pure, clean essentials, the way fire charged through the bush, leaving it desiccated but ready to begin again.

20 THE PRESENT

The wire on the chook shed had to be fixed where a fox had tried to get in. There was washing to do and the bathroom needed cleaning. With the children having their afternoon sleep, she should have been getting on with her chores; instead, Hester sat at the kitchen table and felt the tender place on the right side of her back, near her waist, moved her fingers around the pain. She had taken the kids for their swimming lesson this morning anyway. She had managed.

After a minute she pressed her hands flat on the table, pushed herself up and moved across the room to ease into the big, comfortable chair. Neal's chair. She leaned her head against its high back and closed her eyes. Her fingers picked at a thin fray of fabric on the chair's arm. She turned her head and there was his smell, the familiar, grease-and-sweat, hard-work, close-up smell of him. It was strangely comforting.

When she opens the door to him for the first time there is a palpable surprise, an instant curiosity between them. He is attractive, in a rugged, worn sort of way. She can tell he has worked hard in his life. That first day, he has a parcel for Andy, from his parents, but he comes back the next day with a bunch of flowers hidden behind his back, and blushes to the core when she opens the door. Andy is not there. He is hardly ever at home; when he does make it back he is so out of it he barely notices her.

She invites Neal in. She makes tea but he is ill at ease and stares at his boots while she talks. The next day, he brings chocolates. She suggests they go for a walk. He looks at her then, a direct, clear look that makes her tingle. He sees who she is and he wants her. He doesn't ask questions.

He drives her up to King's Park in his ute. It is winter and the place is almost deserted. She says she doesn't mind the rain. Fat drops fall on them. Neither has a coat and they both get drenched. He walks with the suggestion of a limp and she likes that; he is flawed. Like her. She takes his hand and he responds with a firm, sure grip. She feels safe. She feels safe with him.

He stays away from the farm longer than he should. He drives her up to Mundaring Weir and they stand on the walkway and look at the huge expanse of water. It has stopped raining, but as they walk back to the car cold drops fall from the leaves of the trees. A young couple in a sporty Holden are parked with their windows down and the radio on. Pop music warbles around the car park. Neal lays a hand on her waist and begins to dance with her, right there, in an awkward, out-of-time waltz that doesn't fit with the music. He lifts her hand and indicates that she should spin around. She spins. He smiles, throws back his head and laughs a short, gruff laugh. She knows that he will ask her to marry him. And she will accept.

Something made her open her eyes — a vague noise, a stir of birds. She levered herself out of the chair and went to the window. Dom was there, at the end of the track, walking towards the house. Shit. She did not want him here. Not today. She was tired. She needed some peace.

177

He had seen her at the dam. He would have questions, even if he was too polite to ask them. She wondered how many of them Andy had already answered. God, Andy too. Why now? Why the hell did he have to turn up now? As if Neal didn't have enough to cope with already.

There was a light tap on the wall. She wished he would just knock, hard, announce himself. He was so bloody English sometimes.

'Hello?'

'Hi, Dom.' She kept her voice quiet. 'Come in.'

The door squealed open. She frowned and put her finger to her lips for a moment. 'Kids are asleep. Tea?'

'No, it's okay. A glass of water would be nice though.'

He settled an old shoe box on the table and dropped a half full plastic carrier bag next to it.

She poured him a glass of water from a cold bottle in the fridge.

He drank it in one go. 'Thanks Hester. I hope I'm not —'

She dismissed his pleasantry with a wave of her hand.

'I've been clearing out. Brought some things over for Neal.' He patted the plastic bag. 'School reports. Certificates. A few photos. Thought he might like to have them.'

'Thanks. I'll give them to him.' Or would she just burn them in the kitchen fire, pretend Dom had never been here? It would be easier.

Dom's neat hair was tousled now, unkempt. She realised that his skin had already changed from its pallid English hue, darkened by the sun. She folded her arms across her chest. She didn't offer him a seat, but he wasn't ready to leave.

'Lizzie took me into Marrup to pick up my car this morning. Thanks for giving me a lift yesterday.'

'No worries. How's the hangover?'

He smiled, lowered his head in a chastened way. 'Much better after a swim in the dam. Really clears the mind.' He tapped his middle finger on the table in a quiet rhythm. He looked up. 'I'm sorry if I said anything … out of order.'

She shrugged. 'You were drunk.'

He nodded and seemed to want to say more.

'Look, Dom, I've got a lot of chores to —'

With two decisive movements Dom pulled the lid off the shoebox and pushed the box along the table so it was in front of her. She frowned and eased forward to peer in. An elegant necklace lay on a bed of red velvet. Diamonds. Were they diamonds?

She was curious, despite herself. 'Huh. Wow. You held up a jewellers or something?'

'I found it in Mum's bedroom. In the wardrobe. Look, there's more. Lots more.' Gently, he lifted the layers, setting them on the table. There were bracelets and brooches, necklaces and earrings, all exuding an undeniable, rich beauty.

'Bloody hell. Is this for real? I never knew Marjorie had this sort of stuff.'

'Lizzie Bohan says it's the family jewels. Mum and Lizzie used to wear them to dances in Marrup, apparently. Must be worth a bit, Hester. A good bit.'

'Dances at Marrup? Hard to imagine. God, look at this thing.' Hester picked up a three-tiered necklace of diamonds

179

and glittering blue stones. She held it to her throat. 'Amazing. What's the blue stone?'

'I'm not sure. Sapphire's blue, isn't it? Turn around, let me do it up.'

She couldn't resist. Just for a moment. She was captivated. She wanted to feel the heavy, fragile beauty of it on her body. She turned too quickly and winced in pain. She didn't try to explain and Dom said nothing. When he had done up the clasp she went to the kitchen window, in front of the sink, and stood looking at her reflection in the glass.

She smiled. 'Sapphire.' The word slipped through her lips like silk. She touched her fingers to the necklace, tilted her head to one side. She felt a sudden excitement, a flush of recklessness, as though the necklace was transforming her into someone else from another time; royalty perhaps, or a rich European woman, dressing for a ball. A contented farmer's wife, going to a dance.

'You look beautiful.' His soft accent washed over her. He moved around to stand near her. Close enough to touch. 'Have it, Hester. It's for you.'

The room seemed to refocus itself. Everything was sharp and clear; the worn lino, the yellowing ceiling, the dirty, fraying wire in the flyscreen door. Now she was anxious about the boys waking up, about the work she had to do. About Neal returning.

'What? Oh, no!' She fumbled with the clasp of the necklace and tried to keep her voice down. 'Don't be bloody mad. Where would I wear it, for God's sake?'

Dom's fingers brushed her neck as he undid the clasp for her. His hands rested lightly on her shoulders for a moment. The necklace dropped and crumpled into a solid weight in her hand.

'No, Hester. All of it. It's all yours. I want you to have it.'

She could see his reflection in the window next to hers.

'This is for you. You and the boys. I've thought about it a lot and I've decided. You can sell it, do whatever you like. Leave, Hester. Make a new start. I want this jewellery to do some good.' His voice took on an angry edge. 'You deserve better.'

She shook her head, turned, brushed past him and began to pack the jewellery back into the shoebox.

'Please, Hester, it's the least I can do.'

'Dom. No.'

'Hester, Neal has no right to —'

'Stop it,' she hissed. 'Just stop. What would you know about it, eh? Neal changed everything for me. He saved my fucking life. Can you imagine that? Do you have any idea?' She leaned in towards him, steadying herself with one hand on the table. 'You know nothing about Neal. Nothing. He might not be perfect, but he's ...' She felt her anger drain out of her and slumped against the table. She breathed deeply, willing herself not to cry. 'He's my husband, Dom. He's having a bit of a hard time at the moment, that's all. A hard time.'

She handed him the box.

'Listen, Hester —'

'Dom, please —'

'I just need to know one thing. Neal, was he … with Mum … I mean, he didn't treat her badly, did he? He didn't …?'

'What? Jesus, Dom. His own mum? He'd never — He thought the world of Marjorie.' A trapped fly buzzed at the window. Sweat tickled the skin behind her ear. 'I'll see you later, Dom.'

She moved to the flyscreen door and eased it open for him.

When Alex and Billy got up she made them toast and vegemite and drinks of cordial. They sat at the table and ate while she pulled clothes out of the ancient, clunking washing machine. She knew they would dry stiff and scratchy from the cheap soap powder and the bore water that was verging on brackish.

After the boys had finished eating, she hung the clothes out on the line strung along the side verandah, while they handed her plastic pegs from an old ice-cream container, counting them out. When she had finished, she sat with them and they counted how many pegs were left in the container. Billy helped Alex sort them into colours. There were yellow, blue and green ones. Billy squeezed a green peg open and stuck it on one of Alex's toes. The smaller boy squealed and cried. Billy cuddled him, after Hester had taken the peg off, and said he was sorry. She took the boys to the shed with her to find some wire to fix the chook shed. They collected the eggs in their delicate way — they rarely broke any — while she twisted and pulled at the wire with pliers, holding herself against the pain.

She was beginning to get tea ready when Neal stamped into the room, trailing dust from his heavy boots.

He always took his boots off. He never wore them inside.

He brought the coarse smells of hard work and earth with him. And there was something else; a pungent aroma, so rich it sickened her. The smell of blood and fresh meat.

The rifle hung loosely in one of his big hands, with the barrel pointing towards the floor. He clutched a white plastic fertiliser sack with the other hand, the sinews in his arm showing like taut wire. The boys called out, 'Daddy!' but they stayed where they were. Neal dumped the bag on the table. It spread with an oozing sigh as the weight of its contents settled.

'Might be a bit of a tough old bastard, this one, but you'll make it nice, Hes, won't you? You always do.' His voice was unusually loud.

'I do my best.' She tried to smile.

A trickle of dark blood meandered along the table from the bottom of the sack towards the plastic bag that Dom had left. How could she have forgotten about it? She moved to pick it up but Neal's hand, with a quick, smooth movement, clamped over hers, pinning it to the table. She could hear the water for the potatoes come to the boil. It chugged and spat and began to overflow the saucepan.

Alex started to whine, then to cry in earnest.

Neal twisted around to look at his son. He released her hand. 'What's the problem, eh, my little man?' he crooned, scooping up the boy. 'You want your tea? Won't be long now. Shh.'

That night, her husband hit her hard, twice, on both sides of her face, one after the other, so her head whipped round and her neck felt like it might snap. He pushed her back towards the bed and she stumbled and cried out, without meaning to. A noise, a call, came from the boys' room and Hester and Neal became quiet and still, as though they had just been chatting about getting cheap wood from John Miles, or half a dozen new chooks. Whichever boy it was went back to sleep.

She couldn't stop shaking. He stroked her hair, took her arm gently and helped her to sit on the bed, as though she were a child he'd rescued from an accident. She used to relish his touch, the clearest way he had of showing his feelings for her. Now, she tried not to flinch when he came near her. Sometimes, she felt sick.

Her stomach tightens when Callum's damp hand squeezes her knee at the breakfast table. He smiles and says, 'Cheer up my lovely, it might never happen.' They are going to get married, her mum and Callum. They have been together for six months. He is a medical rep her mother met at the doctor's surgery where she works as a receptionist. He is much younger than her mother. His hair is slightly greasy and his clothes always look crumpled, as though he's pulled them straight out of a suitcase. Callum takes her mother to the Chinese restaurant and waltzes her around the kitchen to pop songs on the radio. Her mother says she's never been so happy.

Hester is fourteen. Her father has been gone more than two years. She has never replied to his letters. In his last one, three months ago, he said he was moving to Queensland with his new girlfriend, and would send an address when they were settled. They are going to have a baby.

One night Callum comes into Hester's room and strokes her hair. He whispers that he just wants to say good night, although he's woken her. He holds her down and clamps a sweaty hand over her mouth. His body shudders when he's finished and he drops his head onto her shoulder. His hair smells bad, like clothes left damp in the washing machine too long, and she gags. He puts his face up close to hers in the dim light of the room and whispers that this is their little bit of fun to share, their secret. Her mother would be destroyed if she found out. Not that she, or anyone else, would believe her anyway. He pats her cheek as he leaves. Each time, after he has finished, he pats her cheek. She feels her skin burn where he has touched her.

He is right. Her mother doesn't believe her; she calls her daughter a lying, jealous little slut. And a few more things. Hester doesn't bother telling anyone else. In the end she leaves. She is fifteen. Something has already begun to harden in her; before she goes she demands money from Callum. It is not much — just enough to get her started, in the city. She will forget all about her parents, about Callum's night visits, the vile, sickening smell of him. She will make her own life. She will.

Neal lay still, with his back to her. Hester listened to the rhythmic pull and whistle of his breath. Outside, parrots rasped early morning greetings. Somehow, she had slept.

She eased back the bed cover and crept to the bathroom. New light glazed through the dusty window. She lifted off her nightdress and turned on the shower. Water spluttered from the rusting shower head, then settled into a thin stream.

They were supposed to have showers only at night, for no more than three minutes. But this morning she didn't care if she was breaking the rules. She closed her eyes and let the warm water soothe her neck, drench her whole body. For a moment, she craved something to block out the pain, the sadness. She remembered how good it was to not feel.

She made herself touch her shoulders, press her hands to her breasts, stomach, thighs, tried to banish the revulsion she felt for her body. It was hers. She had to carry it around, and all the things that had been done to it. She had to live with it.

She touched her neck, felt the hard collarbone below it. She thought about the jewellery Dom had brought for her, the glittering richness of the stones on velvet, the way the necklace had felt against her throat. It had seemed, just for a moment, with the cool weight of the jewellery on her skin, that anything might be possible.

21 LOCKED, BOLTED

He couldn't concentrate on *Finding Inner Peace*; he turned over the corner of the page he was on and closed the book. The blue car shimmered in the mid-morning sunlight. Dom had gone off to the dam, again.

Since Dom's little over-indulgence at the pub his friend had been distracted and uncommunicative. Andy was worried about him, but he had other things on his mind too. Seeing Hester yesterday had been hard. His internal, nagging voice of judgement that he thought he'd put to rest had been stirred up — if he'd been a better person before, if he hadn't been so selfish, things would be different now. Hester wouldn't be stuck out here for a start, with some controlling bastard who hit her. He made himself think the words clearly: he hit her. The prick hit her.

Then there was his dad. How long would it be before he caved in and allowed Andy into his presence? It was like some cruel punishment. Hadn't Andy waited long enough? He needed to get things sorted out with his dad. Until then, he could not draw a solid line under his old life, move head-on, full swing into starting afresh.

He closed his eyes and rested his head against the wall. He must have drifted into a doze; the sound of an engine jolted him awake. The book slipped off his lap. He blinked, disorientated, and watched the ute drive slowly past the house. Neal. It was Neal, staring at him. Andy stared back. The ute turned into one of the front paddocks and bumped away towards a distant water trough.

He had not been shot at. Neal hadn't even stopped. Still, he thought, it wouldn't hurt to make himself scarce, for a while. Now would be the perfect time to put into action the plan he'd been considering.

The car keys were on the kitchen table.

The driver's side door handle was so hot he flinched when he touched it. The seat was comfortable, but too far forward — he reached under and adjusted it with a lever, made room for his long legs. He was going to see his dad. He would be back before Dom even knew the car was gone.

It felt good to drive again. There wasn't much chance of him getting caught here for not having a licence. He whistled to himself and fiddled with the air-conditioning. The little car felt agile and smooth. He pushed up through the gears and down again when he came to the track that led to the farm. He drove past the simple wooden sign, fixed sturdily into the ground: BOHAN.

From the outside, the house looked just the same; tidy and pleasant. Familiar. A hardy climber clung to a trellis on one side of the verandah and the fibro walls had been recently painted. White, again. His dad's ute was tucked into the shed. Andy parked and got out. He strode towards the house. Taking control of the situation had given him a buzz of exhilaration. He felt sure of himself.

His mother appeared on the verandah, a tea-towel trailing from one hand. She smiled in a wary, anxious way. 'Andy. I — I thought it was Dom.'

He stood at the bottom of the steps. 'No, Mum. Just me. The house looks good. Climber's doing well.'

'I try to take care of it.'

'Mum, I'd like to talk to Dad. Is he here?'

'Andy.' She shook her head, a frown of concern biting into her craggy brow. 'Please. It isn't worth it. Believe me.'

'Mum.'

'I know it's hard, but sometimes you have to —'

'Mum, I'm not trying to cause trouble. That's the last thing I want. I know you've tried and I appreciate it, but I need to do this. Don't worry, it'll be alright.'

Lizzie moved cautiously to the edge of the verandah, as though it were a precipice, and eased herself down. She sat with her feet on the steps. Her face crumpled, gave way, like paper being screwed up. She raised a hand to hide her tears. Her sobs were noisy and deep. Andy couldn't remember seeing his mother cry like this before. Ever. It was terrible.

'Mum.' He shuffled around, flapped his arms uselessly. 'I didn't mean to upset you. I just want to talk to him, that's all.' Shit. He had made his mother cry. Perhaps it was him, the way he was. The carrier of misery.

He wanted to go to her, to comfort her, but he couldn't. He had to keep his goal in focus. He couldn't be distracted, now.

Lizzie fished in her apron pocket for a tissue and blew her nose.

'You alright?'

She nodded and tried to smile. 'Sorry. Turning into an over-emotional old biddy.' She bunched her hands on her thighs and stood up, with a humph of effort, or pain. She seemed old suddenly, almost frail.

'Why don't you come in for some tea and cake? I've got raisin loaf, made yesterday. Turned out good.'

Andy glanced at the ground and pushed at a stick with one foot. 'Where is he?' He tried not to sound demanding.

They stood for a few seconds, each stilled by the force of their own fears and needs.

Lizzie's shoulders sagged. 'Down the back, somewhere. Checking the fence, on the bike.' She sounded resigned. 'Some of John Jameson's sheep are missing.'

Straight away he was remembering the landscape, plotting the route in his head as he strode past the shed towards the wide, dirt track that ran along the side of the paddocks.

'Andy!' his mum called, before he was out of sight. He stopped and turned. 'Watch out for snakes, eh?'

The track was flecked with shade from the thin stretch of gums and scrub along its edge. The drumming buzz of invisible cicadas surrounded him.

Once they were face-to-face, his dad would mellow out. It would be a relief probably, for both of them. Anyway, why shouldn't it be him, Andy, who made the first move? It was fair enough really; it had been him who'd fucked up. Nicking anyone's wallet wasn't exactly a polite thing to do, but your own father's — well, that was just nasty. He had been desperate, but still. No excuses.

It was peaceful here. He began to feel relaxed, almost jaunty. His mum didn't need to remind him to look out for snakes; this was his place, he knew the land. Where you grew up wasn't something sloughed off when you left, like an outgrown skin. The farm, the bush — it was part of him. He felt at home here. He felt like himself. It was good to be back.

He came to a stretch of bare paddocks on his right, where wheat used to grow. He stopped. There was no wheat there now. Nothing. Of course, it wasn't quite the same place he grew up. Would the land ever recover, the yearly rhythms of planting and harvesting ever be restored? He wondered how bad the salinity was across the farm. It was something he wanted to ask his dad, once things were sorted out between them. He had avoided putting the question to his mum, in case it upset her — he'd already done enough of that.

He looked around at the waist-high grasses and untamed scrub pushing at the boundaries of the empty paddocks. There'd been no burning-off for a while. As a kid, it was the event of the year for him, the annual burn. His dad always took him along, allowed him to be involved, even when he was very young. When he was older, not even a teenager, he was trusted to take the kero. He learnt exactly how much to splash, where to drop the lit match onto the tindery grass and scrub. The flames crackled and fizzed and rolled away to the edge of the ploughed fire break. It was tense and exhilarating. The smell of kero clung to his hands and stuck in his nostrils. Smoke blanketed the clear sky for hours, changing day into a strange, hazy twilight. Chickens went to roost in the middle of the day and sheep bleated and milled together in confusion. The men carried heavy hessian bags and shouted and whistled, guarding the flames as though they were murderous criminals bent on escaping. It only took a spitting spark, a tiny breath of wind in the wrong direction, to cause disaster. When a fire got out of control everything speeded up, became loud and urgent. It was exciting. Of course, he had no concept then, of what it would really be like if the worst were to happen.

It felt like he had been walking for a long time. The trees were sparse now; there was little protection from the growing heat. His shirt clung to his back, wet with sweat. Flies tried to crawl into the corners of his eyes. He was thirsty. He hadn't brought any water with him. Stupid. He dug a stick of minty chewing gum out of his pocket and felt the moisture spurt into his mouth, savoured its fake freshness.

He stopped where another thin track sliced across the one he was on and hesitated; it was so many years since he'd been down here. He looked around, narrowed his eyes against the glaring red of the dirt tracks. He thought for a minute, then carried straight on towards the stretch of bush which marked the edge of the farm.

He held his breath against the sickening stench of a rotting sheep carcass crowded with crows. They flapped and hopped but did not fly away as he passed, only feet away.

When he reached the bush he stood still and listened. He knew there was a clearing on the other side between the bush and the fence which marked the Jamesons' property. His dad would be along there somewhere.

He plunged into the mottled shade, through the clusters of spindly mallees and the scatter of the leafier, straighter Joondyne type, their rich red bark peeling back in long strips like scalded skin. The scrub was high and thick in places; unruly branches and spear-sharp leaves jabbed at his arms. He drew back at a rustle, a dark movement, but it was only a lumbering goanna.

As soon as he emerged into the sharp light he saw the motorbike in the distance, to his left, leaning on its stand. His dad was squatting down at the fence, near the bike. Andy wanted to call out, but held himself back. The gum he'd been chewing was tasteless and soggy now, doing nothing for his thirst. He spat it out.

His dad stood up. Andy saw him look in his direction and tip his hat back on his head. After a few seconds he straightened his hat and squatted down again.

Andy stopped ten feet away, near the motorbike, but his father did not pause in his work; he did not acknowledge his son's presence in any way. He took a thick metal staple that he held between his teeth and hammered it into the fence post, pinning down the wire.

'Thought you might want some help.'

The older man rose from his squat without looking at Andy. He yanked at the taut fence wire, testing its strength. 'If I wanted help, I'd ask for it.'

It was a relief to hear his dad's voice. He tried again. 'So he's still running sheep, old Mr Jameson? How is he these days?'

His dad moved a few steps away, pulled at the wire again. He said nothing.

'Dad —' As Andy moved forward his dad stepped back, almost cringed away, the hammer half-raised in his hand, as though he was frightened, preparing to defend himself.

He lowered the hammer slowly. 'I don't know what you're doing here, what you could possibly expect from me, but whatever it is, I can't give it to you.'

'Dad, I know it's hard for you to believe that things have changed. But you'll see. Everything's different now, I really feel like —'

'I don't want to be talking to you at all,' his dad cut him off, 'but I'm not uncivilised. Since you're here, I'll tell you that I don't want anything more to do with you. Ever.'

'Look, I know the last time —'

'It's not about last time. Or the time before that. It's all of it. It's you. I used to be ashamed of you, but now I don't care. I don't feel anything.' He lifted his chin slightly and moved his gaze to a spot above Andy's head. 'I don't wish you ill. I just want you to leave us alone. You don't know what you've put your mum through. All those years. There's something wrong with you.' He shook his head. 'Look at Dom. He's got somewhere. His mum was proud of him. And Neal. His father, God rest him, would have been proud too. Neal's kept that farm going. It hasn't been easy.' It sounded like a speech, something he might have rehearsed in his head many times, or practiced out loud, alone. 'And your sister of course — Gillian's done well for herself. But you? You've done nothing but squander your life and cause everyone misery. No more. No more.'

'Jeez, Dad, come on. Don't you think you're being a bit melodramatic? I know I've done some bad things, but that doesn't mean I'm a bad person. People can change!'

'Humh.' His dad snorted. He picked up a pair of pliers from the top of a fence post and put them in a grey toolbox, placing the hammer next to them, neatly.

Andy clenched his fists and fought back tears.

His father strapped the toolbox onto the back seat of the motorbike in silence.

'Dad!'

He swung a leg over the bike and flicked the stand up with the heel of his boot. He hesitated, with his fingers on the key, for a flicker of a moment, before the bike roared into life.

'And I fucking hate you too!' Andy screamed at the receding motorbike before it turned and disappeared down a track through the bush that he hadn't even noticed before.

Lizzie must have been watching out for him. She came down from the house to meet him, waited near the blue car as he trudged around the side of the shed. His dad had kept going, she told him. He had gone out somewhere, on the motorbike. Andy lowered his head. His sweaty feet throbbed, entombed in his cheap trainers.

'Don't worry about him. He's just a stubborn old bastard.' She patted his arm. 'Come inside,' she said.

He drank three glasses of water but could not eat the cake she offered. He told her he should get going, take the car back to Dom. She wrapped the chunk of cake in silver foil. She wouldn't let him leave without it.

From the farm track, he turned left onto the road, instead of right, and drove into Marrup.

The pub door eased open. A man in work shorts and dusty boots swaggered out unsteadily, squashing a battered hat onto his head. A dog stirred itself from its shaded place against the wall and followed when called. The door swung closed.

The air inside the car was heavy and hot. Sweat trickled down Andy's neck. His breath came fast and shallow. He closed his eyes and imagined the pub door closed; locked, bolted, covered with steel so hard that nothing could penetrate it. He pictured the windows the same way. There was no way in. He could not get a drink. It was impossible. Even if his life depended on it, he could not get one.

This was his test. His first big test. If he had one drink, he would have another and another. And once he was on the road to oblivion, he would have no reason, no reason at all, not to slide back to where he had come from, to seek out something so much better at destroying feeling, something potent, all-consuming. It would be so easy.

Going to see his dad had been a mistake. He should have known, should have listened to his mum. But he had not been able to stop himself.

He gripped the steering wheel so tightly his arms began to tremble. How could he have been so stupid? It was just like him, blundering along, never thinking through the consequences of anything properly. He was hopeless. He groped for the door handle and pulled. It clicked open, but he stayed sitting in the car, one hand still tight on the steering wheel.

He looked at the pub across the road. It was all very well to imagine the place to be impenetrable, but he knew that if he chose to get out of the car now and go in, the front door would swing open welcomingly, that slimy bastard Jamie McFadden would greet him like his best friend. What was the point of all the books he'd been reading if they couldn't help him now? Righto, he thought. He needed control. But where did it come from, how could he keep it within reach, have it there to pull out when the going got rough? He had to look within. Believe in himself, that was the key. Not let other people's shit get to him.

What was that he'd read? He couldn't remember which book it was from, but it was a good bit of advice: *You can't change other people*. Not bloody rocket science, but it wasn't rocket science he needed right now. Just because he'd got clean and was sorting out his own life didn't mean he could change anyone else. Hester was still in self-destruct mode, choosing to stay with her fucker of a husband; Dom couldn't show his feelings and was obviously full of worries and hang-ups. And his dad. His dad had decided to live the rest of his life minus a son. There was only so much you could do, then you had to let go.

He whacked the steering wheel with the heel of his hand. He'd tried his best! If his dad couldn't forgive him, that was his dad's problem. He wasn't worldly, his dad — he was a simple country bloke. And he wasn't getting any younger; perhaps he was even starting to lose his marbles. Andy felt sorry for him really. Of course Andy was ashamed of things he'd done, the way he'd messed up, but wallowing forever in the past wouldn't achieve anything. He was not a bad person.

He did not need a drink.

He wiped the sweat from his face with his T-shirt and sat up straight. Luckily his old mate was around. Thank fuck for Dom.

He pulled on his seatbelt and reached for the ignition. He stopped. Neal. Would Neal be lying in wait for him at the Big House? Nothing had happened when he'd driven past this morning. He'd probably forgotten all about his threat anyway. It was a long time ago. It was all in the past.

22 HOPE

Hester waited until the boys were quiet in their room before edging down the passageway towards the study, turning her head to look behind her even though she knew Neal had gone to the O'Briens about the salt on their land, and wouldn't be back until tea time.

She wanted to go in.

The door clicked open. She eased it half-closed behind her so she could hear the boys if they needed her. Light seeped in through the part-open slats of the venetian blinds.

The room smelt of grease and stale air. She looked around. The desk was dirty, strewn with tools and small metal parts from some mechanical thing, or things, like a work bench. The beautiful wood had been scored and scratched, gouged in places. She was surprised by her shock and sadness at the state of the desk; tears stung her eyes. She shook her head, exasperated by her own sentimentality. The door of the gun cupboard was locked. She padded over to the window, pushed down one of the slats with a finger and saw the side of the shed, sun glaring off the tin, the blank paddock behind. When she turned back it took a few moments for her eyes to adjust. She blinked. A messy pile of papers was spread over the floor near the chest of drawers.

She slunk over and squatted down next to the pile. Letters. Nothing but letters. She tucked a loose clump of hair behind her ear and checked the postmarks on the envelopes at the top. They were dated this week. She rifled through the pile. They did not seem to be in any particular order — it was just mail, haphazardly dropped as it came in.

A corner of an envelope stuck out from the bottom drawer of the chest. She eased the drawer open. More letters. Unopened. Ignored. She dug her hands in, felt right to the bottom. Whatever Neal had been doing in here, he hadn't been reading his mail.

She lowered herself to the floor, sat hugging her legs, looking at the pile in front of her. Stiff white envelopes, formal brown ones, shrieking red address windows. So it was this bad. He had given up. Stopped caring. She got up and took a few letters from the top of the pile, rearranging the rest more or less as she had found them.

At the kitchen table she sat with a view through the window. Just in case. There was an electricity bill in the first envelope she opened. A final demand for payment. They wanted hundreds of dollars. She put it to one side. Next was a huge bill for diesel, from Johnson's garage, and a notice from a company she didn't recognise giving seven days warning that they would be taking legal action. It seemed to have something to do with sheep feed. When she opened the letter from the bank a wave of shock stopped her breath for a moment. They had written about overdue payments on a loan. When had Neal taken out a loan? She could hardly register the amount. It was thousands. Thousands and thousands, he owed. They owed.

She'd had no idea it was so bad. A surge of confused fury that Neal had let things fall apart like this, had hidden so much from her, flattened out and gave way to something like pity.

The drought was not his fault. Everyone was in trouble. His behaviour was not surprising, she thought, with the worry of all this hanging over him. He was being pushed to the limit.

The last envelope in front of her was small and white, handwritten. She tore it open and unfolded the thin sheet of paper inside.

Marrup Hotel
Bar tab — Oct 2010
Johnny Walker Red Label 1 bottle — $25

She almost laughed out loud. Jamie McFadden, the tight bastard, was calling in old debts before he left. She could vaguely remember picking up that bottle after Graham at the Store had reminded her it was Mr Collingwood's birthday. She knew the old bloke had a soft spot for the stuff. Neal had taken it out to him. It had been the poor bugger's last year, too. Well, this bill at least would be paid, she resolved. She'd use the housekeeping money; even if it meant rabbit stew all week, she'd pay the damn thing. She would not have Jamie and his stupid wife taking gossip to the other side of the country about how Neal and Hester Connor did not pay their bills.

But what about the rest of it, all the other debts? What would happen to Neal if the bills were not paid, the bank not satisfied? What would happen to them all? Hester felt a flash of craving, like yesterday under the shower, a sudden urge to block out everything, to stop thinking, feeling, caring. To forget.

She doesn't do badly when she leaves home, considering she is not quite sixteen. She stays in the city with some people she knows from surfing, finds a job at Coles. Later, she moves into a flat with a girlfriend and starts studying part-time, so she can finish her schooling properly, get into university. Her dad always said she was bright. She wants to do a degree in Public Policy or maybe Education. Something useful. She makes friends, but doesn't have any serious boyfriends. It is hard for her to get that close to anyone.

The same year she starts uni — she has chosen primary teaching — she discovers heroin, at a party. Just once, she thinks. But it is a revelation, a miracle, this instant panacea for the confusion and self-loathing that are always with her, just below the surface. It makes perfect sense for her to keep taking it. Even when she loses her job, stops studying, has nothing else in the world except the next hit, it still makes perfect sense.

By the time she meets Andy she has finally had enough. She has sunk so far she wonders if she can go any further. She wants to be able to think again. They both do. Their intentions are good. Andy gives her the comfort of a gentle, honest love, but it isn't enough. The life he has been living is so ingrained, he doesn't know how to give it up, runs around in frantic circles trying to punch out an exit. She has to take a leap to escape, leave him behind. It is the only way.

She is lucky. She finds Neal. He comes to her at just the right time.

Hester propped her elbows on the table and dug her fingers into her hair. She fought to focus, to translate her craving into action. There was some State help being offered to people in drought-affected areas, but Neal was too proud, too distrustful of the government, to consider anything like that. Anyway, from what she'd heard, it was hard to get and wouldn't begin to help with this sort of debt. There was no way she could … the jewellery! She sat up straight. Of course. Dom had offered it to her, hadn't he? Why shouldn't she use it to save the farm, see them through this rough patch? After all, the jewellery was Neal's, as much as it was Dom's; it belonged to the family. And if Neal got rid of this terrible burden, the stress and anxiety of all these debts, he would calm down, be his old self again. She owed it to him. And to the boys.

Yes. She had to try. She would not give up.

There was no point sitting around waiting for Dom to show up again. She checked the time. The children had already been lying down for nearly fifteen minutes. Could she make it to the Big House and back before they got up? Maybe. Billy had been more tired than usual since his birthday. But she would have to go straight away. Now. Yes, now! She felt inspired, responsible for something vital and urgent. She pushed the bills under the folded tea towels in a drawer where Neal would never look and stuffed the envelopes into the fire. She listened at the boys' bedroom door for a few seconds. There was no sound.

The flyscreen door squeaked as she eased it open. She grabbed her sandals from the verandah, pulled them on, and ran.

Thanks, Marjorie. She kept up a steady jog, feeling the rough ground through her sandals, trying not to let her determined excitement descend into panic. I know the jewellery is a precious family thing, passed down for however many generations, but I'm doing this to save the farm. And your son, who is not coping. And for your grandchildren's futures. A few good causes, then. Trust me, I wouldn't even think about it if I had any other choice. This is everything I've got, Marj. Everything. She could hear her blood pumping, feel the hot air pull into her lungs. The fence posts at the side of the track wavered and danced through the film of sweat that stung her eyes. I didn't get to say goodbye properly at the funeral. I was preoccupied with Neal. And uncomfortable. Too many strangers. But you probably would have liked it. It would have been what you wanted. There was a big turnout, everyone poshed up. Solemn. We didn't have a wake or anything. I don't think Neal was up to organising it. He wouldn't let me. Maybe it was the money. Lack of. Anyway, no-one seemed to mind. People expect less, these days.

I'm sorry you're gone, Marjorie. I miss you.

Marjorie would have been happy, grateful, that Hester was trying to save the farm, to help her beloved son. Of course, her mother-in-law wouldn't have heard a word against Neal; she wouldn't have stepped up to defend her daughter-in-law if it had meant challenging him. But in her own way, Marjorie had been on Hester's side. She accepted Hester's story about her mum being dead, her dad long disappeared, without question (though the last part was pretty much true). After the first telling, the subject of Hester's history was never mentioned again. She was grateful for that. They had been bound together, her and Marjorie, like shipwreck survivors, by things known but unspoken, and through the man who was the focus of both of their lives. They hadn't seen a lot of each other, but had developed a comfortable closeness over the years.

204

Christmas was the best time. Neal relaxed his usual rules on when she was allowed to go to the Big House, and she and the kids were given free rein for a couple of weeks to spend time with Marjorie. Sometimes, Marjorie and Hester sat together with their tea on the verandah while the children slept or played nearby with Neal and Dom's old wooden toys that Marjorie stored in a box in a spare room. Hester liked Marjorie's easy acceptance, her simple, solid company, how it mattered that the pavlova was crisp and the sponge cake springy. Hester soaked up her mother-in-law's baking skills, spent hours with her in the kitchen, ignoring the dragging heat. As they got older, the kids helped with the trifle, splodging quivering red jelly on top of sodden cake at the bottom of the bowl. They always made a separate trifle for the kids, with fruit juice instead of sherry. Neal had that trifle too — he wouldn't touch alcohol, in any form. It was one of the things she'd always liked about him. The other farmers seemed to respect him for it too. It marked him out as serious, dedicated. In control.

At the Big House on Christmas Day the boys were allowed to watch TV — there was always some sort of Disney film on. The picture was fuzzy because of the bad reception, but they didn't seem to care. Later, when the boys were in bed, the adults played Canasta or Scrabble. Marjorie's set was old but in perfect condition. None of the tiles were missing.

On Boxing Day, Marjorie put on a big do for friends. Lizzie and Colin always came. Usually there would be three or four other neighbouring families too, though last year it was quieter. The Morrisons were gone. The Reillys and the Carmodys had left, too. But the O'Briens had come and the Dodds, with their older daughter on holiday from her boarding school, who played with the boys and read to them when they got tired. There was orange juice and sweet fruit punch with ice, and beer and wine. Even with the depleted numbers, Hester felt part of something. This was hers — her place, her family. She was someone. On the farm, she belonged.

Things could not keep getting worse forever, could they? Someone would find a way to control the salt. They had to. Eventually the drought must break and people would stop leaving. Others would come to take the place of the ones who'd left.

But Marjorie would still be gone. What would Christmas be like without her?

She leaned on the rickety verandah post for a few seconds to flick a stone out of her sandal and let her breathing slow. She could not see Dom's blue hire car anywhere. There was a noise, like someone calling; she tensed and listened but it was only a crow, with its flat, nasal caaww dropping low, as if in disappointment. She wiped the sweat from her face with her sleeve.

The kitchen door was open. She tapped on the wall next to the flimsy flyscreen and went in.

Andy was not there. She stood in the doorway between the kitchen and the lounge and wondered, for a startled second, if it was really him she had come for. Her old mate. She missed their friendship, the way they had talked, shared their problems, their hopes and fears, tried to work things through together. Still, in the end, it had just been talk.

She spotted the shoe box, right there in front of her, on the lid of Dom's suitcase on the far side of the room, as if it had been waiting for her, and sprung back into motion. She felt the weight of the box and peered inside. Yes. It was hers. She did not believe things were ever meant to be, in some sort of mystical, hippy way that Andy would go for, but finding the jewellery like that, so easily, reassured her that she was doing the right thing.

She paused at the kitchen door on the way out and looked around for a pen and something to write on. On the table she found a till receipt from the General Store and scribbled on the back: *D — Took up your offer thanks — H.* Then she was out the door and running, as best she could, pounding down the track with her precious package.

Her face was scarlet with heat and exertion, her hair soaked with sweat, by the time she got back. The house was still quiet. She bundled the box in an old tracksuit top and lay it on the bottom of the washing basket in the bathroom. She gulped a glass of water, pulled the tie out of her hair and ran water over her head at the kitchen sink.

Billy appeared in the doorway, tousled and pink-cheeked. She had made it back just in time.

He blinked at her. 'Your hair's all wet, Mummy.'

Hester smiled at him. Her beautiful, perfect son. She bent down with her face inches away from his and shook her head, so water from her hair flecked over him. He squealed and laughed and tried to run off, but she lunged after him, picked him up and hugged his wriggling body to her.

Hope. Andy was right about that at least. You had to have hope.

23 CYCLONE

Driving up the track, Andy kept a careful lookout, half expecting a last-minute ambush. He didn't want to be frightened of Neal, but he was. Even as a kid he was wary of Dom's quiet, unsmiling brother. After the time Neal gave him a good punch in the stomach for feeding the sheepdog chocolate biscuits, he'd kept well out of his way.

But Hester's husband was not waiting for him with his rifle. Relieved, Andy parked the car and hurried into the Big House. He dropped the car keys onto the kitchen table.

'Dom? How's it going, mate?'

His friend knelt on the lounge floor, surrounded by a mess of papers, books and toppling stacks of magazines, in front of a cardboard box that had once transported bananas from Carnarvon. He looked up.

'Hope you don't mind me borrowing the car. Spur of the moment thing. You know.'

'No problem.' Dom went back to his sorting.

'You went to the dam. I waited for ages.'

'It's fine.'

Andy flopped onto the sofa, closed his eyes and puffed out air slowly, through his lips. 'Had a sudden urge to see the old man. Bad idea.'

He leaned forward, hands loose between his knees, and watched Dom sorting and packing. There were bundles of envelopes, tattered files, a hefty bible. The red cardboard lid of an old Scrabble game was held on with an elastic band.

'Didn't go well?' Dom packed the scrabble into the box.

'Nah. I'll tell you about it later. But it doesn't matter. I'm over it. What doesn't kill you makes you stronger, eh? How about you? Been clearing out?'

'Yeah.'

'Want some help?'

'No thanks.'

'You still going to take stuff to the Op Shop in Joondyne?'

'I suppose so.'

'I can help. Don't mind driving even. If you don't mind me driving, that is. I'm not strictly legal, but I'm sure —'

'I'll decide later.'

Andy leaned back on the sofa. This distant, negative mood of Dom's was starting to get on his nerves. He could have done without it; he was trying to be positive here! Why was his friend so touchy? Perhaps he was having trouble coping with his grief. Going through his mum's stuff must be upsetting. Was he pissed off about Andy taking the car as well, but too polite to say anything directly? Full and frank communication certainly wasn't one of Dom's strong points. No wonder England suited him — he always had been on the reserved side. Dom was more like his brother than he thought.

Andy hoped he hadn't outstayed his welcome already. He felt good about seeing Dom again, reconnecting with his past — the bit before things had gone so wrong. He'd thought Dom was pleased to have him around too. Well, he would only stay another night or so, anyway. See his mum again, then head off. There wasn't much reason for him to be here now. And there was no point pushing his luck with Neal.

He would have to decide what to do next. He needed to make a plan.

But first, there was food.

'You want a cuppa? Hey, we could go into Marrup and see what delights we can rustle up from the Store for tea.' He rubbed his hands together. 'Saw some sausages in there last time that looked just about edible, or eggs — I could do an omelette. You ever go vegetarian? I tried for a while, but ended up living on chips and baked beans. And beer, of course.'

'Andy.' Dom gripped the sides of the cardboard box, his head lowered.

'What?'

Dom looked at him.

'What is it, mate?'

'Something's gone.'

'What? Something important?'

'Jewellery. Old stuff, an heirloom. I found it in Mum's room. In a shoebox.'

'What, like the family jewels?'

'It's just disappeared, Andy.'

'Where was it? Have you looked everywhere?'

'It was here this morning. I know exactly where it was. I — I can't understand it.'

'But how could it just ... Whoa. Wait up. You don't think — listen Dom, I didn't take it.'

'I didn't say that.'

'It's what you're thinking.'

The wood-burl clock ticked a few seconds away.

'Well — I don't know, I suppose I wondered if you —'

'You wondered? Really?' Jesus, he thought. Why fucking bother with people at all? Even so-called friends didn't seem to know the meaning of trust. A bit of trust wasn't too much to ask, was it?

He was furious. 'Ha! The junkie strikes again. Is that it? Thought I'd pissed off back to the city to sell it and find some gear, get it up my arm as quick as possible? Once a junkie, always a junkie, eh? You can't trust us, oh no.' He launched himself off the sofa and began to pace the room.

'Andy, please. It's just gone! No-one else has been here. What was I supposed to think?'

'Oh, I know what you think. You think I'm a bad person. Deficient. Wrong at heart.' He jabbed his finger at his chest. 'Maybe you think I'm not even quite a person, in the same way you are. I was a junkie. An alcoholic. An addict.' He spat the word like a bad taste held in his mouth for too long. 'And Hes. You fancy her, don't you? Eh? Think she'd still be up for it, because that's how she used to make a living? Because she was a prostitute?' He savoured the confusion in Dom's face. It was not like Andy to want to hurt someone else, least of all an old friend, but right now he was determined to do damage, to throw back all the terrible feelings spinning wildly inside him like a cyclone gathering force. He was alone in the chaos, panicked, frightened.

'Come on Andy, there's no need —'

'Oh yes there is. There is a need. Because I didn't take your fucking jewellery and I'm fed up.' He might have been crying. 'I'm fed up with people like me and Hes being treated like we're nothing. Like shit on the shoes of fine upstanding citizens. Like another species that normal people would like to see bred out of existence. Except you can't do that. It isn't possible. Because we are normal. We're like everyone else. No. Everyone else is like us.' He came close to Dom and leaned down towards him. Every muscle in his body trembled. 'Things could go horribly wrong for anyone, you know. At any time. Even for you, Mister Fucking Perfect. Even for you.'

He heaved his backpack over one shoulder, rushed into the kitchen and snatched up the car keys. On his way out he grabbed four cans of Swan Lager, left from a six-pack, from the worktop near the door.

He wrenched the car into gear and sped off down the track. His hands trembled on the steering wheel. In the rear-vision mirror he glimpsed Dom on the verandah.

He drove for a while, away from Marrup, before turning down a nameless gravel track that stopped abruptly in a clearing, screened by trees, a short way off the road. He fumbled at one of the cans of beer and pulled up the silver ring-pull. A sighing hiss escaped. Froth foamed up and spilt over the edge of the can like creamy lava. Andy put his mouth over the opening and sucked, tipped the can and drank until it was empty. He opened the second can straight away and drank that too, then the third and fourth, quickly, gulped the fizzy liquid like a man dying of thirst.

24 BEAUTIFUL STUFF

Neal had shot a couple of scrawny rabbits and was showing the boys how to skin and gut them. Hester watched from the kitchen window as she got the tea ready.

They were squatting in the shade of the salmon gum, the two boys with their small heads lowered, following the movement of Neal's hands, the knife. Their arms lifted now and then, as they batted away flies. The boys had never been squeamish about blood and guts — they were used to it. She could imagine Neal's low, patient voice, explaining what he was doing, his quiet way of involving his sons: you think this would be a good way to cut it, or is this way better? This way? Right. Know why?

While she peeled potatoes, Hester thought about what she would say to Neal later, when the boys were in bed. She was tired, after her earlier frantic rush to get the jewellery, and the problem of putting her plan across to Neal was sinking in. She splashed the cut potatoes into a saucepan of cold water. Had it been a stupid idea? It relied on Neal not only agreeing to sell the jewellery, but actually doing it and sorting things out with the people he owed money to, and the bank. Neal, who could not even open his own mail. The more she thought about it, the more her hope ebbed away.

She held the peeler tight and stripped rubbery carrots of their blotchy skins. She chopped them into pieces and dropped them into a bowl. Outside, Neal threw a morsel of rabbit guts to the dog. It gulped them quickly then sniffed closer. Neal made a sharp noise that carried across to Hester in the odd, delayed way that sound moved through still, empty spaces. The animal slunk away.

She put golden syrup, butter and sugar into a saucepan, and set it on the edge of the stove. She had decided to make golden syrup dumplings. It was Neal's favourite sweet, and the children's — one of the things Marjorie had taught her to cook, up at the Big House, her first Christmas here. Hester had hardly known how to boil an egg then.

She shook flour into a bowl for the dumplings and cut chunks of fridge-hard butter, rapidly softening, into it. She rubbed the flour and butter together, feeling the perfect softness of the flour, like her children's skin, on her roughened fingers.

She had no appetite herself; her stomach was tight with anxiety. What could she possibly say to Neal? Even mentioning his brother's name was a risk. She wiped a hand across her forehead and leaned against the cool stainless steel of the sink, watching the dog wolfing up the remains of the rabbit. Neal carried the prepared carcasses towards the house, the boys skipping around him.

Alex called out, 'Sywup dumplings, sywup dumplings, yummmm!' which made Neal smile. He was in a more buoyant mood than usual. He praised the rabbit casserole she'd made. She began to feel more hopeful.

Once the boys were in bed and she had read to them, she finished the washing up and made two cups of tea. Neal did not go straight into the study. Instead, he sat at the table with the big torch in pieces in front of him and a couple of screwdrivers, trying to fix it. She couldn't have arranged a better opportunity.

She brought the shoebox into the kitchen and put it on the table. 'I forgot, Dom dropped this off. He found it when he was clearing out the house. Said he wanted you to have it.'

He tensed and paused at the mention of his brother. She carried on, lifted the lid off the box, nudged it towards him. She watched him frown and look inside as she sat down at the end of the table with some sewing — a pair of Billy's trousers with a rip at the knee.

'Beautiful stuff, eh? There's loads of it,' she said. 'Must be worth a fortune.' She leaned back in her chair and flattened a thick square of cotton over the tear in the trousers. She jabbed the needle through the two layers of material, only half watching, and stabbed her finger, releasing a tiny ball of blood. She sucked the blood away.

Neal put down the screwdriver he was holding. He reached in and slowly lifted out a diamond and ruby necklace, held the bright thing against his large, calloused palm, as though supporting a baby's head. 'Huh. Think I remember Mum wearing this.'

'Do you?'

He stared at the necklace. She waited for him to go on, but he said nothing more. She realised she was holding her breath. She exhaled, took a slow breath in. She had to keep it going, move things to where she wanted them to be. She pushed the needle into the trousers and leaned forward, delved into the shoebox and brought out a pearl choker. 'How about this, eh?'

Neal tilted his head and considered the choker. He shook his head, a spare, brief movement, and lay the necklace in his hand back in the box. She was going to lose him.

'Neal, it could help us, all this. It must be worth a lot. Dom doesn't want it. We could do something with the money. For us. For the farm. I'm sure your mum would understand.' She could not say more; probably, she had said too much already.

The screwdriver made a clunking sound as he rolled it on the table, backwards and forwards, with his fingers. He looked up at her and smiled. 'We don't need any help, Hes.'

'Neal. Please.'

'We're alright, aren't we?' She couldn't help flinching as he reached out a hand, but he only stroked her cheek, cupped her face in his rough palm.

While she stood in her nightie, folding her clothes onto the chair, Neal put the shoebox under the bed. She tensed with frustration and anxiety as he shoved the jewels, the diamonds and pearls, the rubies and pure, blue sapphires out of sight with his foot. She had to say something, had to give it one last try, couldn't help herself. She touched his arm, eased out his name gently, asked him what he was going to do with the jewellery. She told him that Marjorie would have wanted them to use it. Had probably been saving it to give to them, anyway. He turned to face her slowly and she tilted her head, summoned a smile, tried to read his dark eyes in the shadows of the room. She waited, as the seconds moved by, for a softening, or some sign of uncertainty. But there was none of that, only a kind of tremble, a tightening of his body that

217

alerted her, too late, to the fist in her chest, sudden and hard, knocking the wind out of her, leaving her breathless, gulping for air, drowning. She collapsed onto the floor and his face loomed over her, his voice a furious hiss, spraying flecks of spit. 'Shut up, just shut up,' telling her that she was mad, stupid, an idiot. 'We're alright, Hester.' His chest heaved. 'I told you, we're alright.'

Hester lay next to her husband, felt the pull of pain in her chest as she breathed, the tender spot where his fist had been. The thin doona felt heavy, a burden on her body. Her mouth drooped open, as if some sound from inside her might leak out. Nothing did.

In the deepest part of the night she turned and clung to him, pushed herself close, twined her legs in his, felt the muscle and sinew and bone in his arms and body, searching for a way to sink back, to believe Neal's truth, his version of reality, where everything was alright because it had to be. It had to be.

25 PERSPECTIVE

Andy drained the final frothy drops from the last can of Swan Lager and tossed it onto the passenger's seat. It clanked against the other empties and tumbled onto the floor. He pulled a shaking hand across his damp mouth. He needed more beer. Or something stronger; whisky or vodka. Anything would do. He was desperate. He needed to be drunk, as rip-roaring, utterly, obliviously pissed as it was possible to be.

He fumbled with the keys and started the engine. Joondyne was too far. It would have to be the Marrup pub — there was nowhere else.

He wrenched the car into gear and swung into a three-point turn in the clearing. Halfway around, his stomach began to heave. He fumbled at the door and pushed it open just in time; the contents of his guts splattered onto the hot ground. He spat a few times, wiped his mouth with a scrap of paper from the floor and dropped it onto the yeasty puddle. Four quick cans of gassy beer on an empty stomach. Bad idea. He wasn't used to it anymore.

There was a bottle of water in the back of the car. He wasn't sure whether it was for the car's radiator or for drinking, but he rinsed his mouth out with it and drank some. It tasted okay. He let his head fall back on the headrest. Fool. Fucking idiot! What kind of a stupid, mindless worm was he?

Late afternoon sun glared through the windscreen. He noticed a tiny chip in the glass, circled with minute cracks, suggesting it might expand with time. His whole body felt weary, his mind fogged, blinkered; some kind of vital knowledge danced at the edges of his vision like a shadow puppet — if only he could see it clearly! But it stayed out of sight, hiding, teasing him, feinting, just out of his reach. He cried, sobbed out his lonely frustration. Strings of snot dripped from his nose and tears fell into his gasping mouth. He cried until his chest hurt and his eyes were so swollen he could barely see, then dragged his exhausted, shuddering body onto the back seat, closed his eyes and fell asleep.

It was night when Andy woke, dark except for the light from the star-sprayed sky and a chunk of moon. A bitter taste coated his mouth and he was thirsty. His arm hurt where he'd slept on it, and his ribs felt sore. The glowing numbers on the car's clock showed nearly nine. He had a drink of water and put on his jumper.

He walked around the small clearing, stretching out the aches in his body. Twigs and fallen bark scrunched underfoot. His stomach had settled. He searched the car on the off-chance there would be something to eat and smiled in triumph when he discovered a couple of packets of airline peanuts in the glove box, along with a pair of flight socks and a sleeping mask, still in their plastic wrappers. Thanks Dom.

The peanuts were rich and salty. He sat in the passenger's seat and savoured each one. Dom hadn't deserved the tongue-lashing he'd got, poor bugger. What he'd needed was help to find the lost jewellery, not have some furious tirade hurled at him. Andy must have been piling up a volcano of resentment and frustration without realising it — the stuff with his dad certainly hadn't helped. Still, it shouldn't have happened and he had to take responsibility, to accept that his behaviour had been out of order. It was only natural that Dom would be suspicious, if he thought Andy was the only one who'd been at the Big House. And Andy had never been a saint. With his past, people were going to label him, even those who wanted to believe better of him. The only way to show that he had changed was by changing. Living it. Outbursts like that didn't help. Bloody hell, he had a long way to go. But he did not want to sink into self-recrimination and misery. He had no desire for a drink now. None at all. It was just a blip. It meant bugger-all in the greater scheme of things. These were difficult, testing times, but he was strong. Wasn't he?

He sat with the car door open, looking up at the sky. The night's expanse of stars were awesome and comforting.

He rummaged in his pack and pulled out a small book. The car's interior light was dim, but bright enough to read by. He felt calm and clear-headed now. It was up to him to look for the answer — it would expose itself, gradually, in time. He had to learn, work hard to find his way.

As a book, it didn't look particularly impressive. *Buddhism and Meditation* was a thin, seventies paperback, with the same musty smell of all the books he bought from the bargain bins and rickety bookshelves of the city Op Shops. There was a psychedelic-style drawing of a Buddha on the front, with an orange background. According to the cover it was number two in a series of three called *Buddhism for All*. He knew a bit about Buddhism and had practised sitting still and trying not to think hundreds of times, so he assumed he'd be okay skipping the first one. Andy gripped the paperback in both hands and smiled. He'd been looking forward to getting his teeth into this one ever since he'd set eyes on it. What better time than right now?

He exchanged his own sweat-stiff socks for the flight socks from the glove box, pushed the seat back as far as it would go, reclined it and settled down to read. He was comfortable in his little space, his place in the universe. He had an inkling that this was exactly the way it was meant to be.

The racket of the birds woke him. Andy pulled off the eye mask and put the book away in his pack. He'd read it right through, carefully, before going to sleep. He'd slept soundly.

He clambered out of the car, rinsed his face in a handful of water and had a long drink. The waking bush gave off a fresh, astringent smell. He spent five minutes on slow Tai Chi moves that he hadn't done since he'd left Jules and Summie's place.

A vehicle growled past on the nearby road, obscured by trees and scrub. Andy sat cross-legged on the bonnet of the car watching parrots flicker through the trees. When he was ready, he settled into the driver's seat and started the engine. It wasn't quite time to re-enter the world yet. First, he had some work to do.

He headed north east, calculating there was probably enough fuel in the car to get him to Yarlopin, about a hundred and fifty kilometres away, where there would, he hoped, be a garage. After Yarlopin there was nothing, as far as he knew, except the vast, empty, arid centre of the country.

The steady rush of fresh morning air through the open window tingled on his face. He focused on the straight road ahead. When he drove past the BOHAN sign, neat and proud, at the top of the track to the farm, he was tempted, for a moment, to call in to see his mum. She had stuck by him, no matter what. He wondered if he would even be alive now, without her. He pulled an uncharitable thought to the surface; she should have been harder on his dad, stood up to the old bugger. But no. That was unfair. She'd done her best. Sometimes he expected too much of others. People were flawed and that was no bad thing — it was what made them interesting. Human. His own goal was self-acceptance, not perfection. Just as bloody well, he thought and smiled.

He carried on, straight through the sad remains of Marrup, towards the desert.

26 Without a Trace

The land was appearing around him like a photo developing, pale colours turning bright and deep, paddocks and fences becoming clear and solid. Sitting on the verandah, Dom sipped a mug of sweet black tea; there was no milk left. He'd spent a restless night, full of odd, half-remembered dreams and long periods of anxious wakefulness. Andy was still not back. He'd been gone for two nights now. All yesterday Dom had expected him to turn up, but another night had gone by without a sign of him. What was the fool trying to prove?

Accusing Andy of taking the jewellery had been wrong — he should have shown more trust, been a truer friend. They were different kinds of people, but Dom had been genuinely happy to see Andy again, to have him around over the last week. They shared a real, comforting closeness. It was the stress, Dom allowed himself, and the strangeness of the situation that had clouded his thinking. He was tired.

Yesterday, when he discovered Hester's scribbled note on a till receipt he was about the screw up and throw in the bin, his first feeling was relief — of course Andy didn't take the jewellery! Only after he read the words over a few times — *took up your offer, thanks* — did it begin to sink in; Hester was leaving.

He was glad about her change of heart. Yet even as he told himself it was the right thing for her to do, there was no escaping a sense of loss, a sadness that she was going out of his life so soon. And something else — a strange remorse, a weight of guilt. His brother was a bastard, but was it Dom's place to interfere? Would Neal ever see his sons again? Well, it had been Hester's decision, not Dom's. He was not responsible.

But Hester couldn't have gone yet — he would have heard the ute. How else could she leave? He thought about going up to the cottage to say goodbye, but decided it might be awkward for her. He'd done enough. As much as he wanted to see her, and Alex and Billy, it would be best if he kept out of the way.

He wondered where they would go, Hester and the boys. His nephews.

It crossed his mind that something might have gone on between Andy and Hester, that they had made some plan to leave together, but it seemed unlikely. Andy had got angry after some kind of confrontation with his dad, and then Dom's stupid accusation that he'd stolen the jewellery, and stormed out. There was nothing pre-meditated about it.

It wasn't the first time he'd seen Andy get worked up. Once at school, about grade six or seven, he lost it with some kids who were teasing a boy with a red birthmark on his face. Andy had broken someone's front tooth. There was the time in High School when he'd been upset by news stories about the cruelty of exporting live sheep by sea. He stormed out of a classroom when a teacher refused to discuss it, flinging down his book and kicking over a chair for good measure on the way out. He tried to get a petition going, but it went nowhere — he was in the wrong place for political agitation of any sort. Most teachers were there on sufferance, doing a required rural stint, keeping their heads down. Some of the kids had never even seen the sea. None of them thought much about the outside

225

world and those who did, like Dom, considered it with a level of awe and in the context of themselves and how they would fit into it, not how the world should change for them. Dom signed the petition because Andy was his friend. Looking back, he admired Andy's conviction, his lonely determination.

Somehow, Andy had been ahead of everyone else. He understood things, put two and two together in a way Dom was incapable of until he got away, had been out in the world for a good while.

Perhaps Andy understood too much for his own good. Cared too deeply. Was that why he'd gone off the rails with the drink and drugs? Had he been looking for some respite, a place to escape, a bit of solace?

Dom was sure Andy would forgive his lack of trust; forgiveness was in his nature, too. That was why Dom was so worried. Where was he? He might have gone on a bender — he'd taken the beers and been in a wild enough mood — and wrapped the car around a tree or something. No. Andy knew how to look after himself. He'd survived this long, hadn't he?

But he wasn't here, and Dom could not go and look for him. Without the car he was stuck at the Big House. Alone.

He slung the dregs of his tea over the side of the verandah.

Two nights and a day. What should he do? Phone the nearest hospital? Was there still one in Joondyne? He could call from the phone box in Marrup, and get some food while he was at it — all he had left was a bit of stale bread and a couple of eggs. But he would have to walk there.

He got up and paced the verandah for a minute, jumped the few feet off the edge and went around the side of the house. A pair of shorts and a T-shirt he'd rinsed through yesterday were draped on the rotary clothes line. The plastic pegs in the linen bag hanging on the central handle had gone brittle in the sun and crumbled uselessly in his hand.

He doused himself under the cold shower — the ancient wood-chip heater looked too dangerous to use. How had his mum managed? He got dressed, made more black tea and used the last of the bread for toast with clumpy strawberry jam which glowed an unlikely, vibrant red. He took his breakfast out to the verandah.

The land was clearly visible now, fully formed in the new daylight.

He had to decide what to do. Should he go to see Lizzie? He didn't want to worry her unnecessarily. He wondered how long it would take to walk to the Bohans' farm — an hour? Twice that, at least, to get to Marrup. If he was going anywhere on foot it would have to be soon; later, the heat would be too much to bear.

As he chewed the toast, a noise crept up on him, the drone of an engine, growing louder. He scrabbled up and stared down the track, but there was nothing. It was not Andy. He looked the other way and saw a smudge of dust, caught a flash of the ute turning down the track towards the dam. Hester and the boys didn't usually drive to the dam. Neal? He watched the dust subside. There was transport around here. He didn't have to walk. He could go into town, stock up on food, ask about Andy. Use the phone box, if he needed to. Fuck it! Neal was his brother. Why shouldn't he borrow the ute?

There were no voices, no shouts or laughter, as he came closer to the dam, only the ringing echo of slow hammering. The ute was parked in the shade of a tree, near the edge of the adjoining paddock. The red dog sprang from somewhere, sniffed at him and wandered away again. He checked that the keys were in the ignition and strode to the dam.

Neal lay on his back with his knees raised under the base of the windmill, on the far side of the dam. Hester couldn't have left; a man who had just been abandoned by his family would not be doing chores. Then again, he thought, this was Neal. Who could tell what was really going on with him?

Dom walked around the dam and stood near his brother. 'Trouble with the pump?'

The hollow sound of metal on metal rang out. Neal's body tensed as his arm moved.

'I need to borrow the ute.' Dom raised his voice.

Without looking up, Neal put down a hammer. He felt on the ground and picked up a spanner.

'Neal —'

'I'm busy.'

'I know. Sorry to ask, but I —' He paused. 'I really need it.'

Neal pushed himself up on one elbow and scowled at Dom. 'You bloody deaf? Said I'm busy.' He went back to working on the pump.

The water in the dam lay still, like a crisp crust. It would have felt good to plunge in, crack the surface and glide through that muted, secluded world.

'Look,' Dom said, 'I won't be long, okay? Couple of hours at the most.'

The ute started first try. The red dog scampered up and jumped into the tray. There was a thick smell in the cab, of oil and sweat.

Dom already had the ute in gear when Neal came charging towards him. He resisted the urge to wind up the window and lock the door. Neal leant both hands above the driver's side window. He was breathing hard. His eyes were bright against the dark skin of his face. Dom noticed that his stubble was flecked with grey.

'Jesus.' Neal yanked the door open. Dom's heart raced with sudden fear, but his brother only flicked his head for him to move over. 'I'll drive,' he muttered.

It wasn't exactly his plan, but it would do. Yes, it would do; he'd taken control, stood up to his brother. Neal was driving him into town.

It felt strange, sitting so close together. He thought he could feel the heat radiate from Neal's sun-seared body. They drove past the Big House and onto the bitumen. Now he finally had an opportunity to try to talk to his brother, he didn't know where to start.

'Where's that blue thing, anyway?' It was Neal who spoke first.

'The Nissan? It's — it broke down. Colin Bohan's working on it for me.'

'Colin's working on it?'

'Uhu.'

Neal flexed his fingers and shifted his grip on the steering wheel. Shit, Dom thought. Couldn't he have come up with a better lie? What if Andy, and the car, were in Marrup? He snuck a glance at his brother's impassive face. Did he know Andy was back?

He watched the scrub at the side of the road, the useless, bare land flash past, and said nothing.

As they drove into Marrup, Dom scanned the street. He checked the pub car park as they went past. There was no sign of Andy, or the car.

He asked Neal to park outside the General Store. He bought cheese and bread and milk, biscuits, a pack of bacon and some tinned fruit. He wished he had an Esky. Graham Walker looked curious, when Dom asked him, but he had not seen Andy.

He put the bag of shopping on the floor of the ute and told Neal he wouldn't be long. His brother tapped the steering wheel with a finger. Dom hoped he would wait. The dog lay in the tray, its head resting on it paws.

At the pub, he pushed open the heavy door and blinked into the dim interior. Jamie was on his own today, sitting behind the bar with a cigarette between his fingers, staring at a small portable television. He turned the sound down and stood up when he saw Dom. He smiled and shook Dom's hand vigorously, said how good it was to see him again. With a raised palm Dom declined the whisky Jamie shoved at him, despite the publican's insistent wheedling. He really was a slug, Dom thought. He didn't know how he could have let the bastard get him so drunk the other day. He'd fleeced him of a good few bucks too.

Jamie raised his eyebrows when Dom asked about Andy. One side of his mouth lifted in a sardonic, unpleasant grin.

No, he hadn't seen him recently, he said. Not in years. But he used to spend a lot of time in the pub, before. When his mum and dad had brought him home, to detox.

'Detox,' he repeated and chuckled so that his belly wobbled.

Dom had a sudden, furious urge to ram his fist into the idiot's face. He shook his head and walked away, ignoring Jamie's pathetic pleas to come back that night for drinks on the house.

Back in the dazzle of daylight, Dom was relieved to see the ute still parked in front of the General Store. Halfway up the street he stopped at the phone box. He could call directory enquiries, find out about hospitals. He patted his pockets. Damn. He'd forgotten to bring change for the phone. What now? He couldn't even call Lizzie. Should he ask Neal to drop him at the Bohans' farm on the way back? Bloody Andy. Where the hell was he?

'Stop! Stop here!'

Neal pulled the ute to the verge at Dom's sudden demand, scattering dust. Just ahead was a turn-off, marked by a battered mail box. Through a cluster of trees, a house was visible, with broken windows and a crack in one of the fibro walls.

'Wasn't that the Carmody's place? It looks empty.'

'Yep.'

'How long have they been gone?'

'Few months.'

'The Carmody kids were the same age as us. I wonder where they are now.'

Neal shrugged.

'Let's go down there.'

'What?'

'Go on. I want to have a look at the house. Just five minutes.'

Even as Neal eased the ute forward, Dom could not be sure what his brother was going to do, but at the very last second he pulled the wheel towards the track that led to the house.

Dom walked slowly across the turning circle in the delicate stillness of the deserted property. The gate at the top of the path slumped to one side. He heard the ute door click open. Neal followed him up to the house.

A plastic draining rack next to the sink in the kitchen held a single, upturned mug and a stiff washcloth. The woody remains of a plant stalk stuck up from a terracotta pot on the window sill. He could smell something pungent, a strong odour of rat or possum.

Dom moved from room to room. Neal's slow footfalls echoed behind him. Scraps of foam from a chewed cushion were scattered on the lounge floor. In a bedroom, a pair of shoes lay as if they had just been kicked off. The bed base had no mattress.

Dom felt ashamed of his intrusive curiosity and the odd feeling of reassurance the abandoned place gave him — the Carmodys had been successful people, well thought of. Anyone could fail. Anyone.

But he felt a pinch of fear too.

In the bathroom, a half empty shampoo bottle sat on the edge of the bath. There was a plastic razor and a cake of pinkish soap, cracked and brown along the centre, on the dust-drenched washbasin.

Spiders' webs formed thick clusters in the corners and gaps of the half-enclosed back verandah. He trod down the back steps. From the shade of a salmon gum behind the house he could see that strips of tin sheeting were missing from the roof, exposing the skeletal rafters at the back. Would the Big House end up like this — tattered and abandoned, utterly forgotten? He wanted to cry.

Neal appeared at the back steps. He thumped down and stood in the full sun, feet wide apart, arms folded across his chest, frowning up at the house. Dom felt a flash of connection, a reminder of childhood closeness. He wondered whether Neal had a clue his wife was about to leave him. His wife and kids.

He flinched as a cat skittered past, disappearing under the house between missing base boards. It must have been a pet left behind, gone, or going, wild.

'Got work to do.' Neal unfolded his arms and began to move away. A rush of panic swept over Dom. There was so much to say. He couldn't lose this chance.

'Neal!'

His brother stopped. Dom looked at his tight, work-hardened limbs, his clenched fists. The first thing in Dom's mind was that night. What Neal had done.

'Look, Neal, there's something I have to …' The words wouldn't come. He licked his dry lips and tried again. 'I know it was a long time ago, but when we were … I …' He couldn't do it. He took a few steps towards the dilapidated house, squinted up at the shock of sky above him.

Neal gave him an irritated frown.

'Mum was in hospital, wasn't she?' Dom spoke quietly. 'Why didn't you tell me?'

Neal's fingers spread and curled back into fists, over and over, in the same way Dom remembered from years ago. His brother charged forward, faltered, and stopped. 'I didn't think she'd go and bloody die, did I?' His chest heaved, as if he'd been running. 'I didn't think she'd bloody die.'

On the way back, hot wind chopped through the open windows of the ute. Neal drove, staring ahead, silent again. Dom didn't even notice when they passed the turn-off to the Bohans' farm.

'I should have made more of an effort, with Mum.' He had to raise his voice above the rumble of the road noise. 'Come back from London a few times, at least. I was a useless son.' He stared out of the window, away from his brother, blinking into the hot air. His eyes watered. 'I couldn't have done what you have. Stayed here. Kept the farm going.'

Neal said nothing.

'You took on a lot.'

The ute swerved around a pothole in the road and the bag of food from the Store tumbled against Dom's foot. He pushed it away. He hoped the cold things would be alright, after being in the heat for so long.

'Neal,' Dom turned to his brother, 'I know things are bad here, for everyone. What will you do if the farm —?'

'It's my farm. Nothing to do with you. Just keep out of it.'

'But Neal, I ...' Dom wanted to remind his brother that he had grown up on the farm, explain that it was part of him, who he was. It was his too! Frustration boiled in him, then eased away. Neal was angry and upset; this was not the right time.

Would there ever be a right time?

He stared out of the window.

Did it matter what he had seen, years ago? He could never know, for sure, whether his Mum had forgiven Neal, or even — no matter what Hester said — if his brother had repeated his behaviour. Or worse. His mum was dead. But even if she had lived longer, he did not think he would ever have been able to ask her.

27 THE SURPRISE

The boys played on the verandah while she went to the laundry at the side of the house for a few minutes, to scrub a patch of grease from one of Neal's shirts in the cement trough. She could hear them while she moved the hard-bristled brush over the soft cloth. After rinsing the shirt, she brushed at it again and inspected her work. The black mark was nearly gone. She realised she could not hear the boys anymore and assumed they had gone over to the swing under the tree to play. She scrubbed for another minute before drying her hands and going out to check on them.

The boys were not at the swing. She scanned around her, listened. 'Billy? Alex!'

She ran inside and checked through the empty, silent rooms, trying to stay calm. She remembered the cubby under the house they had made out of cardboard boxes and old bits of material, where they liked to hide sometimes. She warned them all the time to check for snakes and redbacks before they went in there. She scrabbled under the house, where the baseboards were missing. The dirt smelled dank, of chicken shit and rats. She stretched herself flat on her stomach and reached out to pull back the old towel they had used as a doorway. The boys were not in the cubby. She pushed herself back, stood up, and brushed off the dirt.

'Boys! Where are you?' she called, as loud as she could, churning bursts of dust around her legs as she turned. 'Billy! Alex!'

She spotted them, away in the distance, near the edge of the strip of bush in the back paddock. The two boys and Neal, with the dog. Her voice must have carried — she could make out their little arms waving to her. Neal had his rifle slung over his shoulder. From this distance, it was impossible to notice his limp. He didn't turn around.

She watched, panic churning her stomach, as they disappeared into the bush. What was Neal doing? He'd been working in the shed, before. Why hadn't he told her he was taking the boys? Why hadn't she heard him come up to the house? She looked around, as though there might be something there to give her an idea, someone to help, pressed her hands to her head, trying to think. She rushed up the verandah steps, fumbled to get her sandals on, and sprinted across the open yard. At the side of the shed her foot caught in a loose strand of wire and she sprawled, skinning the heels of her hands. She scrambled up, wiped the dirt and grit off the grazed patches of skin and kept going. She had to get to her boys.

When she reached the bush she stood in the frail shade of the trees and tried to steady her breathing so she could listen properly. She thought she heard movement, off to her right somewhere. She wanted to call out, but held herself back.

Picking her way through the trees and scrubby undergrowth, she paused and stood to listen again. Nothing.

'Billy! Alex!'

A shot echoed through the trees, then another. She threw herself towards the sound, manoeuvring around fallen branches, not feeling the scrub whip at her legs and arms. She caught a flash of colour and she was there, in a small clearing, her hair dishevelled, gasping for breath.

Billy's arm was marked with a dribble of blood from the limp rabbit he held up with both hands. He frowned at her in annoyance. 'Mummy! You're not supposed to see.'

'See what?'

'Rabbit for tea. It's a surprise!'

'Ah. Sorry, love.' She tried to smile.

'Daddy's a good shot. There's another one over there.'

She could see Alex with the dog a little further into the bush. She brushed the hair from her face. Neal barely glanced at her; he showed no surprise at her sudden appearance. No emotion at all.

Alex came into the clearing, the dog at his heels, struggling with another rabbit. He stopped when he saw her. 'You going to shoot a rabbit too, Mummy?'

'No mate. I just — I came to see how you were getting on.'

Neal took the rabbits from the boys and turned back towards the house.

'Daddy's going to let us skin the rabbits.' Billy was keen and proud. 'He says we're old enough now.'

'Does he?'

An uncontrollable sickness flooded over her and she bent her head low and retched, dropped to her knees and spat out a mouthful of bitter liquid. Billy rushed over to her. Alex stood back and started to whimper.

'Mummy?' Billy's voice wavered. He bent and pushed his face close to hers, patted her back. 'You sick?' She wiped her mouth with the back of her hand and sat back on the ground.

'I'm alright, love. Think I just ate something bad, that's all.'

'Was it your toast?' Alex came to stand near her, watching her closely.

She reached out and pulled him to her. 'No, I don't think it was my toast.'

Neal stood watching them, the rabbits dangling from his hand, their front legs outstretched as though they were still aiming for a giant leap to safety.

On the way back, she trailed along behind Neal and the boys, the dog slowing to trot next to her from time to time. The boys skipped and ran to keep up with their father. When they lagged behind, Neal didn't slow down; he kept going, his head lowered, as though there was something on the ground in front of him that he dared not take his eyes off.

28 The Old Pond

A few ramshackle houses strayed along the potholed road, their dull tin roofs barely spitting back the sun's glare. Wooden telegraph poles, some tilting precariously, held up drooping wires. As Andy had hoped, there was a garage with a small shop. He pulled into the garage's forecourt and stopped the car next to the bowser. He'd made it to Yarlopin.

He got out of the car and stretched. There was a smell of petrol. A scrawny dog appeared from the sprawl of tyres and car bodies in varying states of disrepair at one side of the garage. It padded towards Andy before stopping halfway, as if it had lost interest, scratching itself half-heartedly with one leg and wandering back to the edges of the wreckage to lie down and bite at its fleas.

A burly man swaggered out of the shop, his overhanging beer gut almost covered with a blue singlet. 'G'day mate. Fill her up?'

While the man filled the car Andy went into the shop. It was thinly stocked, but had what he needed. He piled three large bottles of water, a couple of cans of baked beans with ring-pull lids, a packet of Granita biscuits and a bag of raisins on the grimy counter. There was no need for anything fancy; this was a Retreat, not a party.

The man pulled open the flyscreen door and went behind the counter to tot up Andy's things on an ancient cash register. 'So what brings you out this way? Don't get tourists much these days, since the church went.'

Andy remembered then, coming here as a child, on school trips. The attraction was a small stone church, the remains of an early, misconceived settlement past the town, on the very edge of the desert. The church had been painstakingly built with stone brought from the other end of the state, by the first settlers. The first white settlers, that was. In Andy's childhood, first was always applied to the settling white people. The original inhabitants were only mentioned as an aside, when they'd got in the way. It always pissed him off. In High School once, when he was meant to be regurgitating some white settler story in history, he'd written instead about the massacres of the Aborigines. His teacher had dropped it back on his desk, with a *0* and *You did not answer the question* in red pen. It probably wasn't very good anyway — the only information he'd had to go on was a TV programme he'd seen once, and some stuff his mum and dad had told him. People knew more now. For all the good it did.

The church had totally disappeared a few years ago, the man told him. Buried under sand. It couldn't survive the desert forever.

'Not even bloody God could save it,' his mouth twisted into a grin, and Andy smiled too. The man's grin faded when Andy told him he wanted to find somewhere quiet and remote for the night; a suspicious look crossed his face, then passed, as though he, like the dog, couldn't be bothered.

'No hotels, nothing like that 'round here mate, if that's what you're after. Plenty of quiet, but. No shortage there. Used to be pretty lively when the boys came up from the sheep station on pay day to get a skinful. Had the Abos here too, from the reserve, a hundred kays up the way. That was before the fucking government took my licence away. Made a buck or two in them days, I can tell you.' He paused and tilted his head to give Andy a considering look.

'Course, don't mean I can't have a drink myself. Might even have some left over to … give someone.'

Andy assured him the water would do. He checked his money and added a pastie and a Mars Bar from the small chiller; apart from the peanuts last night, it was ages since he'd eaten. He was hungry. Behind the counter haphazard stacks of cigarette packets and pouches of tobacco caught his eye. It wouldn't hurt, he decided, to treat himself. A cigarette now and then was hardly going to turn his life upside down.

While Andy packed his purchases into a plastic bag, the man leaned a hand on the counter and rested a fist on his hip, facing towards the window. 'Road to the church's gone. Only the one paved road out of here, if you want to keep heading east. Goes for a while, fifty kays or so, then you got a couple of dirt roads.' The man squinted at the blue car, dubiously. 'Wouldn't be going too far in that, mate. Even the paved's not too flash.' He raised his eyebrows and sniffed, offhand. He stood up straight. 'Course, it's up to you. You can do what you want. Free country, so they reckon.'

The Mars Bar was sticky and delicious. He gobbled it as he drove, before devouring the pastie. He wondered what Jules would say if she could see what he was putting into his body. She'd give him a hard time, no doubt. But they would be proud, her and Summie, of the way he had taken control of himself yesterday, called a halt, pulled himself back from the brink.

He cranked up the air-conditioning.

The earth was redder out here, the light more pure. The narrow road cut through the endless flat, scattered with Spinifex and stubby Mulgas. It was mesmerising. Primeval. It felt strange, dreamlike, being in his air-conditioned bubble on a shimmering strip of tarmac, as though he were floating through this timeless place.

There were no other cars. Not a single one.

A mob of roos not far off the road brought him back into the landscape. He slowed to look at them. They moved their ears at the sound of the car, and bounded languidly away. After half an hour, when the drive was getting rougher, he picked a spot and pulled off the road. He eased the car a few feet to a clump of Mulgas that were hardly taller than the roof.

At first the heat outside made his head spin. He stretched and wandered around for a few minutes, had a piss behind a Mulga, though he knew there was no-one to see him. With his book and a bottle of water he sat in the meagre shade of the trees. He crossed his legs and closed his eyes, adjusting, tuning into the place. It was quiet, but not without distractions; the scrub nearby rustled and flies pestered him. He knew snakes kept away from people unless provoked, or frightened. He wasn't sure about scorpions.

He swigged from the bottle of water and shifted around on the hard earth, trying to get comfortable. He was tempted to sit on his jumper, but that would have felt like cheating.

He tried to clear his head, push his thoughts and worries aside. He opened *Buddhism and Meditation* at page one. It was time to concentrate. He wanted to understand, to focus completely, absorb the spirit of the book. He would read it over and over, a hundred times, two hundred, if that was what it took.

The old pond.
The frog jumps in.
Plop.

The frog makes things happen to the pond — it creates circles in the water, changes the way the light falls on it. The frog goes under the water. Yet none of these things matter. The essence is the moment of the frog going in. Only this. This is Mindfulness: the core, the centre. The essence.

The flies stopped bothering him. He hardly noticed the scuffle of desert rodents. He absorbed the wisdom of mindfulness, karma and loving-kindness. He read about calm and insight, the hindrances of restlessness and worry, sceptical doubt, desire, sloth and ill-will.

When Andy blinked his eyes open, the sky was charged with the rich pinks and purples of sunset. He felt strange at first, as though he were coming down to land from a great height. He flexed his stiff legs and stood up. The land around him was flat and featureless. A place of nothingness, but far from empty, like an extension of the place he had been in his mind. He drank some water and walked around. Kangaroos moved in the distance, lifting and dropping like choppy waves.

He ate a can of beans and some biscuits. Night descended quickly. It was cold. He pulled on his jumper and wondered about lighting a fire, but it worried him — he wouldn't want to start something he couldn't stop, out here. Besides, there was not enough wood close by.

Wild dogs called to each other.

It was so bloody cold.

He moved to the back seat of the car, pulled the flight socks on over his own and squeezed his shoes back on. He lit a cigarette and smoked it slowly. It made his head spin, but he didn't feel any warmer. He huddled on the back seat and hugged his arms around himself. Why hadn't he realised it would be so cold out here? The man at the shop in Yarlopin should have warned him. He pulled himself away from feeling anger; ill will would get him nowhere. Nor would regret. He would have to deal with it.

He tried to meditate to take his mind off the cold, but he was shivering too much. In the end, though he didn't like to disturb the peace of the desert, he started the car and turned the heater on, full blast.

'Eh, mate! You alright?'

A regular rhythm echoed into Andy's consciousness. Someone was knocking on the window. He struggled awake and pushed the door open. The air in the car was stifling and dry from the blasting heater. An Aboriginal man with a pouchy face and a battered leather hat stepped back. On the road behind him a Land Rover was parked, its engine whirring, with another man at the wheel, watching.

'Saw the car. Worried, you know. Don't see too many cars out here. Not ones we don't know. Sleeping it off, eh?'

Andy turned off the car's ignition. 'Nah, nah. Just sleeping.' He struggled out of the car and coughed and spat on the ground. He guzzled water and wiped his mouth with the back of his hand. 'Bloody freezing last night so I put the heater on. Must've knocked me right out. Nice of you to stop, mate. Appreciate it. Any idea what the time is?'

'Bout eight.'

Andy nodded. He spotted the cigarettes on the floor of the car. 'You want a smoke?'

The man considered. 'Yeah, alright. Ta, mate. Name's Jimmy.'

'Andy.' They shook hands. Jimmy called something in a language Andy didn't understand and gestured for the man in the Land Rover to join them.

Andy sat on the ground with his back against the car, while the two men squatted near him. The other man introduced himself as Bob.

'From the Reserve?'

'Nah,' Bob wrinkled his nose. 'Up there the other day, but. Took 'em a heap of building stuff from the boss. He's a good bloke. Me and Jimmy, we work on the sheep station, that way,' he waved a hand. 'Wilgarnoo. Been there a long time.'

Andy shared his cigarettes and the rest of the biscuits with the two men. They told him a bit about their work on the sheep station. He parodied himself being taken by surprise by the cold the night before and made them laugh.

Jimmy explained that they went up to the Reserve from time to time, but he didn't like going there. It was rough, he said. A mess. But getting better. Some of the old ones there had sobered up and were teaching the others the traditional ways, how to look after themselves — track animals, find water.

'At least they got water. Good water. You white fellas, you really fucked up this time, eh? All that salt!' Jimmy smiled broadly and tapped Andy on the leg with the back of his hand. 'You losing your water, mate.'

'I know.'

'In the end, you'll fuck it up for us too, but. Be no water for anyone.'

'Yes. You're right.' He had an urge to apologise but hesitated, in case it sounded lame or patronising, and the moment passed.

Jimmy and Bob shook his hand before they left. 'Any chance you got a beer on you, mate?' Bob threw in. Jimmy frowned at him. 'Just asking,' he muttered. 'Baz in Yarlopin, he charges a mint, you know. Whoa! Daylight bloody robbery.'

Andy shook his head. 'Sorry. No beer. Can't help you there.'

When the men had gone Andy sat under the Mulgas and chewed on raisins. Perhaps there were no perfect endings, but he could still strive towards his goals, appreciate what he had: friendships, his health. He'd managed to hang onto his sanity, more or less. He closed his eyes and thought about who he was, and could be, tried to imagine what the next stage of his life would be like.

Before he left, he wandered around for a while, feeding off the strength of the stark, uncompromising landscape.

He hadn't reached Nirvana yet, but he didn't feel too bad. He didn't feel too bad at all.

29 FORGIVENESS

Dom rushed to the verandah as the Nissan, dull with red dust, pulled up in front of the Big House. Andy bounded from the car.

'About bloody time!' Dom went out to meet him. 'I'd just about given up on ever seeing you again. Or the car, for that matter.'

'Mate, what can I say? Sorry, sorry, sorry.' Andy dropped to his knees and hugged Dom's legs. 'Can you ever forgive me?'

Dom laughed and held up his hands. 'Not if you don't let me go right now.' But Dom had already forgiven his friend. The confused, melancholy mood that had crept over Dom since Neal had dropped him off a couple of hours earlier had started to lift as soon as Andy appeared.

There were explanations and apologies on both sides. When Andy found out that Hester had the jewellery he nodded and smiled. 'It's the time for change, mate. The time for change.'

Dom gave his friend a clean pair of boxer shorts and a T-shirt. He listened to Andy's exuberant off-key singing and strange chants from the shower while he made cheese sandwiches and tea. When he handed him the food, Andy pushed back his damp hair and took the offering with weighty gratitude.

After he'd eaten, Andy told Dom about his last couple of days; Yarlopin and the bloke at the shop, the desert and the Aboriginal men he'd met that morning. From the green sofa, Dom watched his friend wander around the room while he spoke, some part of his body always in movement; running a hand across the curtain and scattering a stream of dust, tapping his fingers on the mantelpiece above the fireplace, now bare since Dom had cleared it and packed up his mother's ornaments. He made Dom laugh describing how he stumbled out of the hot car looking like — in Andy's words — some messed-up, wasted zombie.

Then Andy wiped the dirt from his pack, rearranged its meagre contents, and prepared to leave. He was going again. He had called his mum from the phone box in Marrup on his way back from Yarlopin. She was arranging for some local farmer going to Perth to pick him up from the General Store at five-thirty. Dom tried not to show the depth of his disappointment.

He needed to go, Andy said. He was ready.

Dom offered to drive him into town, but Andy insisted he had time to walk, and didn't care about the risk of running into Neal.

'This is the beginning of a new journey, Dom.' Andy pulled him into a tight hug. 'I'm ready to take on the world! I'm not scared of anything.'

Dom could smell the astringent freshness of his own shampoo.

'Take it easy, eh, Dom. I'll leave you in peace now, but I promise to keep in touch.'

Dom watched his friend stroll away down the track. He did not want to be left in peace — he wanted to talk, about his brother and his mum, about Hester and his nephews, have some help to work out if he had done the right thing with the jewellery, with everything. His life. He wished he knew how to explain to Andy that he needed him to stay.

Andy's tuneless whistling carried back to Dom on the still air. He envied his friend's easy conviction, his focused determination. It made him feel humble.

Even when Andy disappeared onto the bitumen road, Dom kept staring down the track.

That night Dom couldn't sleep. He spent the next day wandering around the house, bored and lonely. In a daze he shuffled outside, trod up and down the verandah, drifted back inside again. In the evening, he ate a couple of sandwiches. He had no appetite. He tried to read a musty-smelling Lucilla Andrews novel but couldn't concentrate, and gave up when he discovered half of page nine missing.

After another sleepless night, he threw off the clammy sheet and dragged himself to the shower while the birds were still noisy. With his feet planted on the rubbery plastic of his mum's non-slip mat he let the cold water drench his hair and body until his skin tightened and tingled. The thought of another blank, lethargic day was unbearable. He would have to do something.

He started with the rubbish from the bag behind the house, which had been strewn around again by inquisitive, hungry animals. He collected up bits of torn black plastic, a yoghurt pot, shrivelled potatoes. A few feet away from the bag, the bowl that had been full of mouldy leftovers was empty, cleaned-out. He took the rubbish back into the house, encased in a fresh bag, and dumped it in his childhood bedroom. He closed the door.

Once he had begun, it was easier. He kept moving — tidying and sorting, bundling, stacking and piling. He carted the hoards of his mother's papers and magazines outside, ignoring the sweat crawling down his sides and dripping into his eyes. His sense of purpose built with each load.

He prepared a fire.

30 THE BILL

For the next two days she got the boys up in the morning, fed them, took them swimming. She cooked and washed clothes and made Neal cups of tea when he came in from his work. Once, while she was feeding the chooks and he was fixing the tractor at the side of the shed, he threw a spanner to the ground and walked in circles, muttering. But mostly he was quiet, hardly there. She didn't think. She withdrew into chores, routines.

Billy complained about his hair. He was always peering out from behind it, brushing it from his eyes. She set him up in a chair on the verandah with an old towel around his shoulders. A chook flapped up the steps, clucking softly. She shooed it away.

'Nice and still, please.' She rested her hands on Billy's shoulders as he jiggled and fidgeted. Alex bumbled around in front of his brother, trying to make him laugh.

'Listen, mister, don't forget you'll be next in that chair.' She brushed Alex's sides in a playful tickle and went to get the scissors from the tea-towel drawer in the kitchen. She took them out and slotted her fingers through the holes in the cold metal, moved the blades open and closed. They were stiff. She ran a finger lightly along one long, open edge, right to the sharp point. Outside, the boys were giggling. She pressed her finger down on the point. The rush of pain felt good. She pushed down harder, but soon it was too much. The indent left in her flesh slowly eased away.

After she had swept the black chunks and wisps of the boys' hair off the edge of the verandah she put the scissors away. As she shoved them to the back of the drawer she felt the crinkle of paper. The bills. She pulled out the top one, the bill from Jamie McFadden at the pub — *Johnnie Walker Red Label, 1 bottle — $25.* She felt a jolt of wakefulness, remembering her resolve when she'd first seen the bill. She would pay it. Yes. Tomorrow when she went shopping she would pay the bill.

She hadn't planned to stop — all she wanted to do was sort out Jamie's bill, get the shopping, go home — but as she neared the Big House she slowed the ute. She would like to see Dom. Just for a minute. Neal would never know.

She pulled the ute up behind the blue car, but kept the engine idling. How would she explain to Dom that she hadn't left, even though she'd taken the jewellery? Perhaps she didn't need to. Dom wasn't the kind of person to pry; he was too polite to ask tricky questions. She turned off the engine.

He pulled open the flyscreen door before she had a chance to knock. 'Hester!' His hair was messy and patches of sweat marked his T-shirt. He held a plastic container of clear liquid in one hand. She could smell kero.

'I was on my way into town. Haven't got long.'

'Come in, come in.' He held the screen door and stepped back for her to pass. Her hand brushed his arm.

'I found your note. I wasn't sure if ...' He paused and blinked, moved the kero to his other hand.

'I wanted to say thanks, Dom. When the time's right I'll ...'

'Of course. It's yours, Hester.'

'So how's things?' She made her voice bright.

'Oh, not too bad.' He ducked his head. 'Well, to tell the truth, I've been at a bit of a loss the last couple of days. Andy went back to Perth.'

A dip of disappointment coursed through her. Andy was gone. 'Was the mad bugger alright?'

'He seemed good. Full of the joys of life, after a couple of days out in the bush meditating or something. On a real high.'

'Hmmm. When you're up like that, you've got to worry, don't you, that the only way is down.' She raised her arm then lowered it in a dive.

'I hope not.'

'Yeah. I hope not too.'

Dom tilted his head at the container he was holding. 'Kero.' He put it down against the wall, near the door. 'I'm making a bonfire. Decided it was time to get rid of Mum's old papers and stuff.' He shrugged, in a way that looked apologetic. 'It seemed like a good idea.'

'It is a good idea. She was a terror for keeping things.'

'She sure was.' He wiped his hands on a tea-towel. 'I haven't even offered you a drink, Hester. Tea? I've got coffee too, some God-awful instant stuff.'

'Oh, no, thanks. I'd better get going.'

'I've just put the kettle on.'

She glanced through the flyscreen door at the ute. 'Righto.' She smiled. 'I'll go for the tea, then.'

Arms folded, she leaned against the door frame between the kitchen and the lounge, watching him make the tea. She could smell kero on his hand when he gave her the mug.

They sat together on the rickety back steps. At the bottom of Marjorie's old garden Dom had piled sticks and half-rotten fence posts within a circle, six foot across, edged by a narrow firebreak. Nearby, half a dozen stacks of paper stood, like strange protrusions from the earth, glaring white in the sun, each topped with a small rock to act as a weight.

Hester put down her mug of tea and wandered over to the circle, ambled around it, drawn to look inward as though the wood was already spitting entrancing flames. Dom got up and stood next to one of the stacks of paper. She was aware of him watching her.

She stopped. 'You'll be careful, won't you? With the kero, and everything so bloody dry.'

'Yes. I think it's far enough from the house.'

'It's not so much the house I'm worried about, you bloody galah — it's you.'

She came to where he stood, lifted the rock from the stack of paper and pulled out a sheet. She studied it for a few seconds. 'Jeez. Electricity was cheap in 1994.'

Dom tilted his head to look at the old bill. 'Why do you think she kept all this?'

'I don't know.' Hester lifted the rock again and lay the paper back on top of the stack, neatly. 'I suppose it made her feel safe. Connected her to the past.'

'Well, there's a lot of past here.'

Hester weighed the rock in both hands. 'It must be hard for you. Your family have had this place all these years. Now ... everything's changing.'

'It would have been harder for Mum. Things getting worse all the time, not knowing what would happen. Did she say anything?'

'No. Not to me. But, Dom, I have to say, she didn't give too much away. A family trait, eh?'

He laughed, a short, dry sound.

'Sorry.' She screwed up her nose. 'Was that a bit blunt?'

'No, no. I'd tried to convince myself I was different, but you're right. It runs in the family.'

'Well, some things are hard to talk about.'

They stood close to each other, both looking towards the unlit fire. She thought she could hear the gentle thrum of the pump at the dam. She placed the rock back on the stack of papers.

'Going through Mum's stuff has made me think,' Dom started, hesitant, 'about how different my life has been from hers. I've had so many choices. And I can't help wondering if I made the right ones.'

'Everyone wonders that sometimes.'

He looked stricken, as though realising he might have said something terrible, offended her.

'Hester.' He reached out and touched her shoulder. She felt the warmth of his fingers through her cotton shirt. He brushed his hand down her arm and her skin tingled. She stepped forward and leaned her head on his chest. He held her. His T-shirt was soft against her cheek. She closed her eyes and smelt the sweat of him, the sharp linger of the kero. After a minute, she moved back. His arms eased away, fell to his sides. He let her go.

'I suppose Andy the Spiritual King would say it's never too late to do the right thing,' she said.

'And how are you supposed to know what's the right thing?'

She pursed her lips and shrugged. 'Your guess is as good as mine.'

He shook his head in mock disappointment. 'Andy would have had a snappy answer.'

'He would. But I suppose us mere mortals will just have to keep on guessing.' She brushed gritty dust from the paper on top of the stack.

It was time to go.

As she drove away she saw Dom in the rear-vision mirror, standing on the verandah, watching her leave.

The ute pulled up in a stir of dust next to Jamie McFadden's station wagon. She would get this out of the way before she did her shopping.

Inside, she let her eyes adjust to the gloom. She hadn't set foot in here in years. The pub's stale, smoke-infused stench assailed her. She tapped the white envelope against her thigh. All she had to do was hand it over.

Jamie McFadden stood up behind the bar, a leery smile spreading across his face as she came forward. She had never liked him. He'd pinched her arse and breathed some sleazy comment into her ear once, when she and Neal and Marjorie had come to celebrate her birthday. It was before the kids, when Jamie's wife still did meals; overcooked meat and soggy vegetables.

The other man sitting at the bar turned to stare. It was Charlie, the useless boozer who used the drought as a convenient excuse for his own failure as a farmer. There was no-one else in the place.

'Well, well. Mrs Connor. This is a treat! To what do we owe the pleasure of your lovely presence?'

Hester's sandals stuck and gave on the tacky floor. She handed Jamie McFadden the envelope across the bar. 'Just paying your bill.' She wanted to get out of there. She was already running late, after spending so much time at the Big House, and wanted a bit of time alone to let the confusion of her emotions settle after being with Dom.

'Phhh,' he waved the envelope away. 'Not much, is it? Forget it. Let me get you a drink while you're here. On the house, of course. Gin for the lady? Or would you prefer a beer?'

'No, nothing thanks. I'm in a hurry.'

'What? But how can you say no on this historic occasion, Hester Connor?' He opened his arms wide, his belly straining against his shirt. 'Final days of the once great Marrup Hotel.'

'You want to get me as drunk as you got Dom the other day, for a laugh?' There was a sudden silence. Jamie's face set hard for a second or two, before he tilted his head and looked offended.

'Now, now.' He lifted the wooden bar hatch and came through to stand next to her. She shuffled back a step. His breath was heavy with the stink of whisky. 'I didn't force the bloke to drink. Come on, just have the one. I wouldn't want

259

pretty young ladies wandering the streets drunk in the middle of the day, would I? Give Marrup a bad name.'

'I just came to pay the bill.' She pushed the envelope at him, but instead of taking it he grabbed her wrist. The envelope dropped to the floor. She tried to pull away. He gripped her wrist harder. He lowered her arm and pulled her into a small, sideways step, so her back was towards the bar.

'Let go of me.'

He released his fingers slowly from around her wrist, but moved right in front of her when she tried to step forward. He stood between her and the door. She could see the spidery red veins on his face. He reached out and squeezed her shoulder and she jerked it back to get rid of his hand.

'I don't really need the money. Won't make much difference now. But there are other ways of paying debts, eh? I'm sure a city woman like you knows how to give someone a good send-off.' A glaze of sweat had broken out on his upper lip. His breath was too fast. Charlie was off his stool, moving towards her, cornering her.

'Fuck off.'

She shoved Jamie in the chest with both hands, but he grabbed her wrists and held them together, tight, pushed her back against the bar so her spine hit the hard wooden edge, pressed his lumbering body against her, clamped his free hand on her breast.

'Get the fuck off me!'

Then his hand was over her mouth.

'Eh Jamie, come on,' Charlie said.

She pulled her knee up, hard, into Jamie McFadden's groin, and got him again on the chin as he doubled over, holding himself. He grunted and swore. Before he could recover, she reached across the bar, felt blindly, grabbed the first thing to hand. She swung the half-full whisky bottle and brought it down on the side of Jamie's head. He staggered to the floor. The other man stepped back and just missed the force of the bottle as she whipped around.

Jamie groaned and pushed himself onto his knees. A tiny line of blood trickled down the side of his face. 'You little cunt. Fucking whore,' he panted, his face a furious red. 'As if you don't want it. Everyone knows what you really are. You've always wanted it, whoring bitch.'

Hester cracked the bottle down hard on the edge of the bar. It shattered and spewed whisky. She tightened her grip on the jagged remains of the bottle.

Charlie moved around in a wide arc, to help Jamie to his feet.

They watched her while she manoeuvred towards the door brandishing her weapon, kicking over stools and chairs as she went, setting up obstacles in case they followed. She backed out of the door into the blasting daylight, the bottle still gripped tight in her hand, and ran to the ute.

She fumbled with the gears and roared away, her body shivering, her mind crowded with nothing but escape.

31 LOSER

Dom paced around the fire, prodding at the charring paper with a long stick. Wisps of blackened ash charged into the dusky sky and hung there. His hands were grubby, his hair thick with grime. Sweat soaked his shirt. It almost felt as though he was doing real work.

He dropped another bundle of paper onto the fire and watched it shrivel and disappear. In a perverse way it was gratifying, this destruction, a relief to watch the ancient electricity bills and CWA leaflets, the receipts for groceries and tedious letters he'd sent his mother, curl and blacken and dissolve into nothing.

It was better to be rid of it all.

She was gone.

The fire spat a spark across the firebreak. He rushed over, stamping, kicking dirt, hitting at the ground with his stick. His hands were shaking when he stopped. He told himself to calm down. He drank water from a plastic bottle balanced on a stack of paper nearby, then added a handful of old bank statements to the flames.

He wondered if Hester might have been right; perhaps it was never too late to do the right thing, to make amends, of a sort. Being here, trying to make sense of it all was a start, wasn't it? But he couldn't forget that his mum had suffered, alone and ill at the end, in some impersonal hospital (he didn't even know where), the house she'd lived in for over forty years neglected, the farm she'd poured everything into practically useless. One son lived far away, unmarried, while the other said little and beat up his wife.

Should he have tried harder, done more? Would things have been different if he hadn't left, if he had stayed in Perth, or at least in the same country, gone to Melbourne or Sydney?

Who was to blame? Who was to blame for any of it?

As he patrolled the fire, persuading wayward scraps of paper back into the flames with his stick, he heard noises, glanced movement behind him. He turned. Someone was coming. He planted the long stick firmly on the ground, gripping it with both hands, like a spear.

If Neal had been on his own, Dom would have been frightened, but the two boys were there, flanking him, skipping and running in bursts to keep up with their father. Neal stopped a few metres away from his brother. He was holding something.

The shoebox? Did Neal have the jewellery?

Billy overtook his father and ran up to Dom, with Alex close behind. 'What're you doing, Uncle Dom?' Their voices broke into the haze of Dom's solitary focus.

'Hi there kiddos. Just tidying up. Getting rid of some of Gran's old papers.'

Alex tore his gaze away from the fire to look at Dom. 'Can we do it, too?'

'Put something on the fire? If it's okay with your dad.' Both boys, and Dom, looked to Neal.

'If you're careful.' Neal's gruff growl seemed quieter, less convincing than usual.

Dom gave the boys some paper each. They edged close to the fire, cautious but entranced. When they leaned forward and threw their paper, the blue-tinged flames lurched. He shepherded them back to a safe distance. The boys stood next to each other and watched the fire. Smoke churned and drifted.

'Dom?'

He turned, curious, at the strange, unexpected sound of his brother calling his name. He ambled over, not wanting to appear too quick to respond, too eager.

Neal thrust the shoebox towards him. 'I don't need it. Keep it. It's yours.'

Dom took the box, confused. Fine ash drifted down and came to rest at their feet.

'I need to borrow the car.'

'The Nissan? What for?'

Neal didn't speak, at first. He looked away, towards the boys and the fire, shifted his feet wider apart. 'Hester,' he managed, finally. 'She went shopping. She always … she hasn't come back.' His face was tight and anxious. 'She's not at Lizzie's. I called. She wouldn't leave the kids for so long. It's not like her. Nearly dark.' He shook his head, bewildered.

'I'll go.'

Neal said nothing. The boys were lively, jumping around, waving their arms in the air, making noises mimicking the crunch and spit of the flames. Neal's head seemed to sink down on his shoulders. He looked worn and beaten.

'Just bring her back. Please.' His voice wavered. This desperate stranger seemed as far removed as it was possible to be from his mean, aggressive brother.

Dom let the boys throw one more handful of paper into the flames, then gave them a biscuit each and a drink of water. He watched the trio wander away, like a tiny band of refugees.

He threw spadefuls of dirt onto the fire. Inside, he put the shoebox in his suitcase, washed his face and hands, and left for Marrup.

It was dark enough to need the headlights on. Their pale beam caught a flash of movement — a roo escaping into a paddock. The acrid smell of fire smoke had stayed with him, infused in his hair and clothes

Why did Neal have the jewellery? He seemed to think Dom had given it to him; perhaps he'd found it and Hester had to make up a quick lie. Was she on her way out, leaving, when she called in to see him earlier? Could she have decided to go, without the jewellery, or the boys? The jewellery maybe, but not the boys. He couldn't believe she would leave without them. Besides, she would have told him what was happening. She would have said.

Maybe the ute had broken down. An accident? But surely she would have been found by now. He pictured himself pulling Hester out of the upturned ute, rescuing her, taking her to safety. He shook his head, disgusted. Was that the true reason he wanted her to have the jewellery — so he could play the saviour, make her eternally grateful? It would have been easy to keep holding her today, to tell her he'd take care of her, make her safe, always. But he let her leave, put no pressure on her. He got that right, at least.

The car bumped over a pothole and he gripped the wheel tighter. All that mattered was that Hester might be in trouble. He had to find her.

He cruised slowly up Marrup's main street. The General Store was still open but the pub was closed up and dark, which surprised him. He wondered if Jamie McFadden had already left. There was no sign of the ute.

The fuel gauge sat on the red line marking an empty tank. Had Andy thought the car would run forever on nothing but his newfound enthusiasm for life? Dom drove through Marrup to Johnson's Garage. The garage was deserted, though the forecourt and shop were dimly lit. He got out of the car and paced towards the shop. The sound of TV voices leaked out to him, and the smell of something greasy cooking. The large woman appeared in the shop doorway calling, 'watch the spuds, will you?' behind her as she came through.

She smiled at Dom. 'G'day. How's it going?'

'Fine, thanks. I wasn't sure if you were open.'

'Yeah, course. We're always open.'

She filled the tank and tilted her head on her rubbery neck. 'What're you up to then, out and about?'

'Oh, just going for a drive. Get away from the house for a bit. Hadn't realised the fuel was so low.'

The bowser clicked and churned.

'Not long until you're back overseas, is it? Leaving all us poor buggers stuck out here.' She tried to sound dramatic but laughed, her bosom heaving.

Dom smiled but wished she would hurry up. 'I hope the drought breaks soon,' he said.

She shrugged and clicked the nozzle back into the bowser. 'Oh, don't worry about us. I'm sure we'll survive.'

Dom drove back towards Marrup, hoping to find out from Graham Walker if Hester had been at the General Store, but the Store was closed. He swore and wondered if he should go to their house behind the Store. If he did, the whole district would probably be involved in no time.

He noticed a movement in the pale light of the phone box — someone was there. Dom pulled over and a lanky figure stepped out. Andy smiled. He held up a hand in greeting and loped across the road. Dom unwound his window. Andy!

'You still around? Thought you'd be long gone by now.'

Andy leaned down to the window. 'Bloody lift never turned up. So unreliable, these farmer-types,' he said with mock exasperation. 'Anyway, Graham let me stay with them. Been helping out in the Store, stocking shelves and stuff. Good fun really. Mum's been trying to sort out another lift, but I can't hang around anymore. I'll get up early in the morning and start hitching. Or walking, more likely. Just called Mum to say goodbye.' He tilted his head towards the phone box. 'Dad answered — sounded quite happy until he realised who it was. Anyway, what brings my best mate into Marrup on this fine evening?'

'It's Hester, Andy. I'm looking for Hester.'

Andy quickly collected his things from the Walkers' place. He told them he was going to stay with Dom that night and head off in the morning.

Dom eased the car away from the curb and drove slowly out of town. The two men talked over possibilities, wondering what to do. They could drive aimlessly, searching, or go to Joondyne, to the police station, and report her missing. But what if she didn't want to be found?

'How about that roadhouse on the way to Joondyne?' Andy suggested. 'They might have seen —' He steadied himself with a hand on the dashboard as Dom jerked the car to the right, down a narrow road.

'Sorry. I just thought — Dog Rock.' He nodded towards the faded signpost as they passed. 'I'm sure I remember Hester saying something when we were there about — what was it? — disappearing, or getting lost. I can't remember exactly. Might be a long shot, but it's worth a try while we're close, isn't it?'

'Why not?'

Dom kept his speed down — this time of night was bad for roos, and the road to Dog Rock was poor once the tarmac ran out. The car bumped down the track towards the rise of the rock, its outline looming grim and huge against the night sky. The ute appeared in the choppy beam of the car's lights, parked sideways behind the clutter of gums. The men glanced at each other.

'Jesus,' Andy murmured.

Dom switched off the engine. He left the lights on.

The ute's windows were up. Dom tried the driver's side door. It was unlocked, and the keys were in the ignition. There was a smell of alcohol.

'Hes?' Andy called. 'Hester!'

'Hester!' Dom's voice echoed. 'It's Dom! Dom and Andy!'

They listened.

A hint of movement, a swish of sound. The light from the car's headlights bored into the night, then dropped away.

Andy went to the car and rifled around in his pack. He came back with a tiny torch. The two friends shuffled forward, calling, listening. The torch was not much use, but the stars were bright and their eyes soon adjusted. They moved faster, following the slow squeak of movement.

Dom could make out Hester's form before they reached the playground. She was there, on the swing, her legs dangling. As they came closer she jumped up, shoving something in front of her; a broken bottle.

'Hes,' Andy said. 'It's us.'

She lowered her arm to her side, still gripping the bottle. Her face was a pale moon. She stared at them.

Dom took a step closer. 'Are you alright, Hester?'

'I just went to pay the bill. I only wanted to pay the bill. That's all.'

They told her they would take her anywhere, but Hester was adamant; she wanted to go home. Back to her boys. She didn't know how she could have left them for so long, she said. Every bit of energy and will had drained out of her and she had closed down, gone blank, as though a heavy door had slammed shut on her mind.

Dom offered to go and get the boys for her, take them all to Lizzie's, or Joondyne or somewhere, but she walked away seeming not to have heard him, and dropped the remains of the bottle she was carrying into the bin. It made a heavy, hollow noise when it hit the bottom. Andy helped Hester clear away fragments of glass on the front seat of the ute, while Dom held the torch.

He drove her back in the ute. Andy would follow in the car.

Hester sat up straight, staring ahead. Dom's fury rose in the silence. That bastard Jamie McFadden! Who did the stupid redneck think he was? Poor Hester. He wanted to comfort her; touch her, hold her hand. He knew he couldn't.

The faint, lingering smell of whisky disgusted him.

When they were close to the farm, he glanced across. 'Neal gave me the jewellery back. It's still yours, Hester, if you want it.'

She didn't move. 'I thought … I hoped Neal might use it to …' Her voice was so subdued he strained to hear her. She lifted her chin and spoke louder. 'It could have helped, Dom. With the farm, with — everything …'

So that was what had happened, Dom thought. She hadn't wanted the jewellery for herself at all. He wondered if she was tied, forever, irredeemably, to his brother. And to this place.

He parked the ute in front of the cottage. Hester turned to him before she got out. 'You're leaving soon, aren't you?'

'In a few days.'

'I'm glad we got to meet, Dom. And thanks. For everything.'

Before he could reply she was out of the ute, walking towards the house. Loss and longing settled on him. Neal had come out onto the verandah with the children — he could hear their overtired squabbling. Hester bent to pick up Alex and kissed Billy on the head. Neal ushered them all inside, then lingered on the verandah, looking towards Dom. He raised a hand, nodded, before following his family in.

Andy was parked in a gateway near the end of the track, waiting to pick Dom up. Dom followed the tiny beam of the torch. He was tired now. Exhausted. He got in the passenger's side of the car.

'Was she okay?'

'I just dropped her off. She went inside.'

'You want to drive?'

'I don't mind. No.'

Before starting the engine, Andy shuffled around in his seat, carefully clipped in his seatbelt, checked the mirrors, ran his hands around the wheel. 'We can't let the bastard get away with it, Dom.'

'Jamie McFadden? Do you think we should go the Police in Joondyne? Hester said she didn't want them involved.'

'And if they were, nothing would happen, mate. Waste of time. Even if Hes wanted to tell them, whose side do you think they'd be on, eh? Let's see, an ex-junkie-pro blow-in, who happened to be at the pub in the middle of the afternoon, or the fine upstanding publican whose family have been here for generations? Shit, Dom, the cop'd probably treat her the same given half a chance.'

Dom noticed that his nails were black and grimy. He hoped he'd put the fire out properly. 'God. Jamie. What a bastard.'

'Yeah. He always was a fucking bully, even at school. How dare he lay a finger on her.' Andy gripped the steering wheel with his bony hands. 'He doesn't deserve to breathe the same fucking air as Hester! He'll leave here, Dom, go off to his wife and kids and live a nice comfy life on the coast. Rape a few girls now and then, when the fancy takes him, like it's his right. We need to teach him a lesson.'

'I don't know what —'

'We can't just let it go, Dom. We can't. Forgiveness has its place, but so does justice.' Andy turned the car around. There was silence, for a minute. 'Are you with me, Dom?'

'Look, you're not planning on doing anything —'

'Trust me, mate. Just trust me.'

The road ahead was lit like a blank runway in the car's headlights. Neither man spoke, but Dom felt a solidarity between them, a tangible sense of purpose. He was alert; his tiredness had passed.

Andy killed the lights before he turned into the pub's car park. The green station wagon was there. They pushed the car doors shut with barely a click.

The pub was in darkness. Dom tried the back door. It was locked. They peered through the nearest window. Dom held up the torch. He could make out the cluttered debris of a storeroom — boxes and cigarette cartons, a kettle and a couple of mugs, some old pub chairs. There was a flash of movement next to him, the brittle sound of breaking glass as Andy's hand smashed one of the thin window panes. A dog started barking. Dom watched Andy unwrap his hand from his pulled-up T-shirt and thread his arm inside, curving it around to lift the catch on the window. Together, they eased the window up. It was stiff. The dog quietened down.

Andy brushed away the broken glass and hoisted himself through. Dom followed, more tentatively. Andy put a chair under the window to make it easier for him.

Inside, the two men stopped to listen. The place was silent. A doorway led into the back of the bar. Dom remembered the sodden, stale smell. There was a crunch of broken glass underfoot. On the bar, yellow dregs of beer wallowed in white-streaked glasses. Upturned chairs and stools littered the floor. The glow from the cigarette machine infused the scene with a harmless, hazy stillness.

They stood and listened for sounds of life, but heard nothing. A car drove past, the beam of its lights scattering wild shadows across the walls. They ducked down, behind the bar.

'He might have gone somewhere else for the night,' Dom whispered.

Andy pressed his finger to his lips and pointed upwards.

They stepped up the wide wooden stairs covered with a threadbare runner. Dom kept the torch beam low. At the top, wide French windows led to the dilapidated front balcony. Doors lined up along landings on either side of the staircase. Despite its shabbiness, there was a grand, reassuring beauty to the place, a graceful gentility.

Andy moved with a sure confidence. Dom slunk along behind. Some of the doors were open — a dusty-smelling clutter of old pub furniture filled one room, another had luminous stars dotting the ceiling and wallpaper, with cartoon animals, peeling in the corners. A kid's room.

Andy moved on to the last door along the left landing, flicking his cigarette lighter to see, while Dom lingered in the doorway of the kid's room. A sudden burst of noise, scuffling cries, jolted him into a frantic rush to the room at the end that Andy had disappeared into.

He stopped short just inside the room and flashed the torch around. There was a loud clatter and something heavy slid across the floor and knocked against his foot. In his fright, he dropped the torch. He groped on the floor and picked up the object at his feet — a rifle, it was a rifle — then felt along the wall for the light switch.

A bare light bulb hung in the centre of the room. Andy stood over a blinking, panting Jamie, a pathetic figure perched on the edge of the bed in a singlet and a pair of slack underpants. A grubby pillow, a deep indent in its middle, crowned the bed. A grey sheet was tangled at the end. The room smelt like sweaty socks and stale booze.

'Thought you'd be ready for us, did you?' Andy's face was red and filmed with sweat. His fists were clenched.

Jamie looked at him with the beginnings of a sneer. 'Mr Bohan. So you are back. And a good evening to you too.' His gaze moved past Andy to Dom. 'And you, Dom.'

Dom separated his feet a few more inches and shifted the rifle in his hands. It was an old twenty-two, like the one his dad had taught him to shoot with, when he was twelve or thirteen. He liked the solid, comfortable weight of it, the cool smoothness of the wooden handle. He'd practiced his aim in the paddock behind the house, with cans on lumps of wood, and sometimes a cardboard bullseye target nailed to a tree. He and Neal went out shooting rabbits together, for a while. But he didn't like shooting roos. When he refused to go, Neal called him a girl.

'Look, what do youse want? Got bugger-all. Just the drink left downstairs. Some fags. Take it.' Jamie waved a hand. 'Take it all.'

Andy shook his head. 'How could you do it? I don't think you're really human, are you? Never quite got there. You're nothing but a fucking animal.'

Jamie turned to look at Andy. 'What? You mean —? Jeez, we'd had a few, mate, you know how it is.' His voice was thick with a wheedling exasperation. 'Been celebrating. Commiserating. End of an era, all that. Might've been a bit out of order, but no harm done, eh?'

'No harm done? You stupid wanker.' Andy's furious voice speared the air.

'Oh, Christ, come on. It was just a bit of fun. She made her feelings known, anyway. Went mental, just about knocked me out.' He felt at a tender spot on his head.

'Why don't we put a bullet in him, Dom?' He looked straight at the man on the bed as he spoke. 'Might as well. Do the world a favour.'

'Don't be bloody stupid.' Jamie appealed to Dom with an anxious, matey half-smile. 'Take no notice of him, Dommie. What're you doing mixed up with him, anyway? He's just trouble. A loser. Always was.'

With a sudden lunge Andy grabbed the publican's flabby body and slung him across the room like a sack of wheat. Jamie staggered and tumbled to the floor. He lay still for a few seconds, before struggling to prop himself up on one elbow.

Andy stood over him, breathing fast. Jamie peered sideways at his adversary, his face, childishly open, contorting with a mix of outrage, confusion and fear.

Andy's jaw moved, clenching and unclenching. He turned away, paced a few steps back towards the bed and lowered his head. His shoulders lifted and dropped as he took even, deep breaths.

Dom watched Jamie wipe his nose with the back of his hand and aim a sneering smirk at Andy's back. The publican began to heave himself off the floor but Dom moved fast, propelled by a surge of rage. He landed a solid kick to the man's side, swung the butt of the rifle, brought it down with a smooth force on the side of Jamie's head, as if he had practiced exactly this manoeuvre many times. There was a cracking sound and Jamie dropped to the floor with a grunt. Dom drew back his leg and kicked again, felt his foot ease into soft flesh.

'Dom.'

Startled, he glanced up, panting with the exertion of his violence. Jamie rocked slightly on the floor like an upturned turtle, his fat belly quivering. He groaned and whimpered a string of words: 'Don't hurt me fellas, please don't hurt me, got a wife and kids, fellas.' Blood matted a patch of his wispy hair.

Dom took a step back and flexed his fingers on the rifle. He raised it, balanced the metal barrel in his right hand and pointed it at Jamie.

'Dom. That's enough now, mate.' Andy's voice was calm. He moved to the bedside table, picked up a glass half full of a pale liquid and sniffed at it. He squatted down next to Jamie, lifted the man's head and put the glass to his lips.

Dom didn't move. Jamie's eyes shifted nervously, looking from Dom to Andy. He put a trembling hand to the glass and gulped at the drink. It spilled and dribbled down his chin and neck. Dom smelt the sharp tang of whisky.

'Now fuck off away to your poor fucking wife,' Andy said in a mild, weary voice. He lowered Jamie's head back to the floor, stood up and walked to the door.

Dom stared down at the publican and gripped the rifle tighter in his sweat-damp hands. He felt rooted to the spot, held there by a churning fury, a force of confusion and frustration that demanded release.

'Come on, buddy. It's time to go.'

Dom looked up. A whining murmur came from the man on the floor. Andy nodded slowly, as though he were agreeing with something Dom had said. Dom took a step back. The rifle clattered loudly on the wooden floor when he dropped it and Jamie let out a frightened yelp. A trail of pungent yellow liquid began to spread across the floor. Dom followed Andy out of the door.

The Big House became a pale backdrop in the night when Andy switched off the car's lights.

Dom opened the car door but didn't get out; the strength had drained from him. He heard the driver's side door shut, an underwater sound, and Andy was there, close to him.

'Come on, let's get you to bed.'

277

With a great effort, Dom swung his legs around so they were planted on the ground. He pulled himself up, one hand on Andy's arm, the other on the edge of the open door, but he could not stand — Andy caught him as he slumped forward.

'You're alright. I've got you.'

Sobbing heaved up from inside him, loud and uncontrolled. He was vaguely aware of Andy murmuring soothing sounds, rubbing a hand on his back. Eventually, he became aware of his own ragged breaths and, between them, the peace of the farm around him.

32 Fire in the Heavens

Sitting on the verandah in the cool of the night, drinking tea with his mate, Andy thought he had never felt so full of peace, so right with himself. He was glad Dom was off the beer.

An outline of the land showed under the sweep of stars, with smudges of fences and trees. There would always be beauty here, no matter what happened to the place. His dad might not want him around, but he could not stop him feeling a connection, a love for this land. He could not take that away from him.

Dom offered him an open packet of biscuits and he took two. He stretched out his legs and crossed them at the ankle. They had worked hard the last couple of days. His body felt pleasantly tired.

Putting Mrs Connor's things back was the right thing to do, something positive after all the shit on Thursday night. Dom had decided he'd destroyed enough of his mum's stuff, and couldn't bear to get rid of anything else. It was a kind of breakthrough, a moving on for him, Andy thought. The emotional meltdown had been a good thing too, a release of all that feeling squashed inside him for so long. Dom seemed strong now.

They had spent hours working side by side, replacing ornaments on shelves, unpacking boxes of crockery and cutlery, taking clothes out of bags and returning them to drawers, fitting them onto hangers in the wardrobe. It was therapeutic, a kind of spiritual act. He was proud of his friend.

Andy hoped Dom would listen to his emotions more from now on, act on his gut feeling. It would do him good.

Dom took Andy's mug and went inside to make more tea.

The lights from the cottage windows were pale in the distance. Andy allowed himself a moment of sadness and regret about Hester. Then he let it go. She had another bad time to add to her pile, but he was sure she would recover, with her strong will and the boys to think about. When they'd found her the other night Andy had indulged in an old fantasy — he pictured her leaving Neal, bringing the boys and going with him, far away. They would be together, have more children. A happy family life, at last. But he knew it was nothing more than a pleasant, selfish dream. Hester would find her own way. And he had other plans.

He heard the bubble of the electric kettle in the kitchen, the click as it switched itself off. A teaspoon clinked against a mug. There was a calmness about Dom today, an ease that had been missing before.

Dom brought out the tea.

'Excellent. Thanks fella.'

'No worries, mate.' Dom drawled in exaggerated Australian. They both laughed.

'You can't even do a decent Aussie accent. You're a bloody Pom now.'

'I suppose I am. Halfway there, at least.'

'You did the right thing, leaving.'

'You think so?'

'No doubt about it. You've made a life for yourself over there.'

'Huh,' Dom tipped back his head. Andy waited, but Dom said nothing. He had guessed that not everything was perfect for his friend in London, but even in his emotional state last night, Dom hadn't given away any details. Communication-wise, Dom still had some work to do.

'You're not thinking about coming back, are you?'

'No. What's there to come back to?'

'Good. I mean, don't get me wrong, I didn't —'

'It's okay.'

'I'd love to have you around, but when you've been away for so long I just don't think you'd —'

'I know. You're right. No offence taken.'

'Phew.'

Dom smiled.

They both sipped at their tea.

'What about you, Andy? You're going back to Perth to stay with your friends.'

'Indeed I am.'

'And then what?'

'Oh, I've got some ideas. I'll keep you posted. Want another biscuit?'

Dom promised that when he got back to London he would find the Christopher Brennan poem Andy liked, 'Fire in the Heavens', and have it memorised for the next time they saw each other. 'I don't know when I'll be over here again, so I suppose you'll have to come to London to hear it.'

'You're on.'

Andy could tell by his friend's vague smile that he was sceptical about such a thing ever happening.

The cottage disappeared into the darkness; the lights had gone off.

Dom went inside again and came out carrying his mum's old Scrabble set. 'How about it?'

'I thought you'd never ask.'

Andy's mum picked him up the next morning, early, before Dom was even awake. She would take him as far as Joondyne.

33 Swimming in the Sea

The bath was nearly full with foamy water. The boys played together, splashing and laughing, with a small family of yellow plastic ducks Marjorie had bought them years ago, for Christmas.

They were overexcited and too loud. They splashed water on the floor. Hester tried to stay quiet and patient, and sound happy. She told them to calm down, but smiled; it was good to see them enjoying themselves. On top of them losing their Gran, they have sensed a shifting in their world over the last couple of days, since she went missing, and have tended to be whiney and demanding.

A cool bath, in the afternoon, for fun. A stupid waste of water, but she didn't care. Neal would not say anything. Since Dom had brought her home that night, something had changed. Neal was even more absent than before. Always a quiet man, his silence was different now — empty, as though he was thinking nothing as well as saying it.

He had stopped playing with the boys. He looked at them vaguely as though he was not sure what they had to do with him. She tried to keep them distracted but she was so tired. An afternoon splash in the bath was a novelty, an easy way to amuse them.

She squeezed more bubble bath — another present from Gran — into the water and swooshed it around. The bubbles foamed up and the boys screeched with delight. She collected a clump of foam on both hands, lifted it like an offering, and blew. The foam quivered and broke up, and landed on the giggling boys. They scooped up the foam themselves and puffed at it, waved it around.

A dizzy, sick feeling came over her and her heart started to race. She pushed herself up from her squatting position next to the bath and pretended to be doing something at the sink while she focused her breathing, tried to quell the nausea. She did not want to break down in front of the children. Was she still in some kind of shock from what had happened? She had thought, a long time ago, that it might have been her, something about her that invited men to treat her that way. But now she didn't believe that. She did not ask for it. Why the hell would she? It was not her fault.

Neal was out. He left the house early, came back late each night. She wasn't sure how he was spending all that time — he didn't seem to be taking any tools with him. Just the rifle. Yesterday, he brought back two rabbits he'd shot, but she had already cooked the tea.

There were no accusations about her disappearance; Neal showed no curiosity about where she had been, though the children had asked as soon as she got back. She told them the ute had broken down, she had got stuck by the side of the road, and Uncle Dom had helped her. There was no question of them not believing her, and this simple lie seemed to mark the end of the matter for Neal, too.

He didn't seem angry. At night, he kissed her forehead and left her to sleep, without touching her. He was strangely calm, as though all the aggression had drained out of him. Had he sensed a change in her? Or simply lost the strength, the will, to even take his misery out on his wife? Not that she trusted this change; it was too sudden, his need too great. She was wary. Waiting.

The bubbles had gone and the boys were starting to bicker. She got them out of the bath and helped them to get dry and dressed. They bleated that they were hungry and she made some toast with Vegemite which they ate while looking at books and building with plastic blocks.

It was nearly three o'clock. Past the boys' usual afternoon nap time. Hester felt an overwhelming urge to lie down with them, to close her eyes, drift into sleep with their perfect bodies close and safe. Billy responded to the novelty of Mummy coming with them and skipped along willingly to the bedroom. She drew the curtains and pushed the two single beds together. The boys snuggled up on each side of her.

She craved stillness and calm but, although Alex fell asleep quickly, Billy was restless and wriggled and jostled. She tried soothing 'Shhs' and 'Quiet nows' and he almost settled, but not quite. He began to huff and whine and woke his brother. Something in her sprang loose and she was angry and shouting and gripping his arms hard, telling him to shut up, just shut up and stop being a little bastard, a fucking little shit. His eyes went wide and gushed tears. He wailed and sobbed. Alex was crying too. Her anger melted away as fast as it had come, and deep remorse instantly took its place. She hugged a resistant Billy to her and breathed into his ear how sorry she was, that she didn't mean it, that Mummy was very, very tired, she was so, so sorry. She hugged Alex to her as well, and they cried together.

She could not bear that this was happening. Something damaged in her had broken free. It was frightening. She wanted her perfect children to know nothing but love and goodness, at least from those closest to them, those who were supposed to protect and cherish them. She had shielded them from Neal's violence towards her. But now this.

It could not happen. She knew she must hold back the part of her that wanted to shout and scream, lash out and tear at her clothes. She needed to think, to work out what to do. The right thing. Whatever that was.

The boys settled and fell asleep. She stayed very still.

She thought about the farm and her marriage to Neal. For too long she had been clinging to a dream of stability and happiness that neither Neal nor the dying land could ever fulfil. But imperfect and difficult as it was, this was the life she had become used to, and all her boys had ever known. Did she have a right to make such a huge decision for them? She had to be sure. Completely sure. Could she really do it? People started afresh all the time, she reminded herself. Even Andy seemed, finally, to have left behind his old, destructive habits. And look at Dom — he began a different life on the other side of the world. She had changed her own life before — why not again?

The boys' breathing was gentle and regular beside her, their small bodies warm. Eventually, she slept too.

She opened a tin of tomatoes and mixed it into fried mince and onions. She took some peas out of the freezer and put a saucepan of water on the stove to boil for spaghetti. The boys were playing outside, chasing the chickens. They would be dirty again, after the bath. It was getting dark. They would have to come in soon.

Through the kitchen window she saw Neal traipsing across the paddock, the rifle hanging loosely in one hand. His shirt had come untucked at the side. It was the shirt that needed patching on the sleeve, where he had caught it on a bit of fence wire. He went into the dark shade of the shed and she could not see him anymore. The children stopped playing and looked towards the shed. Before, they would have rushed to their father, but now they carried on their game for a minute before scurrying back into the house.

She lay awake that night, listening to the background sounds of life all around her. She heard the distant, plaintive calls of the sheep, which had always helped to lull her to sleep, and unexpected things too; the scuttle of a rat in the roof, the scritter of cockroaches between the walls. There was the shuffle and scratch of the one chicken that still laid, as she moved on her roost, with just a thin weave of wire between her and the foxes. Hester's senses had become oddly sharp; she picked out the dense, earthy smell of white ants in the wood, burrowing invisibly through the roof beams, breathed in the sharpness of crushed leaves, caught the muddy scent of the dam water, with the hint of a brackish tang, drifting across the paddocks.

Neal was silent beside her, his eyes closed and his breathing regular. She assumed he was asleep.

She had thought and thought about whether it was safer to slip away in the darkness, when she knew where he was, or try to leave in broad daylight. She could not tell. She just had to go. She had to go now.

Her feet were on the cool lino and she was moving through the dim house pulling on the clothes she had left in the bathroom, taking the rucksack she had packed earlier off the hook on the back of the children's bedroom door — water, torch, biscuits, a few clothes — then waking the children, kissing them gently on cheeks, whispers, fingers on lips, out of bed, quiet, quiet, please, here's teddy, blankie, pulling a jumper over Billy's pyjamas, his bewildered, sleepy whimpering, sandals on feet, shh, don't worry, lifting Alex, carrying him slumped over her shoulder, the pack swung on the other side.

The flyscreen door swooped open soundlessly; she had put cooking oil on the hinges late last night — why had she never thought to do it before? She took out the torch, and hoisted Alex so he was on her back, pulled his arms around her neck, and they were walking away, across the bare circle of ground, past the big salmon gum and down the track, the sound of her footsteps on the ground vibrating in her ears; *dum, dum, dum.* A movement next to her gave her a rush of panic, but it was only the dog. She made a low sound and pointed back towards the house. The dog hesitated, turned and slunk away.

The stars were thick above them. The torch gave a bubble of light at their feet. Just the three of them. Without the jewellery. In a way, she was glad. It was not hers to sell; the jewellery belonged here, to the farm and the family. She was cutting her ties.

Dazed and tired, Billy wondered aloud where they were going, in a whiney voice. She told him they were going somewhere good, but they couldn't take the ute because it wasn't working properly. She would explain later, she promised. He held her hand and trotted along beside her. What choice did he have?

Alex dozed on her shoulder. His breath whistled through his nose, into his tiny chest and out again. She half expected, at any moment, to hear the growl of the ute's engine, its lights exposing them, pinning them hopelessly against the night.

They walked and walked. She tried not to rush in case it panicked Billy. She hummed Twinkle, Twinkle Little Star. Next to her, Billy started to sing the words, softly.

The blue car was there at the side of the track, in front of the house. A gilded chariot. It was perfect. It was all she needed. The back doors clicked open. She settled the sleepy children into the shelter of the seat, clutching their blankets and their teddies, belted them in. She checked, just in case, but the keys were not in the ignition.

She dashed to the house, up the front steps, across the verandah and eased open the screen door. Scanning the room with the torch she spotted the keys, discarded on the table. She grabbed them and slipped them into the pocket of her cotton trousers. As she searched for a piece of paper to write on, she heard a noise and flashed the torch.

Dom raised a hand to shield his eyes from the beam of light. 'Hes?'

'Dom. I was ... the boys are in the car.'

'The boys?'

She nodded. 'We're going.'

289

He stepped towards her so they were standing close in the dark room. Marjorie's old fridge burred around them. Cockroaches scuffled into hiding.

'I'll drop the car off at one of the hire offices in —' She paused, then shrugged. She didn't know where she was going. A city, but not Perth. Somewhere different, where she had never been before.

Dom nodded. 'The jewellery. I'll go and —' He began to turn, but she reached out and touched his arm to stop him.

'No, Dom. It's not mine.'

He breathed deeply, a faint frown on his face, but did not challenge her.

'You'll be okay to get back to Perth?' she asked.

'Of course. Don't worry about that.'

'Thanks, Dom.'

'Hes —'

'Look, I'd better —'

Dom took half a step forward and folded his arms around her. 'Take care,' he whispered. 'I'll be thinking of you.'

She held him too. It felt good, like she was drawing strength from him. She tilted her head back and looked at him. In the dim room, his resemblance to Neal made her tense up, for a moment. She felt his fingers stroke her hair. She kissed him on the cheek. 'I have to go.'

'Wait.' He found his wallet on the table, pressed some notes into her hand. She took the money. She was grateful.

When she turned the key, the petrol gauge rose and rose, until it was near the full mark. She smiled. Andy would say it was a good sign.

After a couple of hundred kilometres she stopped panicking every time she saw the lights of another car behind her. With the kids drooped fast asleep in the back seat she began to cry, silently, tears dripping down her face, tickling and annoying like persistent flies. She would stop crying when the children woke. It was an indulgence, a release of tension rather than sadness. But she would miss Neal, wouldn't she? Her husband. He was a good man, in so many ways. She thought about when they had met, their early days together. The feeling of hope, the expectation of a happy future. Had she ever really believed it would work for her and Neal? Had she truly loved him, or was it only what he had offered her? She shook her head. What did it matter? He was the father of her children. It was complicated. She would think about it another time. It was done. Finished. She would have to make a new life for her and the boys. She was determined to trust herself.

She thought of Marjorie, and imagined her smiling down at her. Worried about her son, but approving. Definitely approving. Would she have done this if Marjorie was still alive? No. It would never have happened. She could not have left Marjorie there, to deal with the consequences.

'Thank you, Marjorie,' she whispered.

She will stop for food in the morning, when they get to a town. She has some grocery money and the money Dom gave her. They will have a cooked breakfast, if she can get it, with beans and eggs and sausages. Something substantial. Milk for the boys, coffee for her. Strong. Later, she will sleep. Later.

They will go swimming every day, in the sea.

34 Connection

Dom got up and pushed back the curtain. The Nissan was gone. He smiled, remembering the feel of Hester close to him. Any lingering disappointment that it was not him she had come for faded away. There was something between them that would always be there. Something important. That was what mattered.

He folded the sheets and tidied the lounge with focussed energy. Hester had done it. She had made her choice. It didn't matter about the car. He couldn't have cared less.

He ate a bowl of cereal standing up, rinsed out the bowl and spoon and left them in the drainer by the sink. He pulled out a few essentials from his suitcase, packed them into his day pack and took the coins he needed from the pile of change dumped on the table.

The shoebox was heavy and solid in his hands. He felt its weight and substance. He knew the jewellery wasn't really his, and never had been. It belonged to Neal. He was the one who had stayed, given his life to the farm. No matter what he'd done or how badly he had treated Hester, whatever Dom thought of his brother, the jewellery was Neal's. A heaviness lifted from him with this acknowledgement, the release of a dragging anxiety, a balance for the guilt he felt about Hester leaving. There was only one thing he could do.

He shrugged the pack onto his back, settled the shoebox under his arm and set off down the track.

From a distance, Dom could make out his brother's form on the verandah. The purity of the light gave the scene — the paddocks, the cottage, the tin shed, the towering gum with its bright, shimmering leaves — an unreal, magical quality, as though he had stepped into a painting.

He walked steadily towards the cottage, breathing in the morning air, with the gentle bleat of sheep around him. He shifted the shoebox to his other arm. When he reached the cottage he stood at the bottom of the verandah steps. Neal was sitting down cleaning a rifle, pushing an oily rag into the barrel with a straight length of wire. He ignored Dom.

He must know they're gone, Dom thought. He would know they're gone, for good.

'Neal? I'm leaving today.'

His brother's eyebrows lifted slightly, but he did not look up or speak.

'I wanted to bring this back.'

He moved up the verandah steps, one by one, as if trying not to startle a nervous animal. He stood close to Neal, waiting for him to take the offered box, but his brother carried on cleaning the rifle, shoving the rag into the barrel over and over. A messy clutter of tins and bottles surrounded Neal's chair. Dom breathed in the smooth smell of gun oil mixed with the bite of kerosene. There were dark drops of oil on the verandah boards. He bent down and put the box near his brother's feet.

He took a step back and watched Neal for a minute, retreating with him into the silence until it became something between them, a connection, a taut, linking rope. It was hard to speak, but he knew he had to.

He sighed out his breath and let his head droop for a moment. 'I never even bothered to wonder if things might have been different, Neal. You staying on the farm, me leaving — it all seemed … mapped out. Inevitable.'

Neal stopped moving. The rifle rested on his lap. One of his big hands clutched the wire with the rag wrapped around it. In the silence Dom heard his own breath, felt his chest move in and out. He tensed in surprise when Neal finally spoke.

'You left us. Me and Mum.' His voice was wilted, without force.

Dom nodded. 'I'm sorry.'

'Now Mum's gone, too.' He looked up at Dom.

For a few moments there was such loss and misery in his brother's face that Dom wanted to reach out to him, to offer him some comfort. 'I know how much you'll miss her.' It was the best he could manage.

A flapping chicken scrabbled around the side of the house, chased by another thinly feathered creature. The tyre swing hung from the branches of the salmon gum.

'What are you going to do, Neal?'

His brother blinked slowly, like someone who could not quite wake up.

Dom wondered what would happen to him. Would he survive here, alone? 'You're still young. You can make a new start. Do whatever you like. Sell the jewellery.'

Neal's body seemed to sag a little in the chair.

'Neal? Will you be alright?'

Dom waited, but his brother said nothing. He would have to get moving soon, before it got too hot. His mouth felt dry and sticky. He could have drunk the water from his plastic bottle and refilled it again at the Big House on the way out, but he had an urge to go inside the cottage, one last time.

'Can I get a drink?'

He slid off his pack and left it near the verandah steps. The flyscreen door opened silently. He was sure it had squeaked before.

Without Hester and the boys the room seemed hollow and grubby. Dom took a glass from a cupboard. It clinked against the one next to it. As he walked past the table he stopped. There were two photos. Dom recognised them from the bag of papers he had brought over for Hester to give to Neal. He put down the glass and picked up the photos. One was of all of them, his mum and dad, him and Neal, at the Show in Merredin that they used to go to every year. Dom was only a toddler; Neal held his hand as they stood in front of their parents. In the background, there was a Ferris wheel, and a cow being led by a rope. The other was of the two boys together, a portrait, all freckles and gappy smiles, and rough, home-cut hairstyles. They were, perhaps, five and eight. Dom and Neal.

Dom's hand shook as he turned on the tap of the filter barrel. He drank two glasses of water and wiped his mouth.

Back outside, he lowered himself onto the edge of the verandah, with his feet on the middle step. He forced himself to look at his brother. Neal sat with both hands gripping the rifle in his lap.

'You know, I only wrote to you when I first went to London because I was lonely.' Dom's voice was a tight whisper. 'I didn't really think about you at all. I didn't think about what it was like for you and Mum, here.'

The red dog padded over from somewhere near the shed and stood at the bottom of the verandah steps, its ears twitching, before slinking under the house.

'The truth is Neal, my life's a bloody mess. I've made so many mistakes. But it could have been different, couldn't it? Everything. Do you think it could have all been different?'

He didn't expect a reply.

After a while, he hauled himself up and settled his pack on his shoulders. His brother didn't move.

'Goodbye, Neal.' He walked away, half hoping that Neal would call out, summon him back. He would have turned around and gone to him.

But there was no call. Dom kept going down the track, planting one foot after the other on the rough ground, squinting against the daze of sunlight. He wondered what had happened to his sunglasses. He couldn't remember the last time he'd worn them. A sheep in the paddock next to him lifted its head. The reek of gun oil and kerosene stayed with him.

The coins clunked into the slot and he pressed the numbers. It rang for a while.

'Hi, Lizzie.'

'Dom? Are you alright? Where are you?'

'I'm fine. In Marrup. Phone box. I just wanted to say goodbye.'

'I didn't realise you were leaving today. We've hardly seen you.'

'I know. I got so busy, somehow.'

They both tried to speak at the same time. Lizzie laughed, then there was a short silence.

'It was good of you to help Hester out, the other day. When the ute broke down.'

'The ute …? Oh. Yes. It was no problem.'

Through the glass of the phone box he saw Graham Walker come out of the Store and set up his A-frame sign on the footpath. The man noticed Dom and raised a hand in greeting. Dom replied in the same way, before turning his back.

'I — well, I wanted to say thanks, Lizzie. Everything you did for Mum. I just wonder, sometimes … I don't know … I wonder if I could have done better.' The phone made it easier for him. He wasn't sure he could have said these things to her face.

'Don't be silly now. We'd all go mad if we thought like that. Bugger regrets.'

'Yes. You're probably right.'

'Listen, Dom, I'm not sure if —' He heard a deep intake of breath. 'She was in hospital before she died, your mum. Did you know?'

'I found out.'

'Neal didn't tell me either. Not the truth. Kept saying it was nothing, a bit of dizziness, she was coming out the next day. By the time I discovered that it was a stroke, how bad it was, it was too late. Oh, I don't suppose she would have known me anyway. But I was upset. Angry, for a while. Not long. I can't hold things against your brother, Dom. Neal has always been … well, he's struggled, sometimes. He was so close to your mum.'

'I know.'

'I won't tell you that you have to forgive him. Just do the best you can, eh? The best you can. Keep making your mum proud.' There was a shuffling, rummaging sound. 'Bugger.' Lizzie blew her nose. 'And Dom? It's been so good for Andy, seeing you again. You'll keep in touch with him, won't you?'

'Of course. He gave me his friends' phone number in Perth. I'll call him before I go.'

'Righto. Thanks, Dom.'

'Lizzie? What hospital was Mum in?'

'Merredin. She was in Merredin Hospital. It's a little place. Nice. As hospitals go.'

'Good. Good.'

The black phone receiver felt large and clumsy in his hand. The fly curtain fluttered in the doorway of the General Store, and a woman came out with a bag of groceries. He hadn't even noticed her go in. For a shocked moment he imagined it was Hester, but the woman turned and he saw she was shorter and older. It couldn't have been Hester. She was gone.

'Is Colin there, Lizzie?'

'Hang on, I'll get him. Look, before you go, write down Gillian's address. That's where you can get in touch, if we're not here. Don't forget us, will you, Dom? You're always welcome.'

He wrote down the address she gave him on a scrap of paper and said goodbye. The receiver clunked down when she went to get Colin. He slotted more coins into the phone.

'Dom. You're going today?' He sounded older, frailer on the phone than he did in person.

'Yes. I never got that tour of the farm.'

'No. Not to worry. Next time, eh?'

'Okay. You're on. Next time.'

'Well, have a good trip back.'

'Thanks. Mr — Colin, you know, he really is a great person, Andy's a good man.' His words rushed out. 'You should be proud of your son; he's one of the best people I've ever known. I wish I was more like him.'

The seconds ticked away with the intimate whistle of Colin Bohan's breath in Dom's ear. He could imagine the older man's straight back, his tight jaw. Dom wondered if he might hang up.

'Is that right?' Colin Bohan pronounced slowly. Perhaps it was meant to be sarcastic, but it sounded like a question to Dom, a real question.

'Yes. It is. I'd trust him with my life. Don't give up on him.'

There was another, shorter pause. 'I'll keep that in mind, Dom. I'll keep that in mind.'

Dom took a deep breath in, pressed his palm flat against the cool glass of the phone box. 'I'd better go now, I —'

'The dog was sick, Dom.'

'What?'

'The dog. She was going to die anyway. I found a tumour on her neck, months ago. Took her to the vet in Joondyne.

Hadn't got around to telling Lizzie when you … she was so attached to the thing.'

'I'm sorry.'

'It was a quick death, Dom. You did us a favour.'

Dom stared out at the deserted street. 'She didn't suffer?'

'No. No. She didn't suffer at all.'

35 ALMOST CHRISTMAS

On the long pedestrianised section of Hay Street some shops were already adorned with gaudy Christmas decorations. Andy thought it was a load of meaningless crap, the capitalist Christmas splurge. Still, the bright displays made him smile. He meandered along, sipping a freshly-squeezed orange juice, amongst shoppers and tourists and workers on their lunch breaks. A white didgeridoo busker with dreadlocks had collected a decent pile of money in a battered leather hat.

Andy was saying goodbye to the place. Making a day of it. Tonight, Summie and Jules were having a barbecue in his honour. Summie had been fishing a couple of weeks back and had a huge dhuie he wanted to grill, with chilli and spices. Andy's job was to pick up some salad vegetables on his way home.

There was a buzz of excitement in the city centre, the expectation of the hot holiday season not far away; long days on the beach, picnics and barbecues and endless sunshine. The Christmas holidays had always been the best time of the year when he was growing up. He'd loved messing about in the water at the Connors' dam, exploring in the bush, riding bikes into Marrup with Dom for sweet icypoles that left their hands sticky. His family had come for the occasional holiday to the coast — they stayed in a caravan at Coogee beach one year, with the raw whiff of the chemical plant when the wind blew the wrong way. Dom was there too, of course. They had a great time.

There'd be no sun and sea for him this year, but he didn't care — what he had to look forward to was so much bigger and more important than just another hot summer; he was heading for a whole new life. He wasn't going to tell Dom about London, and Summie and Jules had been sworn to secrecy. Dom didn't need to feel responsible for some straight-off-the-boat Aussie. Though he hadn't said much, it was pretty clear that his friend had enough on his plate without having Andy to worry about too. It wouldn't be fair. Besides, Andy wanted to make this happen himself, to know that he could do it, without help. He would get a job, set himself up, then get in touch with Dom. It would be an awesome surprise.

He needed to get away from here, the old and stale, the drag of his history. He wanted to be part of a crowd, feel the rush and push of life, the hum of possibility. Dom had done it, and so could he. Why not? He was ready.

He found the right stop on St George's Terrace and waited for the bus to King's Park. He hadn't been there for years, even though it was only minutes away from the city centre. He was looking forward to seeing the fountains and the trees, the city and the river stretching out below him. It seemed a good way to say goodbye. He remembered the time, only months ago, when he'd stood waiting for a bus somewhere around here after he'd come out of hospital, with his Fremantle cap and flimsy slip-on shoes donated by the hospital. He ran his hand through his hair; it still felt strange. Jules had cut it for him again, very short this time, at his request. It had transformed him. He looked, Jules said, almost stylish. If he was lucky, the dentist would be able to fit a bridge to fill the ugly gap in his smile before his flight next week. His mum had paid for the dentist, and the flight. His wonderful mum. Anything you need, she'd said. She had always been in charge of the finances, so Colin did not even have to know. Of course, they weren't millionaires, but she'd assured him money wasn't a problem; they'd been careful, and lucky. She didn't really want him to go so far away, but she understood it was the right thing for him to do.

His dad, of course, would be pleased to see the back of him.

The bus purred to a halt. He stood back and gestured for an older man next to him to go first. The man smiled at him and murmured his thanks.

The fish was delicious and Summie was full of pride that he had provided it with his own hands. Fishing, Andy thought, was obviously going to take over surfing as Summie's favourite pastime. Andy balanced Callie on his knee and shared his desert of coconut ice cream and fruit with her.

'Well, here's to a freezing cold, wet, grey English Christmas, eh?' Summie raised his bottle of beer. 'Cheers, you mad bugger.'

'If you don't keep in touch, I'll never speak to you again.' Jules reached for her beer on the garden table and waved it in Andy's direction. 'Cheers. Now listen, I don't want you coming back with some posh accent and —' She was interrupted by the trill of the phone. She hurried inside.

Callie shoved her fingers into Andy's ice cream and stuck them in her mouth.

'You know,' Summie stretched his legs out in front of him, 'if it's too cold for you over there, or you end up hating it, or whatever, just remember you can always come back and stay here.'

'Andy!' Jules called from the back door. 'It's for you.'

Andy handed Callie over to her dad. He wondered if it was Dom — he was due in Perth about now. Or his sister, again. They'd never been close, but he had talked to her on the phone last night, for more than half an hour. She hadn't gone as far as inviting him to go and see her and her family, but she had asked him to keep in touch. It was a start.

Jules met him halfway down the garden. She looked happy. 'It's your dad, Andy.'

'Yeah, right.'

'No, really.' Her silver bracelets jingled as she reached out and squeezed his arm. 'Your dad's on the phone, mate. Says he wants to talk to you. Wish you luck.'

'Wish me luck?'

She raised her eyebrows and nodded. 'Go on. Phone's on the kitchen table.'

A smile crept onto Andy's face. So his dad had come round, after all. He licked sweet ice cream from his lips and ran his tongue around his teeth. He didn't really mind if he couldn't get the gap fixed before he went to London. He'd lived a life; this was who he was — scarred, a bit battered. Why should he care what people thought? They would have to take him as they found him.

He bounded towards the house.

36 Bloody Shame

The low roadside scrub shivered with the movement of a hidden animal. Cicadas trilled. Dom shifted his pack to make it more comfortable and kept walking, moving with the rhythm of his breathing, feeling the regular fall of his feet through his body. A heat haze shimmered on the road, the sun glinted off tiny chips of stone embedded in the tarmac. He breathed in the bite of hot tar, swung his arms in the endless space. He was leaving. Perhaps he would never come back.

He resisted the wash of nostalgic feeling. The place was beautiful, in a harsh way, but there was nothing left here for him. It was just land, and land didn't remember anyone. It bore scars, or it blossomed. But it didn't care.

While the sun climbed, he trudged along, steering around the occasional fly-ridden kangaroo carcass. He wore his cap pulled down to his eyes. Sweat drenched his hair and made his scalp prickle and itch. At the rumble of an approaching vehicle he brightened and stuck out his arm, but the car swerved to the other side of the road and sped past.

When he reached a side road not far from the main turn off for Joondyne, he stopped to rest in the shade of a clump of Mulgas and searched the road ahead. There used to be a small service station somewhere around here. He hadn't noticed anything when he'd driven in this way, weeks ago, but it had been dark and late. His mouth was sticky and dry and he wanted to drink the last of his water. He made himself leave it. Just in case.

He wondered where Hester was.

He kept going for another ten minutes until he spotted the shimmer of a building, the glint of a tin roof ahead. He smiled with relief and gulped the last of his water. He'd be able to pick up a lift from the service station, he was sure. And get something to eat.

In an oily shed next to the service station shop and café, a man leaned into the open engine of a car. 'G'day.' He looked up as Dom straggled past.

Dom nodded and said hello.

A bell tinkled when he opened the screen door, and a woman appeared at the counter. She turned her head to check out the window, tilted it back to give the exhausted man in front of her a suspicious frown.

'Didn't think I heard a car. Where'd you spring from?'

A fan on the counter buzzed and ticked in a semicircle, just missing Dom with its putter of cool air before it arced back, ruffling the ends of the woman's limp, straight hair. A small bamboo basket full of tomato sauce sachets and a stand-up cardboard advertisement for Mac's Meat Pies sat on the sticky-looking counter.

'I — I'm visiting from England. My car broke down in Marrup and I have to get back to Perth to catch a plane — you won't mind if I wait around here for a lift?'

The woman shrugged. 'Don't see why not. Might have a bit of a wait, but. Not too busy around here these days. Wool trucks, now and then. Families — but mostly leaving. Their cars are always chocka.' She considered for a moment. 'Friday. Sometimes get government blokes, about the drought and that, heading back to the city. Or salesmen been out in the sticks, doing the rounds. Yep, even when we're stone dead on the ground they'll still be trying to sell us some bloody thing.'

Dom smiled.

He doused his head with water at a hand basin in a fly-ridden toilet cubicle at the side of the building. The woman had warned him the water was no good to drink.

Inside, three round tables were covered with plastic floral tablecloths. Each table was decorated with a bottle of tomato sauce, crusted around the lid, plastic salt and pepper shakers with the letters S and P nearly worn away, a glass bowl of lumpy sugar, and an ashtray.

Dom paid for a large bottle of water, cold from the fridge, and took it to a table, along with a flimsy plastic cup the woman sold him for thirty cents. He drank until the bottle was half empty.

The woman shuffled over with a soggy, microwaved pie and a pile of chips. Dom was so hungry it tasted like the best meal he'd ever had. When he finished eating he sat looking out at the empty forecourt through the dusty window. Desiccated flies lay scattered along the window sill.

A local farmer, travelling in the wrong direction, pulled up in a ute. The woman went out and chatted to him while she worked the fuel bowser. The farmer handed her some bills and touched the brim of his hat when he said goodbye.

When she came back in the woman collected his plate.

He smiled at her. 'Thanks. That was great.'

She didn't say anything, but reappeared a few minutes later with a mug of tea and some biscuits on a saucer. She waved a hand when he pulled out his wallet. 'You've had a rough day, love. On the house.'

Her kindness sent a surge of emotion through him, and for a moment he had to hold back tears.

He drank his tea. A couple of vehicles came and went. One was a small refrigerator truck, heading back to Perth. Dom went out to talk to the driver, but he would not offer him a lift. It was against company policy, he said. The woman suggested, as she pulled a squeegee across the truck's windscreen, that no-one would know if he bent the rules, but the driver held up his hands and shrugged.

Dom took his pack outside and propped it by the wall. He scuffed around the forecourt, peered down the empty road. A clatter of tools came from the shed where the man he had seen — presumably the woman's husband — was working on the car. He thought about calling Lizzie again, to ask her to go and see Neal, make sure he was alright. The woman would probably let him use the phone. He went back inside and bought some chewing gum he would never use, but he didn't ask about the phone; it would seem silly and awkward, he decided, to call Lizzie again, when he'd already spoken to her this morning. He would wait until he got to Perth.

He sat down for a while in the shade, next to his pack. What would he do if no lift materialised? Perhaps the people here would let him stay with them the night, and he could try again tomorrow. But his flight was the day after tomorrow — he would be cutting it fine. They might take him to Joondyne. He thought there was a train to Perth from there, the one that went to Kalgoorlie, though he didn't know how often it ran. There might be a bus.

The man came out of the shed wiping his hands on a rag. He nodded to Dom and disappeared into the shop. He heard the man and woman speak a few low words to each other.

He got up again and meandered across the forecourt to the road. He gazed down the blank strip of tarmac. No cars. But there was something — a difference in the constant landscape, a change. What was it? He squinted into the glaring light; a drift of smoke in the clear sky, a tinge of feverish red in the distance.

The woman had come out to the forecourt to empty a bin next to the bowser. She took off the bin's swing lid and pulled up the edges of the bag. He remembered he had never found out what to do with the rubbish at the Big House. He had left the bags inside, in his old room, to moulder and decay and attract rodents.

He asked the woman if he could help.

'I'll be right, love.' She lifted the bag of rubbish out and tied the top tightly in a knot. Noticing the sky, she paused and straightened. She rested the bag against the bowser and came to stand near Dom.

'Is it a fire?' Dom asked.

'Looks like it.' She shaded her eyes and stared out towards the smudge of smoke, the bright patch of sky. 'Close. Near Marrup. Normally someone'd let us know if it was bush. Might be a house.' She lowered her hand and frowned. 'The old wooden places go up, no trouble. Not that many left now. Bloody shame.'

Dom felt dizzy. His skin tingled strangely. He stood with the woman, in silence, while they watched the sky.

After a while a silver Commodore charged into the forecourt and rocked to a halt next to a bowser. A round-faced man in a collared shirt threw open the door and climbed out. The woman went over to the car. Dom vaguely heard them talking. He was, as the woman had predicted, a salesman, a multinational rep pushing a new lime-flavoured fizzy drink around the state's rural backwaters. The woman explained that Dom needed a lift to Perth.

'No problem, mate,' the rep called out. 'Be good to have the company.' He was in a generous mood, heading back to civilisation.

The woman filled the Commodore with fuel and washed the windscreen. The rep went into the shop with her to pay. When he came out, Dom was still standing by the road.

The rep clicked opened the boot. 'Come on, then. Show time!'

Dom retrieved his pack and drifted over to the car.

The rep stuck out his hand. 'Brian.'

Dom told him his name. They shook hands.

'Righto, Dom. Sling your pack in here and we're off.'

The bell on the shop's flyscreen door tinkled and the woman came out again, her gaze drawn back to the sky.

'That a fire?' the rep asked. 'Noticed it before. Glad I'm driving in the right direction — away.' He tapped his fingers on the raised boot.

'It's not a bushfire,' the woman said, a touch of irritation in her voice.

'No?'

'Don't think so. Not yet, anyway.'

'You ready, mate?'

Dom's hand trembled as he adjusted his cap. 'Look, Brian, sorry to mess you around, but I'm not going to Perth after all.'

The woman turned to Dom.

The rep lifted his eyebrows and shrugged. 'Up to you, mate. I'm off.' He shut the boot, slid back into the driver's seat and was gone. In the sudden quiet that followed, Dom could hear the ticking sound of the fan inside the shop.

The woman picked up the bag of rubbish.

Dom settled his pack over his shoulders and edged towards the road. 'Thanks for your help. But I have to get back to Marrup.'

He wanted to be moving, shifting his tired limbs, feeling the solid pressure of the road beneath his sore feet. He could not let himself think. He took a few determined strides away.

'Hold on.'

He stopped and turned.

The woman moved her head, indicating he should come back. 'It'll take you forever without a car. Let me give you a lift.' She took the bag of rubbish to the door of the shop and stood waiting for him. 'It's no trouble. I have to find out about it anyway. The fire.'

It seemed to take him a long time to walk across the forecourt, but the woman didn't rush him — she waited, and pushed the door open to let him through. Flies followed him in, but she didn't seem to care. She pulled out a chair for him. He sat down.

'I'll call a few people, make sure it's safe. Before we go.'

He flinched when she touched his shoulder, but he liked the warmth her hand left when she had taken it away.

He didn't even know her name.